TAKEN
BY STORM

Jennifer Lynn Barnes

Quercus

Published in Great Britain in 2012 by Quercus

55 Baker Street
7th Floor, South Block
London W1U 8EW

First published in the US by Egmont,
443 Park Avenue South, Suite 806, New York, NY 10016

A CIP catalogue reference for this book is available
from the British Library

ISBN 978 1 78087 240 7

13 5 7 9 10 8 6 4 2

Printed and bound in Great Britain by Clays Ltd, St Ives plc.

For Justin.

CHAPTER ONE

I RAN AS THOUGH MY LIFE DEPENDED ON IT. Branches tore at my ankles and legs. My bare feet—caked with blood and mud and who knew what else—slammed into the forest floor, again and again and again. It hurt. Everything hurt.

It didn't hurt enough.

I pushed harder, faster, my lungs on fire and my chest tightening like a vise around my heart.

I couldn't run like this indefinitely. I couldn't keep going, but I couldn't stop. Muscles screaming, heart pounding—any second, my body would give in. Any second, it would be over.

No.

I fought. I fought to breathe, fought to hold on, to keep going, to—

Survive.

There it was: a whisper from somewhere deep inside of me, a familiar feeling creeping up my spine. I tasted copper on the tip of my tongue, and my vision—already blurred—shifted.

Red, red. Everywhere, there was red.

And just like that, I couldn't feel the pain, not in any way that mattered. I ran faster, the burst of energy coming out of nowhere, the need to escape overwhelming, all-consuming...

And then gone.

As suddenly as I'd shifted into the altered state, I fell out of it.

No, I thought. *No, no, no.*

I'd been so close. For a moment, I'd almost had it. I'd felt it. I'd *controlled* it, but now I was just me again: sweating and exhausted and human, as incapable of summoning up my Resilience as I would have been at fighting back the tide.

Spent, I collapsed on the ground, my back against the trunk of an old tree, my lungs and legs and common sense rebelling against the ordeal I'd just put myself through: the physical pain, the strain on my endurance, the panic I'd worked myself into on purpose.

At least I'd managed to get there this time. At least it had worked. If I could flip into fight or flight mode at will on Cedar Ridge land, in the safety of a forest that felt like home, there was hope that I'd be able to do it elsewhere, that I might be able to control this power I only halfway understood.

A large part of me still balked at the idea that some people were born with unnatural aptitudes: psychic knacks that pushed the bounds of possibility. Until I'd run into a coven of psychics bent on my destruction, I'd never identified that way myself. I was just a girl with a habit of surviving things that would have killed a normal person—things like being attacked by a werewolf or set on fire by a coven of psychics.

Just, you know, for instance.

Avoiding a trip down memory lane, I waited for my breathing to even out and ignored the burning ache in my chest. It took a full five minutes for my heart rate to go back to normal, and even then I knew that I'd be feeling the effects of this little experiment tomorrow. This was the third time I'd attempted to jump-start my knack—which typically flared up only when I was in danger—and the first time I'd actually managed to tap into the power, for a few seconds at least.

"Damn fool thing you just did, Bryn," someone opined, from behind me.

I didn't bother turning around. At seventeen, I liked being called foolish about as much as I liked people treating me as if I was some fragile little butterfly, best kept under glass.

"I'll live," I replied. I'd spent my entire life surrounded by werewolves, whose animal instincts didn't always line up with human ideas about "violence" and what was and was not an acceptable form of "conflict resolution." Running in my bare feet wasn't going to kill me.

"I don't know," my companion drawled, coming into view and rubbing the back of his hand roughly over his chin. "That mother of yours might kill you if you come in from the rain looking like that."

"It's not raining," I replied, deliberately sidestepping the older man's point about Ali, which was probably true. My foster mother was not enamored with the fact that, as the alpha of a pack of werewolves—the only human alpha in history—my life was pretty much the textbook definition of *dangerous*. Ali wouldn't take too kindly to the idea that after seven and a half months of relative calm, I was willingly putting myself through the wringer.

For practice.

Beside me, Jed said nothing, letting me mull over his words. Of all the people currently living at the Wayfarer, the old man was probably the only one who could have taken one look at me and known what I was up to—and why. Like me, Jed was Resilient. And human, which put him in the minority around here.

Reflexively, my mind went to a series of numbers ingrained in my very being. *Eight females. Ten males. Two humans.* The rest of the Cedar Ridge Pack was always there in my mind, their names a constant whisper in my subconscious. As alpha, I could feel each and every one of them—four-year-old Lily was waiting impatiently for Katie and Alex to wake up from their naps; Lake was spinning a pool cue around her fingers like a baton; Devon was in the shower, singing into a bottle of shaving cream at the top of his lungs; and Chase . . .

Chase was gone. Not for good. Not even for the night. He was checking in on the peripherals, the members of the pack who'd chosen to live at the edges of our territory instead of at the center. As much as Chase hated leaving me—leaving what we had together—I knew there was a part of him that felt the distance as a relief. He wasn't wired for pack living the way I was.

He was used to being on his own.

"Penny for your thoughts." Jed's voice was as gruff as always, but there was something about the set of his features—old and worn and wrinkled—that made me think he was being generous with his offer, that he didn't need to pay a fictional penny for my thoughts when he understood why I'd been running fast and hard enough that I'd come close to throwing up.

"Things have been quiet," I said finally, answering Jed's question carefully. "They won't always be quiet."

And there it was. The reason I couldn't just sit back on my haunches. There was a threat out there, and every day was like waiting for the guillotine to fall. I had to be ready. I had to do something. The rest of the pack trusted me to be prepared. They trusted me to make the right decisions, even when there wasn't a right decision to be had.

They trusted me to lead, but I didn't trust myself.

Sure, I'd make the decisions, I'd do whatever I could to make them safe, but at the end of the day, I was human. I was slower, weaker, more fragile—and if the previous year's events had taught me anything, it was that to protect my pack, I might need to be something else.

Since I hadn't heard one word from the werewolf who'd promised to Change me into one myself, that left only one option. I had a psychic knack. I had power. I just didn't know how to use it.

Yet.

"Seems to me, a girl like you could think of better uses for quiet time than running around and getting her feet all cut up."

I opened my mouth to reply, but Jed preempted the words.

"Seems to me, you could have asked someone."

"For help," I clarified, since Jed was a man of few words. "Asked someone for help."

There were days when I relied on the rest of the pack as much as they relied on me, and days when the concept of help seemed as foreign as the idea that most girls my age were just starting to look at colleges. Being an alpha was impossible and lonely and bigger than anything my human half might have wanted.

"I don't need help," I said softly, willing that to be true.

Jed rolled his eyes heavenward. "I'm not suggesting you go belly-up and ask your Weres for pointers," he said. "I'd wager the ability works differently once there's another set of animal instincts at play."

Like Jed and me, many of the wolves in my pack were Resilient. At one point in time, they'd been human.

Just like I was.

Just like I wouldn't be anymore, once Callum made good on his promise to Change me.

In the distance, I heard a rumble of thunder. Looking up, I noticed the blue sky turning a dark and ominous gray.

"How'd you know it was going to rain?" I asked Jed.

He snorted. "I've broken just about every bone in my body at one point or another, Bryn. I can feel a storm coming from a mile away."

Jed's body was covered in scars. I'd gotten so used to seeing them that I barely noticed anymore, but his words reminded me he had a lifetime of experience coming out on top of fights he had no business winning.

If anyone understood that a few scratches were a small price to pay for what I was seeking, it was Jed.

"You'll help me?"

Jed nodded, gazing out at the horizon, looking oddly at peace as it started to rain. "I'll help you," he said. "But we'll do it my way."

I was going to go out on a limb and guess that his way did not involve putting myself through hell in hopes of convincing my body I was under attack.

"Fine by me."

Jed gave me a look that said he thought I was constitutionally incapable of doing things any way but my own. Once upon a time, that might have been true, but now I'd do whatever it took to keep my pack safe. To be the kind of alpha they deserved and make sure that what had happened last winter never, ever happened again.

With nothing more than a nod in my direction, Jed began walking back toward shelter, but I just sat there, letting the rain beat against my body and thinking about a broken boy with hungry eyes.

A boy I'd invited into my pack.

A boy who'd tried to kill me.

A boy I'd killed.

Bone-tired and sopping wet, I went home.

CHAPTER TWO

—~—

THE CLOSER I GOT TO THE WAYFARER, THE MORE aware I was of the rest of the pack, and the more aware they were of me. Being alpha meant that the others didn't have an all-access pass to my mind, the way I did to theirs, but even without the benefits of the pack-bond, my friends knew me well enough to know that a quiet Bryn meant Trouble with a capital *T*.

I wasn't altogether surprised to find someone waiting for me at the clearing.

"Halt! Who goes there?"

If ever a werewolf had mastered the art of yelling from the diaphragm, it was Dev. Like a knight guarding a princess's tower, he put his hands on his hips and threw his head back haughtily.

I could so feel a Monty Python impression coming on.

"'Tis I," I yelled back, playing along. "Queen Bryn."

With any luck, I could distract my best friend—and second-in-command—enough that he wouldn't pay much attention to the fact that I looked like I'd been mud wresting—and lost.

"Queen?" Devon repeated, looking down his nose at me. Since he was six foot five, he had a long way to look. "Thou dost not look like a queen."

I rolled my eyes, but amended my previous statement. "'Tis I. Peasant Bryn."

Dev's lips twitched, but he didn't crack a smile, which was not a good sign. That Peasant Bryn line was comedy gold.

"You okay?" he asked, dropping the accent and searching my face for the answer.

"I'm fine," I told him. "I just went for a run."

To a werewolf's nose, those words would have smelled true. I *was* fine—as fine as I could be, given everything that had happened in the past two years.

"You want to tell me why you're not wearing any shoes?" Devon asked, quirking one eyebrow to ridiculous heights.

"Not really," I replied. "Peasant Bryn is a girl of few words."

Maybe I should have given him a real answer, but this was Devon. He couldn't stand to see me in pain. I doubted he'd understand why I'd sought it out.

A twig snapped somewhere behind us—fair warning we were about to have company. If I'd been in a more charitable mood, I might have acknowledged the fact that "company" had probably stepped on the twig on purpose. I knew better than anyone if Caroline didn't want to be heard, she wasn't heard. She came out of nowhere and disappeared the same way. She was the ultimate hunter, a psychic with supernaturally good aim.

We weren't really what one would call best buds.

"Heya, Caro," Devon called, perfectly amiable. I didn't understand how he could call her by a nickname. She'd been a part of the coven that had waged war against our pack. She'd made our people bleed—Devon included.

"Did Jed find you?" Caroline met my eyes and ignored Devon. Dev wasn't the type to be ignored, but for some reason, he let Caroline get away with it.

If you asked me, Caroline got away with a lot.

"Jed found me," I told her. I didn't elaborate, and she didn't seem to expect me to.

"In that case," she said, turning back the way she came, "I guess there's not really anything else for me to say."

As she turned, I caught a glimmer of something in her eyes, and I couldn't help but think of the way Ali looked, gritting her teeth and breathing through the worst life had to offer, the memories that cut her to the bone.

"Wait."

Caroline paused. She waited. I didn't know what else to say to her, didn't want to be talking to her at all, but the resemblance to my foster mother, however fleeting, had reminded me that no matter what this girl had done, she was family. Ali's family.

Her biological family.

"You should come by to see Ali more," I said finally.

That was as close to an olive branch as I could come. Caroline lived with Jed: on our land, but not in the house I shared with Ali; privy to what the rest of us really were, but not a part of the pack. If I'd had my way, the girl who'd shot Devon and—whether she'd meant to or not, whether she'd had a choice in the matter or not—helped kill one of our own would have been living in another hemisphere. But Ali cared about her. She wanted a relationship with her, and I couldn't be the one to screw that up.

Family mattered to Ali the way Pack did to me.

Family. Pack. That combination of words made me think of another person who should have been standing here, but wasn't. A person whose absence I couldn't blame on Caroline in any way, shape, or form.

Maddy.

Maddy, who'd been one of us. Maddy, who'd loved an angry, broken boy.

Maddy, who'd left, because I'd killed the boy she loved.

For a moment, Caroline actually met my eyes, and I wondered if she played Eric's death over and over again in her head, the way I obsessed over Lucas's. I wondered if she felt even an ounce of my guilt, if she sat up nights, staring at the ceiling.

Caroline broke eye contact first. She turned on her heels and left without snapping a single twig.

What happened last winter wasn't her fault, Bryn, Devon told me silently, for maybe the thousandth time. *Caroline never stood a chance against her mother's mind-control mojo. You know that.*

Maybe that was true and maybe it wasn't, but my pack should have had twenty-two people, and it didn't. Eric should have been starting his sophomore year in college, and he wasn't.

Your mother never had a choice when Callum ordered her to beat the crap out of me, I retorted. *But I don't see you rushing out to mend bridges with* her.

That was a low blow, and I knew it. Growing up, Devon and I had both been a part of the same pack—Callum's. Devon's mother was the second-in-command, and the moment Sora had laid hands on me, she'd changed everything—for me, for Ali, for her son.

Suffice it to say, Devon was much less willing to forgive and forget when the person who ended up hurt was me.

For a second after I snapped at him, I thought Devon might turn around and leave me standing there by myself, but he didn't. He put an arm around my shoulder and pulled me close.

"Come on, brown-eyed girl," he said. "Let's get you some food."

I'd never done a thing in my life to deserve Devon. I probably never would.

We passed the restaurant on the way back to my cabin, and Lake—who'd heard us coming—shot out the front door like a jackrabbit. Or a werewolf under the influence of too many Pixy Stix—take your pick.

"Got room for one more?" she asked. Dev inclined his head in a gentlemanly fashion, and Lake was on my other side in an instant, her arm flung around my shoulder, just like Devon's.

Pack. Pack. Pack.

Physical contact sent my pack-sense into overdrive, and my body was flooded with the feeling that this was how it was meant to be. We were together. We were safe. I could feel their wolves, feel the emotion rising up inside of them, the same way it did in me.

And then I felt something else.

Foreign. Wolf.

Devon and Lake went absolutely still, and I knew they'd felt it, too. Each of the twelve packs in North America had its own territory. The last time a foreign wolf had crossed into ours without permission, things had gone badly.

Very badly.

Foreign. Wolf.

Dev stepped in front of me, his jaw granite-hard. Lake's upper lip curled, and I could physically see the growl working its way up her throat.

And that was when I felt it—a tremor in my pack-sense, horror and recognition that whoever had come here without seeking my permission first wasn't just a wolf from another pack.

Wasn't just a threat.

Our visitor—whoever he was—was an alpha.

CHAPTER THREE

ALPHAS DIDN'T INVADE EACH OTHER'S TERRITORIES. They didn't take each other's wolves. The Wayfarer was *mine*. The people who lived here, my pack—they were *mine*. The hairs rose like hackles on the back of my neck, and a sense of foreboding washed over me, one that said there was only one reason for another alpha to come here unannounced.

Our visitor wanted something: my head on a platter, a harem of underage females to add to his ranks—it didn't matter. Either way, if another alpha had broken Senate Law to come here, there was nothing saying he wouldn't take what he wanted by force.

Suddenly, running barefoot through the woods until my feet were bloody and my muscles weak didn't seem like such a good idea. I'd been set on preparing myself for the next confrontation, but I'd assumed that the other alphas would continue playing by the rules.

That if Devon's brother, Shay, wanted to kill me, he'd do it with cunning and subterfuge, staying just this side of the Senate strictures on inter-pack relations.

"If it's him," Devon said calmly, "he's dead."

If Shay had come into our territory without permission, Devon could attack him without fear of reprisal from the rest of the Senate. He could Shift and go for his brother's throat, and the connection between the two of us told me that he wanted to.

That he was on the verge of losing control.

"Wait," I said softly. I wanted Shay dead as much as the next girl, but the Snake Bend alpha had a couple of centuries on Devon and the same solid build. I needed a plan. I needed to think.

"Bryn." The sound of Ali calling my name from just around the bend turned my blood to ice. Besides me, she was the only human in our pack, and she didn't have a knack to fall back on. If Shay had her, if any of the other alphas had her—

"It's okay." Ali's words barely penetrated my brain. "Take a deep breath."

I couldn't take a deep breath. I couldn't even breathe.

Foreign. Wolf. Alpha.

"It's not Shay," Ali called. "It's Callum."

Hearing Callum's name did something to me. My eyes stung, and my insides went liquid and warm. I would have sworn my heart stopped beating, and my fingers curled so tightly into fists that my nails cut into the palms of my hands.

Callum was the alpha who'd brought me into the werewolf world. He'd saved me from a rabid werewolf when I was four years old. He'd raised me. He'd protected me. He'd hurt me. And the last time I'd seen him, he'd promised that he would do the unthinkable.

My mind went immediately to places I didn't want it to go—to memories of the rabid wolf who'd killed my parents, to the sound of their blood splattering against an off-white wall. Werewolf attacks were vicious. Brutal. And unless you had a knack for survival, they didn't end with the wolf's prey turning into a Were.

They ended with the wolf's prey dead.

To Change me, Callum would have to rip me to pieces. He'd have to take me to the brink of death and hope my Resilience would pull me back. I told myself that I wanted this. That I was ready. That I'd been ready for seven long months.

I steeled myself against fear and took a mental hatchet to my reservations. I'd said I would do anything for my pack, and I meant it. I'd die for them. I'd Change for them.

I'd say good-bye to my human life forever.

A gust of wind snapped me out of my thoughts, and beside me, Devon and Lake—oblivious to my train of thought—visibly relaxed, their noses confirming what Ali had said. Like me, Lake and Dev had once been a part of Callum's pack. Intellectually, they might not have trusted him, but instinctually, they did. He'd been their rock, their protector, their alpha for too long for them not to.

Even though I was their alpha now.

As Devon and Lake dropped back and let me take the lead, I realized that knowing Callum was the trespasser didn't completely calm my senses. He'd still come here without permission, and I couldn't push down the part of my brain that said this was a challenge.

He'd challenged me.

Alpha. Alpha. Alpha.

The closer I got to Ali and Callum, the stronger the feeling was—alphas weren't meant to coexist. By definition, there could only be one: one in a given territory, one total, if it weren't for the precarious democracy in the werewolf Senate, which kept each of us in our own little worlds.

Alpha. Alpha. Alpha.

I had to do something, had to fight, had to protect what was mine—

I didn't actively try to call up my Resilience. I didn't have to. One second, I was fine, and the next, I could feel myself slipping, feel an alien power taking over my body, driven entirely by instinct and self-preservation.

"Bryn." This time, Callum was the one who spoke my name, and it played in my mind in stereo, pushing back the haze, as I remembered the hundred thousand times he'd said it when I was a kid.

I looked at him—through the anger and fear and the heady call of letting everything go red again—and I met his eyes. I didn't mean to. I knew his wolf would see it as a direct challenge, and I made it a rule not to get into any staring competitions I couldn't win. But to my surprise, Callum only met my gaze for a second, before flicking his eyes downward and rounding his neck.

Submission.

He stood there, the man who'd made me what I was, a thousand-year-old werewolf with more power than the rest of the Senate combined, and he bowed his head toward me.

Relief washed over my body, then confusion, then awe. My skin thrummed with the power of what had passed between us, and slowly, Callum raised his eyes to meet mine once more. There was no challenge there, only understanding—of everything I was feeling, of everything I was.

On good days, I liked to think that was why he'd agreed to Change me. Because he still cared about me. Because he knew as well as I did that, sooner or later, being human would get me killed.

"The alpha of the Stone River Pack apologizes for this intrusion. I'll accept any sanctions you see fit."

The idea of applying any kind of sanction to someone who had grounded me more times than I could count was just bizarre.

To Callum's left, Ali rolled her eyes. She had no use for werewolf politics, and Callum wasn't exactly on her list of favorite people.

"The alpha of the Cedar Ridge Pack accepts your apology," I told Callum formally. "No sanctions necessary."

I didn't always trust Callum. I knew he had an agenda, that his own knack—an ability to see possible futures—lent itself to manipulating the rest of us a little too well. Callum kept secrets, and he played God, and every time I thought I had him figured out, he threw me for a loop.

But I trusted that he wouldn't have come here without a reason—a good one.

Knowing that, my mind jumped immediately to the promise he'd made me, the unthinkable thing I'd asked him to do—*Teeth snapping. Muscles tearing. Skin and tendons and gristle. Minced, like meat*—I couldn't stop picturing what it would be like to be attacked by a Were, couldn't keep from seeing the people I'd once called Mommy and Daddy reduced to carnage.

But there was no turning back now.

Callum had told me he would Change me. He'd made me wait. And now he was here. It didn't take a rocket scientist to do the math.

"Tomorrow morning," Callum said, his voice breaking into my thoughts, "Shay Macalister is going to call a meeting of the Senate."

That wasn't what I'd expected him to say. In retrospect, math had never been my strong suit.

"Since Shay is the one calling the meeting, the rest of the alphas will be expected to go to him."

As far as I knew, the Senate normally met in Callum's territory, at Callum's house.

Callum shrugged in response to my unasked question. "Normally," he said, "I'm the one who calls the meetings."

Most of the other alphas probably would have been happy to stay in their own territories and forget that Callum existed altogether. For that matter, they'd probably have been happy if *I* didn't exist. The last time I'd been in a room with the entire Senate was the day I became an alpha myself. None of them— save for Callum—had seen it coming. None of them had been pleased.

More than one alpha would have enjoyed bathing in my blood.

"The Senate is meeting," I said slowly, "and I have to go."

I was an alpha. The Senate was composed of the alphas of all of the North American packs. Eleven dominant werewolves and me. In one room.

This could not possibly be good.

"What does Shay want?" I asked. Beside me, Devon stiffened at the mere mention of his brother's name.

"Shay wants what Shay always wants," Callum replied calmly, his voice washing over us, understated and warm. "Trouble. Power. Females. Take your pick."

"So this is a power play?" I asked. "Shay's calling the Senate just because he can?"

I could tell by the look on Callum's face that the answer to that question was no. Shay had a reason for calling the Senate—but Callum wasn't sure I was ready to hear it.

"Tell me."

Callum's lips quirked upward at my no-nonsense tone, more like his than either one of us would have cared to admit. After another long pause, he answered my question. "Whatever Shay's going to tell us at this meeting, there are bodies involved. Human bodies."

Those words hit me like a physical blow. Callum must have known the effect this would have on me, the memories his words would drudge up.

Human lives would never be mere *collateral damage* to me, but the last time the Senate had met, they'd voted to make a deal with the psychopathic werewolf who'd killed my parents, a monster who had been hunting and killing human children—and Changing Resilient ones into werewolves—for years. If Shay was concerned about a few dead bodies, it wasn't because he recognized a value to human life. It was because the Senate's highest priority was keeping the human world from finding out that werewolves existed.

That was the reason werewolves didn't attack humans.

That was the reason a Were who hunted without authorization was normally executed, no questions asked.

I met Callum's eyes, and this time, neither one of us looked away. I knew then what he wasn't saying, why he'd risked trespassing on my territory to give me warning that Shay was about to call.

"It's happening again," I said, my mind going back to the

last time, to a werewolf who hunted humans and the things that he had done to my family, to the kids in my pack, to Chase, and to me. "Shay isn't calling the Senate as some kind of power play." The words stuck in my throat, but I pushed them out. "He's calling this meeting because there's a Rabid."

CHAPTER FOUR

HOURS LATER, WHEN I CREPT INTO THE BATHROOM
and shut the door behind me, a sense of overwhelming relief
flooded my body. Around the others—around Callum—I had
to be strong. Showing weakness to a member of another pack
was not an option, and I couldn't afford to let my feelings
about this development infect the rest of my own pack, either.
Devon would be accompanying me to the Senate meeting
as my second-in-command. Coming face-to-face with Shay,
knowing his brother wanted me dead—that would be hard
enough for Dev. He didn't need my emotional baggage making
it any worse.

Besides, with werewolves, control was the name of the game.

Never flinch.

Never show your anger.

Never let them see you cry.

It was disgustingly easy for me to shove my emotions into
a box in the back of my mind, to slip into alpha mode and
mimic Callum's facial expressions, his posture. But now, with

the bathroom door standing in between me and the others, I could finally let myself breathe. I could remember.

I could feel.

Flipping on the shower, I let the sound of water beating against marble drown out my jagged breathing. I slid slowly to the floor, a mess by every sense of the word. My hair was tangled and matted to my forehead. My feet were streaked with dirt, my earlier wounds ugly and scabbed. Beneath my year-round suntan, my face was pale, and when I caught a glimpse of myself in the bathroom mirror, my lips were pressed into a thin and colorless line.

For a few seconds, I thought I might actually cry. That was so unlike me, I wasn't sure how to respond. Bronwyn Alessia St. Vincent Clare didn't get sad. She got mad. Or better, she got even.

Why was I letting this get to me? I'd known from the moment I'd survived Shay's last attempt on my life that he would have another plan, and another, and another. I'd known I'd have to see him again face-to-face, that I'd have to play politics when I wanted nothing more than to tear out his throat. But the idea of doing it in a room full of alphas who felt the same way about me that Shay did, who had voted to let the last four-legged psychopath get away with it because human lives—my life, Chase's, the lives of innocent children, *my parents'*—weren't worth much when you stacked them up against the secret to making female Weres?

That made me sick.

Natural-born female werewolves were rare enough that the other alphas would have let the rabid wolf who killed my parents keep right on killing, so long as he delivered on his promise to supply them with a constant flow of girls who'd been born human and Changed into Weres.

Now both the Rabid and the secret to pulling off that trick were buried, and as far as Shay and the other alphas were concerned, that was my fault. If they'd had any idea I knew what the last Rabid had known, that Callum knew—

Bryn.

I heard Chase in my mind long before I sensed his physical approach. The closer he got, the further away everything else seemed—the knowledge that this time tomorrow, I'd be headed for a Senate meeting; the unwanted memories; the frustration and rage and worry that wouldn't do me a speck of good. Instead, I felt Chase. His presence. His thoughts.

Even when I shut my mind off to the rest of the pack, Chase was there.

He wasn't strong the way Devon was, or as brash and fearless as Lake. He didn't understand me—or my priorities—the way someone with alpha instincts would have, and if it hadn't been for me, he would have left our little pack long ago—but Chase excelled at being there. Physically, emotionally, he was there and he was steady, and I didn't question, even for a second, that he'd love me just the same no matter what I said or did or felt or didn't feel.

Sitting very still, I closed my eyes and waited. Waited until Chase's presence wasn't just a shadow over my mind. Waited until I could feel his breath on my face, until I could smell him, cedar and cinnamon and *home*.

I opened my eyes. There he was, inches away from me, close enough to touch. The constant hum of the shower faded into the background. I let go of the barriers in my mind. In an instant, everything that had happened passed from my mind to Chase's. My hands found their way to the sides of his face. My palms were warm with the heat of his skin, and I concentrated on that—on feeling him, touching him—and not thinking about what tomorrow might bring.

"Shay's going to call?" Chase asked, leaning into my touch.

I nodded. "Callum said we'll have a few hours after the call comes in before we'll need to leave. Sora will be joining him at the edge of Snake Bend territory. I'll be taking Dev."

Chase didn't stiffen, didn't react in any way, but I could feel in the pit of my stomach that he hated not being the one to go with me. He had no desire to fight Devon for dominance; he would never treat me as if I were some kind of prize to be won, but Chase didn't like the idea of my walking headlong into danger without him.

He didn't like knowing that there were times when he couldn't have my back.

"I'll be fine," I said, and somehow, saying the words to Chase made them feel true. "I can do this."

A rueful half smile cut across the boyish features of his face. "Of course you can."

He pressed his lips into my palm, and I heard the rest of his words in my mind, felt them in the surface of my skin.

But if you don't want *to,* he continued silently.

Chase would never understand that what I wanted didn't matter. Not to me, not the way it would to any other girl.

I'd *wanted* to help Lucas ...

There was no room for emotion in my decision-making process. No wanting, no feeling, no anger, no grief.

"Okay," Chase said softly, murmuring the words into my hair. "Okay, Bryn."

He wasn't pushing, wasn't asking me to change, but I knew he wanted me to have choices that I would never have. I couldn't blame him for that—not when he was willing to give up *his* choices for me.

But it would have been nice, really nice, if being together hadn't required that kind of sacrifice. If neither of us had known, in skin and bones and blood-deep certainty, that I would always come first for Chase, and the pack would always come first for me.

"Love you," Chase whispered, and my lips found their way to his. I rose up on my knees and drove my fingers through his hair. I pulled his head closer, echoing his whisper. Kissing him. Loving him. Heat played on the surface of my skin and the bond between us flared until I could feel it as a physical thing.

Tomorrow, Shay would call a meeting of the Senate.

Tomorrow, I would leave.

Tomorrow, my emotions would go back in their box. I would strategize. I would stay strong in front of the rest of the alphas. I would win.

But today—today wasn't tomorrow. And for this instant, this second, I could be a girl, just kissing a boy.

I could feel.

CHAPTER FIVE

"RISE AND SHINE."

The voice that woke me the next morning was low and gruff—and male.

A man. In my bedroom. Unannounced.

My eyes flew open. My hand went for the knife I kept on my nightstand. Jed caught my wrist halfway there.

"What do you feel?" he asked me.

If he hadn't been well over sixty, I would have shown him exactly how I felt. This was my space—*mine*—and my alpha instincts weren't inclined to take any intrusion lying down. At the same time, there was another part of me that had reacted to his unexpected wake-up call—the Bryn who had grown up around werewolves, the Bryn who knew that most Weres were male, that they were bigger than humans and stronger than humans and fast enough to catch me if I ran.

I was an alpha now, but some lessons were hard to unlearn.

"Pissed," I said finally, locking eyes with Jed. "I feel *pissed*."

"What else?" Jed asked, but he must have seen some hint

of danger in my expression, because he dropped my wrist and took a step back.

"More pissed?" I suggested.

"Before you were fully awake, before you processed who I was or what I was doing here, before you remembered who *you* were and what you're capable of—" Jed kept walking backward, but his voice never wavered—"what did you feel?"

I hated that he was asking me to think about this, hated that even for a moment, even half-asleep, I'd felt ...

Fear.

I could tell, just by looking at Jed, that he was waiting for me to say the word out loud. He'd be waiting a very long time. Even if I hadn't been alpha, even if there hadn't been an entire pack of people counting on me to be strong, I never would have admitted to that kind of weakness.

Fear was something you squashed, something you pushed down and hid and glossed over, because fear was like catnip to werewolves. They could smell it. They could taste it. It whetted their appetite for more—more fear, more of you.

In short: not good.

When I was a kid, Callum taught me how to hide my fear. But not feeling it? That was something I taught myself.

"You ever notice, right before you flash out, that the room gets really small?" The rhetorical question seemed harmless enough, but Jed wasn't done yet. "Maybe you start to feel trapped. A trickle of sweat builds on the back of your neck.

Your heart starts pounding faster, your mouth goes dry. What exactly would you call that, Bryn?"

"Adrenaline," I replied.

Jed raised a brow.

"Panic." I grudgingly let go of that word, because being anxious or frantic wasn't the same thing as being scared. You could panic that you were going to sleep through your alarm or miss your flight or get caught making out with your boyfriend on the bathroom floor.

You could panic about a lot of things, and it didn't taste like …

"Fear." Jed said the word. I wondered if he expected me to flinch, but I didn't. I didn't even blink.

"Claustrophobia. Anxiety. Desperation," I countered.

Jed did not seem impressed with my vocabulary. "Fear," he said again, uncompromising. Certain.

Despite myself, I thought of the way I'd felt in the forest the day before, running and running and working myself into a frenzy. I'd run like something was chasing me. I'd told myself I would die if I stopped.

But had I ever really been *scared*?

Jed smiled. With the scars on his face, it looked more like a grimace, but his eyes were twinkling. "Downright ironic, isn't it?" he asked me.

"What?" I asked, though I had a sinking suspicion what he was going to say next.

"It's ironic," Jed said again, "that if you want to be stronger, the first thing you're going to have to learn is how to let your-self be weak."

Half an hour later, I was sitting in the dirt outside the cabin Jed shared with Caroline, awaiting instructions he seemed in no particular hurry to give. Oblivious to—or ignoring—my impatience, Jed took a seat on the ground beside me and reclined back on the heels of his hands.

"My way," he reminded me.

"Your way," I repeated. I wasn't overjoyed with the prospect of more dirt sitting—or with the way he'd woken me up that morning—but I would have made a deal with the devil himself to find a way to control the power inside me, to make it some-thing more than a defense mechanism.

Someday, waiting for the other guy to attack might get me killed.

"You know how to get there," Jed said finally, breaking what felt like a small eternity of silence. "Deep down, you know. You just ain't admitted it to yourself yet."

He wasn't talking about pain or panic or running like someone was on your heels. The kind of trigger Jed was talking about was something I wanted no part of.

Something I'd spent my entire life training myself not to do.

"Think of the worst thing that ever happened to you," Jed

told me. "Think of a time when you were cornered and trapped and terrified."

Was that really what it took to summon up my Resilience, to fall into that state where nothing mattered but surviving and protecting the people I loved?

Where I was a faster, better Bryn?

"Every bad thing that's ever happened to you." Jed was implacable. "Every moment of terror, every loss, every time you had no power, and someone else had it all. One by one by one, Bryn. That's the way."

I'd said I would do anything for my pack. I'd said I would do this Jed's way. So I did.

I started with recent memories, moments I spent all of my time trying to forget.

The look in Lucas's eyes—hungry and desperate and dark—when he'd challenged my right to rule. The knowledge that had flooded my body in that instant, that a Were—any Were—was physically capable of killing me dead.

Dread built up inside of me, like bile rising in my throat, but I pressed on and thought of another heart-in-throat moment: seeing Devon lying still on the ground, blood pouring from a bullet wound in his heart. I thought of Lake missing a shot in a fateful game of pool and pretending that she wasn't terri-fied that losing might mean spending the rest of her life as the property of Shay.

In the here and now, I was sweating. I was cold. But I wasn't done yet. Forcing my muscles to relax, I went further, deeper, the memories flashing before my eyes at rapid speed.

I saw a man with violet eyes threatening to burn me to death in my sleep. I couldn't fight back, couldn't move—

I felt myself waking up in a cabin belonging to the monster who'd killed my parents, tied to a chair and wearing a frilly white dress designed for a little, little girl. The Rabid had touched me and cooed to me and backhanded me to the floor.

At the time, I hadn't let myself be scared. Didn't ever let myself be scared, but now...

I pictured myself standing still, as the members of Callum's pack circled up around me. I pictured Sora, long and lean, her familiar face devoid of emotion. I pictured myself just standing there, heart pounding, knowing that if I fought back, I might die.

I remembered letting her break my ribs and bloody my lips, blacken my eyes and strip away every illusion I'd ever had that they were my family, that I was theirs.

"No." I opened my eyes. I wasn't going to do this. There was no sense in opening up old wounds when Shay would be calling a meeting of the Senate later today. This wasn't the time for me to be feeling anything that might remind the other alphas of what I was.

Or, more to the point, of what I wasn't.

"Sooner or later," Jed said, opening his own eyes, "you get to the point where you know fear the way you know a lover. You know what it smells like. What it tastes like. How it feels."

Listening to Jed use the words *lover* and *taste* in close proximity to each other was flat-out disturbing. His voice was dark and almost tender, and I just didn't want to go there—on so many levels.

"You memorize that feeling, Bryn, and you build a place for it in your mind. You keep it under lock and key, and when you need to . . ." Jed's pupils pulsed, and an instant later, he was behind me, his arm wrapped around my throat, crushing my windpipe and cutting off the flow of air.

"When you need to," Jed repeated, "you let the dark things out."

He dropped his hold on me before my own power could flare up, and then he took a step backward, his palms upturned, unthreatening. I took that to mean that the lesson was over. He'd made his point. I'd felt the power come over him, an instant before he'd rushed me—stronger, faster, and more sure of his movements than he would have been without it.

For a second, I let myself think of the way fear tasted—like sweat, like metal, like blood.

"It might take some practice, and it might take some time, but you'll get there, sooner or later." Jed ran one hand over the stubble on his chin. "Then again, what do I know? I'm just an old man."

Yeah. And a saber-toothed tiger was just a kitty.

"Caroline!" Jed's scarred face lit up as he said her name. Warily, I followed his gaze over my left shoulder. Sure enough, the Wayfarer's resident assassin was standing there, her blue eyes narrowed at Jed, like she hadn't expected him to clue me in to the fact that she was there.

"Going running?" Jed asked her.

Caroline nodded, her gaze—sharp and guarded—shifting over to me.

Jed cleared his throat. "What do you say, Bryn?" he said, suddenly sounding inept and awkward and old. "You feel like a run?"

I stared at him, trying to decide whether or not he was seriously suggesting that the two of us play running buddies, like we'd never wished each other dead.

"I can run by myself," Caroline interjected. "In fact, I prefer it." She sent Jed a mutinous look that told me he'd be hearing about this later.

Jed, however, was not easily deterred. "It will make Ali happy," he said, playing his trump card. "Won't it?"

I didn't answer his facetious question. Instead, disgruntled, I turned to Caroline. "You'd better be able to keep up," I told her.

She arched one blonde eyebrow at me. "Big words, wolf girl."

She took off running. I took off after her, pushing down all of the memories my session with Jed had called up and banishing my gut reaction to them—the one that said if and when I let the dark things out, there was no guarantee I'd ever be able to put them back.

CHAPTER SIX

◦—◦

CAROLINE AND I DIDN'T SAY TWO WORDS TO EACH other on our run, but at least she kept up. By the time we'd finished and I'd made my way home, I wanted nothing more than to fall back into bed.

You! You! You! Not Pack, you. Want play? Want play?

The voice in my mind didn't belong to someone who was deliberately trying to talk to me, and I certainly hadn't gone looking for anyone else's thoughts, but the littlest members of my pack could never quite contain themselves. Their thoughts—such as they were—were always at the surface of their minds, spilling through the pack-bond whenever I was in range.

Down. Up, down! You!

The content of Kaitlin's thoughts told me that she was in wolf form, playing. Or, more specifically, play-fighting. I didn't realize until I opened the front door and walked into the living that the person she was playing *with* was Callum. He was sitting cross-legged on the carpet. Even that low to the ground, there was still a weight to his presence, a power I never would have noticed before I was an alpha myself.

A power that my baby sister—not quite a baby any longer—gave very little heed as she bobbed up and down on her front paws, lowering her head with a loopy, lupine grin. A second after I came into the room, she pounced on Callum's feet.

He bobbed his own head and reached out to gently tussle her from one side to another.

You! You play! Katie was ecstatic. Out loud, she made a sound that could only be described as a baby growl, and I felt a sudden stab of loneliness—because I was Katie's alpha, and she was playing with *Callum*, because he was Callum, and there was nothing playful between the two of us now.

Bryn? Katie whirled around, feeling my presence as safety and warmth. She came bounding over to my feet and immediately bit my sock, pulling me toward Callum.

No, Katie, I said softly. *You go. You play.*

She cocked her head to the side. *Bryn play?*

Later, I told her. *Bryn play later.*

Satisfied, Katie turned her attention back to Callum. In blatantly unstealthy fashion, she leapt toward him.

Out of habit, I scanned the room for Alex. Where one of Ali's twins went, the other followed. I found him standing in the shadows, intently watching Katie, like a bodyguard keeping an eye on a particularly troublesome client. On the other side of the pack-bond, his mind was steeped in the sensation of togetherness and love and warmth, the way I felt when the pack went for a midnight run.

Alex was here, and Katie was here, and that was all either one of them needed to know that things were right in the world.

Crossing the room, I picked Alex up and settled him on my hip. He snuggled into me, but never stopped watching his twin doing her very best to coax Callum into a full-on wrestling match.

"Rrrrrrrr." Katie issued a particularly fierce baby growl. A few seconds later, my foster mother appeared in the doorway, and I crossed the room to stand beside her. Out of habit, I handed Alex off. Ali took him from me and slipped her free arm around my waist. It was an affectionate gesture, but it also sent a message. Callum might have been the one who'd asked Ali to raise me, but Ali was reminding him that I was *her* daughter and that she would never fully trust him again—not with me, not with Katie, not with Alex.

Not after what Callum had ordered Sora to do to me.

On Ali's other side, her four-year-old shadow—who'd followed her into the room—got tired of waiting for the rest of us to acknowledge her presence.

"Katie," Lily said loudly, "you come over here." She narrowed her little green eyes. "You play with *us*."

When Katie did not heed Lily's "suggestion," Lily walked right up to Callum and kicked him in the shin.

"Lily!" Ali sounded horrified—and horribly, horribly amused. For my part, I was stunned. Lily was all of four years old, and Callum was the most powerful werewolf on the continent. Play fighting with him was one thing, but an actual assault?

I waited to see how Callum would respond, but he just turned slightly, deferring the situation to me.

"Lily," I said calmly. "Come here, please." She seemed to be considering whether or not she could get another kick in first.

Now, I added silently.

She came. But she wasn't happy about it, and as she raised her arms imperiously upward, I caught a hint of a smile tugging at the corners of Callum's mouth.

I picked Lily up, wishing she were a tiny bit less sturdy.

"Sorry about that," I told Callum. "She's four."

In most packs, children were a rarity—prized, protected, precious. There wasn't a werewolf alive who would have retaliated against a pup—let alone a female one—no matter what she did, but it still probably wasn't a good idea for Lily to get the impression that she could shin-kick werewolves ten times her size with impunity.

That could have gone badly, I told her.

Lily hunched her shoulders, ever so slightly. "What if I just kicked him a little bit?" she asked, not bothering to send the question through the pack-bond.

Beside me, Ali choked on laughter.

"You are not helping," I told her.

She grinned. For all I knew, maybe she'd put Lily up to it.

No kicking someone who could eat you in two bites, I told Lily. *Not even a little.*

She furrowed her brow, and a flurry of thoughts crossed from her mind to mine, all of which could be summarized as follows:

I was her alpha—not Callum.

This was our home—not his.

And Katie should have been paying attention to *her.*

Luckily, for everyone involved, Katie got tired of play fighting and picked that exact moment to change back to human form. Naked as a jaybird, she gave Callum a toothy grin and streaked out of the room. With the little streaker's twin still balanced on her hip, Ali took off after her. Ordering Lily to behave, I set her down, and she followed on their heels, leaving me alone with Callum.

There was so much unspoken in the air between us that I didn't know where to start, or if I wanted to start at all. This was the first time it had been just Callum and me since he'd promised to end my human life.

"Ali said you went to see one of the psychics who lives here. A Resilient?" Callum was the one to break the silence. He did a good job of sounding politely curious, but I spoke Callumese well enough to know that polite was always a cover for something else.

"I did," I replied, not offering any more than that. If Callum wanted to know what Jed and I had been doing, he could ask. Just like I could theoretically ask him why he'd waited so long to Change me—why he was *still* waiting—when every day I was human was a day my pack was more at risk than it would be if I were a Were. He'd told me, the day he'd made the promise, that I had some human time left and he didn't want me wishing it away, but if there was one person in the world who should have understood that, human or not, my life wasn't ever going to be normal, it was Callum. If anyone could understand that what I wanted, what I was scared of, who I loved didn't matter—it was Callum.

"Why?" I asked him finally, not putting any more of the question into words than that.

"Because," he replied, rising to his feet and heading for the door. "You need to be human for this."

This?

In the kitchen, the phone rang. Callum tilted his head to the side. "Shay," he said. "For you."

I had no choice but to answer the phone. To ignore the oily condescension in Shay's voice, the undertones, the fact that he'd tried to kill me—indirectly, of course—more than once. I stayed in control. I calmly told Shay that he could count on my presence at the Senate meeting. I said the words *man-killer*, *rogue*, and *Rabid* like they were nothing.

But Shay wasn't the type to let things lie. "I'm looking forward to your, shall we say, *insight*," he said. He wanted me to know that no matter how calm I sounded, he was aware that this issue was personal to me.

"I don't know, Shay," I replied, refusing to take his bait. "I'd bet you know more about the kind of wolf that kills humans than just about anyone."

I could practically feel my words hit their target. Shay wasn't a Rabid. He wasn't out of control, he wasn't an exposure risk, but he *was* a killer—and I deeply suspected that he'd killed more humans than anyone on the Senate knew. Humans who weren't a threat to Shay's pack or the species, more broadly.

Humans like Caroline's father.

I doubted the Senate knew what Caroline and I had discovered—that Shay, unprovoked and in his right mind, had attacked and killed a psychic and exposed himself to the man's coven, with the intent of inciting their hatred against other werewolves. That knowledge was a card in my hand, and I needed Shay to know that I wouldn't hesitate to play it.

"I look forward to your arrival," Shay said, his voice as calm as mine. Still, in the silence that followed, I could practically *feel* him on the other side of the line, his eyes pulsing with bloodlust, hating Callum, hating me.

I said good-bye and hung up the phone.

Fear, Jed's voice suggested from somewhere in my memories, and for just a fraction of a second, I let myself smell it, taste it, feel it.

I let it usher in the red.

And then I let it go.

I turned back to the door, where Callum was standing. I wanted to ask him again why I had to stay human, when going to a Senate meeting in my current state was the equivalent of taunting a bull and drawing a big red target on my back.

But I didn't. Callum wouldn't have answered the question anyway, and I wasn't in the mood to let him tell me no.

"You did well," Callum said.

I accepted the compliment, but didn't dwell on it.

"We should get ready to go," I said, turning to leave. "We'll want to arrive in Shay's territory well before nightfall."

I'd made it halfway out of the room before Callum spoke again. "I know you have questions. I know that you want to know why I haven't Changed you yet."

Those words stopped me in my tracks.

"There are limits to what we are, Bryn. Humans grow. They age, they change, and they *learn*."

I didn't make a sound, didn't give any indication that I'd heard his words, though if he were listening for my breath, he might have realized it was caught in my throat.

"There are reasons, Bryn-girl," Callum said finally. "And the only one you'll be getting out of me is that, sometimes, it's hard to teach an old wolf new tricks."

CHAPTER SEVEN

HOURS—AND AN EXTENDED ROAD TRIP—LATER, I still hadn't made any sense of Callum's words.

WELCOME TO NORTH DAKOTA! The sign in front of me declared cheerfully. DISCOVER THE SPIRIT!

I glanced over at Devon. He held his hands artistically to the side and wiggled his fingers.

Jazz hands? I asked silently.

No, he corrected, jerking his head toward the sign. *Spirit fingers.*

I choked back a laugh. We were getting ready to cross into another pack's territory, and my second-in-command was making spirit fingers. I couldn't blame Dev for injecting some much-needed comic relief into the situation, especially since I knew he'd spent the past few hours thinking about the member of Callum's pack due to meet us here.

Sora. Callum's second-in-command. Devon's mother.

If Callum realized what the idea of seeing Sora again was doing to Devon, he gave no indication of it. Instead, he'd spent the drive here silent and still, his hands on the wheel and his gaze locked on to the road. I'd passed that same stretch of time playing Callum's cryptic statements over and over again.

It's hard to teach an old wolf new tricks. You need to be human for this.

This as in the things Jed was teaching me about being Resilient? Or *this* as in whatever was about to happen with Shay?

There are reasons, Callum had said. *Reasons,* plural, but he'd only given me one—not the whole story, never the whole story with him.

"After you, Bryn." Callum's voice brought me back to the task at hand. I glanced back up at the welcome sign and then stepped forward, out of Montana and across state lines. I expected to feel something as I crossed the border that separated Snake Bend territory from Cedar Ridge: an electric shock, a chill on the surface of my skin, nausea, power, *something*. But there was nothing, no indication that if it hadn't been for the Senate meeting, if Shay hadn't invited us into his territory, stepping over this invisible line would have been an act of war.

Shay wouldn't have forgiven my trespassing the way I had forgiven Callum's. He would have used it as an excuse to attack me. He would have killed me, and he would have enjoyed it.

"My turn." Dev crossed to join me. He bumped his shoulder against mine, a gesture of comfort and solidarity as old as our friendship. His presence beside me calmed the thoughts in my head, slowed the beating of my heart, but as I glanced back over the border—at *our* land, *our* territory, *our* home—I felt a sliver of unease take root in my gut.

Leaving my pack behind felt wrong. Taking Devon with me felt worse. If I couldn't be there to protect them, he should have been. Without the two of us, they were vulnerable, open to attack.

"They're safe, Bryn," Callum said, from the other side of the border. Even without any actual psychic connection between the two of us, he could still read me like a book.

"Are you sure?" I couldn't help the question, because *I* had to be sure.

A change fell over Callum's face. His pupils didn't pulse, but looking at them was suddenly like staring into a bottomless cavern, knowing in the pit of your stomach that something was staring back.

"The day someone takes advantage of a Senate meeting," Callum said, his voice a perfect match for the power in his eyes, "is the day there's no Senate."

This was Callum the alpha speaking. This, my pack-sense told me, was real power—unimaginable, ancient power. Twin instincts battled in my gut—one that wanted nothing more than to offer up my throat and one that wanted me to fight for what was mine, what Callum could have taken from me, from all of us, if he'd been a different man.

Then, as suddenly as the power had started spilling off

Callum, it was gone, and he was just Callum again. The hint he'd shown us of his true power receded, and he strolled across the border looking unassuming and unaware.

Try unbelievable, I thought, but there was comfort to being reminded of who and what Callum really was.

Shay could be snide. He could gouge open old wounds and try to intimidate me, he could maneuver and manipulate and try to give me enough rope to hang myself—but I didn't have to oblige, and at the end of the day, unless Shay wanted to face Callum one-on-one, he'd play by the rules.

If there was one thing in this world that Callum would go to war over, it was me.

"Looks like Shay has moved his pack closer to the border," Callum commented, as he stepped forward. I followed, and a slight breeze caught my hair. As the three of us went farther and farther into Shay's territory, my alpha senses were flooded with power.

"We're not the first ones here," I said.

Callum confirmed my observation. "Knowing Shay, we're probably the last."

Not so long ago, Callum had hinted that the other alphas were forming alliances. I doubted Shay inviting the rest of the Senate into his territory before us boded well. Werewolves weren't designed for democracy. The instinct to dominate was always there, and the moment the Senate imploded, there would be blood.

"Callum." Sora announced her presence—a courtesy meant more for my benefit than the others'. My senses were good, but hers were better, and outside of my own territory, my pack-sense didn't react the same way to foreign wolves.

Here, we were the foreign ones.

That thought distracted me enough that I didn't have to give Sora my full attention. I didn't have to remember playing at her house, eating dinner at her table, sleeping doubled up with Devon in a tiny twin bed. I didn't have to hear the sound of her fist plowing into my face or feel my ribs pop, all over again.

But beside me, Devon couldn't think of anything else. He hadn't seen or spoken to his mother since that day, and coming face to face with her now cut him deep. Without a word, I took a step sideways, until my shoulder was touching his, a reminder that right here, right now, I was fine. I was solid, I was whole, and Sora wasn't a threat to either of us.

In fact, next to Callum, she was probably the closest thing to an ally we had.

"Devon." Sora met her son's eyes, and I could practically see her wanting to reach out and touch his face. Luckily for her, she managed to restrain herself. "It's good to see you, Dev."

"Likewise," Devon replied blithely, but I could tell by the way Sora's nostrils flared that she smelled the lie.

Sora looked at me. "Bryn."

I didn't reply, unsure what I could say that wouldn't just fan the flames. On some level, I knew it wasn't logical to hold Sora responsible for something Callum had ordered her to do. It made no sense that I could ride in a car with him, but couldn't stop the rush of emotion I felt just looking at her. Werewolves didn't have a choice about obeying their alphas—not unless they were strong enough mentally to go alpha themselves. That was how I'd killed Lucas. I'd ordered him to die.

But Sora hadn't even *tried* to fight Callum's order. She hadn't hesitated, hadn't shown even a fraction of regret. Fair or not, it was her face I'd seen in my nightmares right after it had happened. No amount of conceptual understanding about the role that moment had played in setting up everything that had followed could change that. My body knew her. It knew what she had done to me, and "logic" didn't stand a chance at over-riding a thing like that.

For a few brief seconds after she said my name, I took Jed's advice and let myself remember: the smell, the taste, the over-whelming darkness. Then I pushed it back behind lock and key, my jaw set, my mind empty.

"Hello, Sora." It was easy to say—surprisingly so. I wasn't that girl anymore, and I wasn't afraid.

"You've seen Shay?" Callum asked. The idea that his second-in-command would have been to see Shay without him was nearly unthinkable, until I recalled the obvious: in addition to being Callum's second, Sora was also Shay's mother.

She'd given birth to him. She'd raised him, same as Dev.

"I have," Sora replied. "And, no, I don't have any idea what he's up to, but there's something. There always is."

There wasn't any particular condemnation in Sora's voice, and it occurred to me that maybe I wasn't the only reason Devon was no longer on speaking terms with his mother. Parental expectations could be killer, and Devon's brother had transferred into the Snake Bend Pack and challenged its former alpha when he wasn't all that much older than Dev was now.

The last time I'd spoken to Sora, she'd talked about Devon's potential and what he was meant to be—none of which had anything to do with *who* Devon was. As a purebred werewolf—a rarity in our world, since female Weres were few and far between—Devon was bigger, stronger, and more dominant than most, and Callum had groomed him almost as much as he'd shaped me.

But Devon would never be Shay, and while I thanked God for that fact, I wasn't entirely certain that Sora wouldn't have preferred it if he were.

"We should go," Callum said, stepping between Sora and Devon—between Sora and me. "Shay will have felt our arrival, and I wouldn't put it past him to send out a welcome party."

I wouldn't put anything past Shay.

I'll take dysfunctional families for five thousand, Alex. Devon's voice was bright and sardonic in my mind.

I swallowed a laugh. *Seriously, Dev, are you okay?*

Peachy, Dev replied. *You?*

Almost of their own volition, my shoulders pushed themselves backward. My chin went out, and as a sense of detached calm flooded my body, I told Devon exactly what he wanted to hear.

I was ready for this. If Shay wanted to dance, I'd dance.

CHAPTER EIGHT

Shay obviously hadn't been living at this end of his territory for long. The smell of his pack should have been thick in the air. The trees, the grass, the very earth should have absorbed it like soot or smog, but instead, I could make out only the scents of the wolves present. Devon, whose nose was infinitely better than mine, didn't seem to be able to smell much more than that, at least according to what I could pick up through the bond.

Consider me an open book. Dev must have caught me looking at him, because he sent the message straight from his mind to mine. *Mi casa es su casa. Mi nose es su nose.*

Dev was the only wolf in my pack who could choose to completely block his mind from me. We both knew that was a good indication that someday, he might leave the Cedar Ridge Pack to rule his own, but tonight he was telling me—in his own oh-so-Devon way—that there weren't going to be any barriers. I was at a distinct disadvantage, with my human nose and my human ears, in the company of men who had senses ten times as keen.

Devon—strong, solid, sensational Devon—would be my eyes and my ears and my nose.

You're the best, Dev.

If we hadn't been quickly approaching a variety of wolves from other packs, he might have preened. Instead, the expression on his face stayed carefully neutral.

To our left, Callum and Sora held back, allowing Dev and me to enter first. There were fifteen, maybe twenty men spread out on the field in front of Shay's house, none close enough to touch another. Some were smiling politely. Some were playing human. But the two closest to us didn't bother to mask what they were: the weight to their presence, the unearthly grace in the way they moved, the hint of fang in what a regular human girl might have mistaken for a grin.

Those weren't grins, and these men weren't our friends.

They're from the Ash Mountain Pack, Devon told me silently, and I let his senses flood my mind. These men smelled like wild grass and charcoal and dirt. To another person, it might have been a pleasant enough smell, but to Devon—and by extension, to me—it was tinged with something rotten, something sour.

Not Pack. My pack-sense and subconscious were equally sure of that fact. The Ash Mountain alpha and his second-in-command were foreign. They had no allegiance to me or mine. They were a threat.

"Hello, girl." Of the two men, one looked vaguely familiar,

and he was the one who spoke. The last time I'd seen him had been the day I'd become an alpha myself, but his tone left little doubt that he didn't consider me his equal.

I schooled my features into an expression I'd seen on Callum's face a hundred thousand times, one that gave away nothing to what lay underneath. I didn't respond to the fact that the man had called me *girl* or the implicit *little* his sneer had tacked on to the front of that word. I didn't avoid his gaze, but I didn't force him into a staring contest, either.

If these men wanted to be condescending, I couldn't stop them, but if they were looking for a response, they weren't going to get one.

"Hello." My lips quirked their way into a subtle smile. I may not have had Callum's knack, but I knew these men. Not personally. Not by name. But I'd known plenty of men just like them, and it was a good bet that they had never, ever known a person like me.

"You remember Devon," I said politely. Beside me, Devon inclined his head in greeting.

"Charmed, I'm sure," he said, but I doubted anyone else caught the mischievous glint in his eye. The Ash Mountain alpha—and the others, spread out behind him—were too caught up assessing my best friend's size, the way he'd filled out, the power that told them that someday—not too far in the future—he'd be a physical match for anyone here.

Suddenly, their collective gaze shifted from Devon and me to a place just over my left shoulder.

Callum.

He'd hung back, letting me make my own first impressions, letting the others see how Devon had grown, how effortlessly I commanded his loyalty, how I carried myself as their equal in every conceivable way—but from the moment Callum stepped out of the shadows, the other alphas only had eyes for him. Physically, Callum wasn't the most imposing man here, and he made no move to make himself seem bigger. He didn't puff up his chest. He didn't raise his chin. His face was relaxed. His arms hung loose by his side.

"Hello, William," he said, greeting the Ash Mountain alpha and then letting his gaze roam out to the rest of them, standing there watching us.

Watching him.

"Callum," the alpha who'd been taking measure of my mettle returned, his eyes narrowed, his chin jutting out.

"You'll want to be careful of your new neighbors," Callum said, meeting the other man's eyes. "They enjoy hunting and don't pay much mind to property lines."

I realized, belatedly, that Callum was talking about human neighbors, and that the words were meant as a friendly warning about a future the Ash Mountain Pack would most likely wish to avoid.

"I'll take that under advisement," William replied, his even voice at odds with the tension suddenly visible in his neck.

Callum didn't wait for a thank-you. He wasn't expecting one, and he didn't act like anything extraordinary had just passed between the two of them, because to Callum, it wasn't extraordinary. Seeing the different ways the future could play out was as natural to him as breathing—but to everyone else present, Callum's casual words were a reminder and a warning.

Whatever they did, whatever they had planned, whatever they even thought of doing—he'd know it.

"Glad to see you made it."

Shay's voice was louder than it needed to be, surrounded by people with enhanced senses, but as he strode through the crowd, toward Callum—and me—I got the impression that wasn't an accident. This was his rodeo, and he wasn't ceding the spotlight to Callum.

And they say I'm *melodramatic,* Dev commented, with a mental roll of his eyes. Despite the levity in his words, I could feel a change in my friend as Shay approached—like every muscle in Devon's body was hardening to stone.

Like his heart was hardening, too.

"Little brother." Shay came to a stop directly in front of Devon, and I realized that Devon had grown since the last time I'd seen the two of them next to each other.

He wasn't exactly the "little" brother anymore.

Devon didn't reply to Shay's greeting. Instead, he turned his head slightly, deferring to me and declaring for everyone present that I was his alpha and not the other way around.

I was probably the only person present who realized that Devon's deferral had less to do with forcing Shay to acknowledge my status, and more to do with the fact that there was something inside Devon that he couldn't afford to let out. He wasn't about to engage Shay, because right here, right now, with adrenaline high and the collective power of the alphas in the air, Devon had a fragile hold on the desire to introduce his fists to Shay's jaw.

As wild and feral and vicious as the undercurrent of power all around us was, violence wasn't an option. The men in the Senate had chosen to play by certain rules, and Devon knew them as well as I did.

Within a given pack, a person could challenge the alpha for dominance, but inter-pack aggression wasn't allowed. Unless Shay transgressed first, Dev couldn't take a swing at him—not without bringing the wrath of the Senate down on our entire pack. That was the reason Shay couldn't kill me outright.

The reason he'd sent other people—first the psychics and then Lucas—to do his dirty work.

"Hello, Shay." I stepped in between Devon and his brother. "Long time no see."

The glint in Shay's eyes told me beyond a shadow of a doubt that he had never expected me to survive Lucas's challenge. He'd known I would accept the abused boy into my pack, and that as a member of my pack, Lucas would be able to do what Shay could not.

Challenge me.

I was a human, and Lucas was a Were. In a fight to the death, I shouldn't have stood a chance. And yet, there I was. Alive. Shay had to have been wondering how.

Maybe they all were.

"Bryn." From the way Shay said it, you would have thought it was a dirty word. "So glad you could make it."

Like I'd had any other option. This was just Shay's way of suggesting that my attendance here was a farce—that I wasn't really an alpha and didn't have the right to stand side by side with these men.

"Oh, Shay," I said, like he was a child, one I had some level of fondness for. "I wouldn't have missed it for the world."

A muscle in Shay's jaw tensed. I could get under his skin just as easily as he could get under mine.

"You said there was a problem that needed to be addressed, Shay." Callum's voice carried, even when he made no attempt whatsoever to make it do so. "Perhaps we should head inside to discuss?"

Callum's suggestion was every bit as pointed as my response to Shay's taunts, a reminder to everyone present that the Snake Bend alpha wasn't calling the shots, that, officially, all of the alphas were on an even footing.

And that, unofficially, it wasn't even close.

"Of course," Shay said tightly, before turning his attention back to me. "I'm afraid you'll have to leave your protection out here, Bryn."

Referring to Devon as my protection was an insult, implying that I couldn't protect myself.

If Shay thought it was going to get a rise out of me, he was wrong. "Don't worry," I said. "I'm sure Devon can find some way to entertain himself."

Dev didn't miss a beat. Towering over everyone else there and looking every inch the werewolf warrior, he nodded austerely. "I've been considering teaching myself to juggle."

Biting back a smile, I took the first step forward toward Shay's house. Callum followed my lead, and a second later, all of the alphas were breaking off from their backup.

Alpha. Alpha. Alpha. I felt the call, heard it in the air all around us. These men were dominant. They were strong. And each and every one of them was pushing down the animal instinct to fight the others, the whisper telling them—and me—that there was only ever meant to be one.

Alpha.

If the power was this overwhelming outside, it was going to be unbearable with the entire Senate crammed into a single room, but I wasn't intimidated, wasn't frightened.

Something about this moment felt right. Like I belonged here. Like this was what I'd always been meant to do.

The last thing I saw, as we filed into Shay's house, was Devon and his mother watching us go, three feet between them, miles apart.

Game on.

CHAPTER NINE

SHAY'S LIVING ROOM WAS OPEN AND LARGE, BUT where Callum's house was made of stone and wood, Shay's seemed to be all glass and steel: cold and sleek, with sharp edges everywhere you looked. Instead of arranging the furniture around a central hearth, the room boasted a larger-than-life conference table.

In a show of restraint, Shay didn't seat himself at the head of the table. No one did. But from the moment a screen descended from the ceiling, it was clear that this was the Shay Show. If the performance outside had been aimed at making me feel like I didn't belong here, this room had been constructed to make the other alphas feel like artifacts of a different time—and to remind them that in the modern world, exposure wasn't a minor threat. It couldn't be quarantined or contained.

"These images have already made their way to the internet."

Shay clicked through a series of crime scene photos, each more ghastly than the last.

"Luckily, both local authorities and the person responsible

for leaking these pictures seem to believe this is an isolated incident."

Shay paused, and in the space between his words, I could hear the beating of my own heart. The sound of it—and the picture on the screen, blood spread across white walls, like someone had been finger painting with it—made me dizzy, almost nauseous.

"Local authorities are wrong."

This time, when Shay clicked over to the next slide, the images weren't crime scene photos, but they were just as bloody. Just as gruesome.

"These were taken last week, just outside of the southern-most portion of Snake Bend territory and just north of the Arkansas state line."

Years of geography lessons—the kind regular girls never had to take—came pouring back into my mind. The Snake Bend territory reached from North Dakota over to Minnesota, and then down through Iowa and most of Missouri. The Delta Hills Pack had most of Arkansas, Louisiana, Mississippi, and Alabama—but there was an area between the southern tip of Snake Bend and the northern border of Delta Hills that didn't officially belong to either pack.

No-Man's-Land.

There were strips of land throughout the continent that fell to the same classification, places where geographical barriers and state lines didn't line up, or where history might have divided up territories in a way at odds with the present.

No-Man's-Land was the only option for wolves who didn't want to be associated with any pack—and sooner or later, most lone werewolves broke under the pressure of life alone and went Rabid.

"We're lucky that as of yet, Missouri and Wyoming officials are not talking to each other."

Was it my imagination, or did Shay's gaze rest on me a second too long when he said Wyoming? That was where Cedar Ridge territory met up with Stone River. And in between the two, there was another slice of No-Man's-Land.

One I knew all too well.

"You're sure this is the work of a rabid Were?" the Ash Mountain alpha asked. "The Wyoming attack could have been a human, albeit a disturbed one. And Missouri—looking at the body, there's no way to know that wasn't an animal."

I couldn't help staring at the photos, looking for differences. The victims were both decimated past all recognition. They had no faces, no extremities, no visible sign of having ever been a person with a name and a family and a future.

These people were dissected and torn to pieces and devoured, and while an animal might have managed it in the backwoods of southern Missouri, the Wyoming crime scene was indoors. Someone had opened the door to the house, and—it appeared—closed it after they left, but there were clear teeth marks in some of the wounds.

The jugular had been ripped out. The walls had been sprayed with blood, and then hands—human hands—had played in it.

This wasn't just a werewolf who had lost control. This was a monster who enjoyed the control he had over his victim, and whether or not the same person was responsible for the Missouri attack, there was a very good chance that whoever had killed the Wyoming victim was a Were.

Anger bubbled up inside of me, overriding my earlier nausea. Wyoming was near the edge of my territory. This was a threat to my peripherals, my pack, and that someone had chosen to do this so close to the place where the last Rabid had set up camp with his own victims—the kids who now looked to me for protection as members of the Cedar Ridge Pack—felt like a slap in the face.

Or possibly a warning.

"I don't see how this is a Senate matter." The alpha from Luna Mesa had an almost musical voice and a calm about him that made me wonder exactly how old he was. "Two attacks is not a pandemic. Let the local alphas investigate and deal with the situation. I'd venture to guess that neither you nor Callum needs our interference, Shay."

The words reminded me of something I'd known, but forgotten: the Senate wasn't called every time there was a Rabid. The reason Callum had called it the last time was because the man had been hunting across the country, in and out of different territories, for years. Plus he'd done something the others had thought next to impossible: created new Weres.

But one murder in Wyoming and one in Missouri? As graphic as they were, as horrific, the Luna Mesa alpha was right. That shouldn't have been a Senate affair. For a few moments, I thought that perhaps Shay was just trying to undermine Callum—and me. It even occurred to me that he might have sent someone to play Rabid in between our lands, but that didn't explain why he was claiming that a similar attack had happened near his territory, or what he was hoping to gain by going public with this information now.

Nothing could have prepared me for what Shay said next.

"Believe me, Arturo. This *is* a Senate affair." Shay took a seat, like the fight had drained out of him, but I knew better. The look in his eyes told me he was about to deliver a lethal blow—though to who or what, I wasn't sure.

Beside me, Callum looked straight ahead, staring at a fixed point in the distance. His facial expression never changed, but my stomach plummeted, and my heartbeat became audible once more.

Shay looked at me, only at me. "I have reason to believe that this Rabid is going to strike again. And I have reason to believe that she's female."

CHAPTER TEN

—⌒—

THE SILENCE FOLLOWING SHAY'S PROCLAMATION WAS deafening. The undercurrent of power in the room surged, unmistakable and violent. Muscles tensed. Pupils pulsed. The air, thick with unspoken emotion, was hot in my lungs. I felt like I might suffocate on the unbearable intensity of it all, and even though I'd known objectively that I was in a room full of people who weren't human and didn't live by human laws, the beasts inside them were much closer to the surface now.

Close enough that if even one of them Shifted, I could easily find myself in a room full of wolves.

"A female Rabid?" The alpha from Shadow Bluff—a man I knew only by reputation, one that said he had a habit of going through human wives like Kleenex—recovered first. "There's no such thing."

Just like there wasn't such a thing as a female alpha. Just like there was no such thing as a werewolf who was born human, but Changed.

"You can't honestly expect us to believe that a female

is responsible for this." That was from the Ash Mountain alpha—William. I didn't know whether to be insulted or flattered that he didn't think my sex was even remotely capable of committing this kind of violence.

"I think females are capable of many things." Shay let his eyes linger on my face, my body for a second too long. "Does anyone in this room doubt that my mother could kill? That she has killed?"

There wasn't an individual in the Senate who hadn't taken a life—myself included. Sora had been around for centuries—at least—and she was one of the most dominant wolves in the Stone River Pack.

There probably wasn't much she wasn't capable of.

"You're not suggesting that your mother is responsible for this." The Luna Mesa alpha—the one who'd challenged Shay to prove that this Rabid was Senate business at all—was incredulous. Of all of them, he seemed the least taken in by Shay's performance, the most skeptical.

"My mother," Shay said, glancing meaningfully at Callum, "is otherwise occupied. But this Rabid *is* female, and I think you'll all agree that complicates things."

That was putting it mildly. The standard operating procedure with Rabids—with the exception of the one who'd managed to bargain with the Senate—was immediate execution, brutal and absolute. But there wasn't a man in this room who would willingly kill a female werewolf. There were too few of them. Even with the addition of the six females in my pack who had been born human, there were fewer than two dozen female Weres in the country.

I wasn't sure Shay's pack had even one.

"What evidence do you have that our killer is female?" Callum asked. If he'd seen this turn of events coming, he gave no visible indication of it, but there was no surprise in his features, either.

Shay leaned forward and delivered the answer to Callum's question. "The police in Wyoming have a witness that puts a female between the ages of sixteen and twenty-one at the crime scene. No one knows where she came from or where she went, but there's an indication that she may have been living in the woods."

A female werewolf. Living by herself. In the unclaimed land between Callum's territory and my own.

No.

I didn't want to give purchase to the thought. I didn't want to consider that it might be possible. It *wasn't* possible.

"I trust that no one here is missing a female?"

At Shay's question, every single person in the room turned to look at me. More than a third of the female werewolves in the country were members of my pack, and if anyone else had been in possession of a female Were in that age range, they almost certainly would have kept her close to home.

"I'm not missing any wolves," I said firmly. I wasn't. My

pack only had twenty members, and each one was accounted for.

But Maddy...

Maddy wasn't.

"You have two peripheral females." Shay played those words like a trump card. All eyes were on me, and this time, I didn't just feel the power—I felt the *animosity*. The violent, animal rage that I had something they wanted. The suspicion that I might not be protecting that most valuable of resources.

The Ash Meadow alpha, the alpha from Flint Creek, Shay—none of them would have let a female live on the edges of their territories. None of them would have given her that kind of freedom. Even Callum had probably only let Lake live in Montana when she was a part of his pack because her father lived there, too.

"The Cedar Ridge Pack has two peripheral females," I said, my voice steely and utterly unapologetic. "And I know exactly where they are. At all times. Always."

Not because they were female. Because they were Pack.

"Phoebe and Sage haven't been anywhere near Wyoming," I said, allowing the others to smell the truth in my words. What I didn't say was that Maddy could have been there, and I wouldn't have known it. She'd broken off from the pack, and I'd willingly withdrawn my mind from hers. I had no idea where she was, or what she was doing, or if she was even okay. She certainly hadn't been okay when she'd left. She'd been heartbroken and bowled over by grief and angry—at me, at Lucas, at herself.

And I'd let her go.

I couldn't let myself think about that, couldn't risk a tell working its way onto my face. Unless Shay specifically mentioned Maddy, I could answer his questions in a way that would smell true to the other alphas, without giving a hint to the fact that I knew more than I was letting on.

I just had to bank on the likelihood that none of the others, Callum included, would ask if I'd withdrawn my claim to one of the females in my pack. I had to hope that none of the men in this room would consider that possibility, because they never would have entertained the idea themselves.

Most alphas didn't even like losing males. The larger a pack, the stronger the alpha, and werewolves weren't naturally inclined to make themselves weak.

"If you deny that one of your wolves is responsible," Shay told me, lingering on the word *if*, "then we have to consider the possibility that Samuel Wilson may have Changed at least one additional female of whom we had no knowledge up to this point."

Samuel Wilson. I'd never even heard his first name before. In my mind, he'd always been "the Rabid," the monster who had killed my parents and haunted my dreams. But now, we were dealing with another Rabid, and the monster from my nightmares had a name.

"You think Wilson made another female Were?" the Flint Creek alpha asked, his eyes alight with hunger.

"So it would seem," Shay replied.

I wanted to latch on to the possibility—wanted to ignore the reality that Maddy was missing, and a female had turned up in the middle of a murder investigation in a place she might well have gone. But I knew my pack. I'd been in their heads, and they'd lived with good old *Samuel Wilson* for years. He'd been power hungry, abusive, psychotic. He wouldn't have let a female wander away from the fold any more than Shay would have.

That meant that if there really was a female Rabid, in all likelihood, it wasn't some unknown girl, who'd never had a pack. It was—

No.

I wasn't going there. Not here. Not now.

"And if there is a new Were out there on her own?" Callum met Shay's eyes, and though there was nothing aggressive in the motion, I could see Shay actively fighting the urge to turn away.

"If there's another female," Shay said, his voice a whisper that cut through the air like a snake through the bushes, "a *lone* female, then there's a question of what's to be done about it."

The Ash Mountain alpha was the first to catch on. "It goes without saying that we can't kill her, Rabid or not. But if she's out there, without a pack, it's our duty to offer her *protection* and *guidance*."

I didn't know which was more sickening—the way he said the words, or the expression on his face.

"If there is a female Rabid in Wyoming, she's between Callum's territory and Bryn's." The Luna Mesa alpha was the first one to actually say my name at this little meeting, the first one to openly acknowledge that I had territory, that I was one of them.

"Are you suggesting that we give this girl to Callum or Bryn?" Shay's counter caused a rumble of discontent to pass through the room—audible and animalistic.

Threat.

It was there, in the air, and there was no mistaking the fact that it was aimed at me.

"Shay's right."

Those two words should never have exited Callum's mouth. Under any circumstances. Ever. Silence fell on the room once more, and the sinister edge in the air receded, like a wave being pulled by the undertow back to sea.

"There's no reason that either Bryn or I should have special privilege here. If there's a female, and if she's unclaimed, Senate Law says that whoever gets to her first is free to claim her." Callum leaned back in his seat, in a motion that looked almost human, but not quite. "Of course, Senate Law also says that neither Bryn nor I has to grant you access to our territories, and I'm sure you'll understand, given the circumstances, if I'm reluctant to do so."

Callum wasn't claiming special privilege. He wasn't forcing his will on the rest of the Senate—but if this Rabid really was in Wyoming, even in No-Man's-Land, there were only a few ways to get there.

You could go through my territory.

You could go through Callum's.

Or you could go through a sliver of particularly rough terrain that belonged to Shadow Bluff.

"We don't know if she's still in Wyoming," Shay said, and I thought about the case in Missouri—the one that may have been the work of the same Rabid.

If it was Maddy, what was she doing that close to Snake Bend territory? How had she gotten there, without passing through a hostile alpha's land?

Stop it, I told myself, hating that I could even think a thing like that. Angry or not, grief stricken or not, alone or not— Maddy couldn't hurt another person.

She wouldn't kill someone.

Would she?

"It's entirely possible that the Rabid we're looking for is no longer in Wyoming," Callum said, "just like it's entirely possible that this whole thing is some kind of mistake, but I'm fairly certain, Shay, that if you thought there were a lone female anywhere near Snake Bend territory, this meeting would never have been called."

As subtle as the accusation was, it worked, and the rest of

the alphas fixed their weighty stares on Shay. The Snake Bend alpha hadn't called this meeting out of the goodness of his heart. He knew that this girl—if there really was a girl—wasn't within his reach, and he was hoping to change that, hoping to mobilize the Senate in a way that might give him access to this femme fatale.

"If this Rabid continues killing, if there's a threat of exposure..." Shay let his words hang in the air.

"This could become a Senate concern," the Flint Creek alpha finished.

If the risk of exposure was imminent, if the Senate felt that the local alpha or alphas weren't sufficiently dealing with the threat a Rabid posed, if this girl killed again and the authorities connected another murder to either of the first two...

Callum met my eyes across the table, and a wealth of understanding passed from his mind to mine. He would forbid the rest of the Senate entry to his land as an alpha, but if Shay could make a case that this girl was a real exposure risk, if the Senate voted to intervene, Callum would either have to cede to the vote or fight them all.

A year and a half ago, I would have wondered why he bothered with democracy when he could have taken control of it all by force, but now I knew. Without the Senate, Callum would have had to kill Shay. And William. And anyone else dominant enough that they would refuse to submit.

Sooner or later, Callum would have had to kill every man in

this room. And if I wasn't careful, he might have to kill me, too.

"If this girl becomes a real problem," Shay said, eyes glittering with a desire I didn't want to understand, "I'd like to bring a motion that the Senate intervene."

They were voting on a future that I hoped would never come to pass—but it was one that most of the men in this room would welcome. Forget the risk of exposure. They wanted a loophole, a legal reason to demand equal access to the person responsible for the corpses on the screen.

She's not a person to them, I thought. *She's not even a monster.*

This Rabid was a prize.

"The Flint Creek alpha votes in favor of this proposal."

"The Ash Mountain alpha votes in favor of this proposal."

"The Delta Hills alpha votes in favor of this proposal."

Callum and I voted against it, as did the Shadow Bluff alpha, who must have thought he stood a better chance at getting to the female through his land than he would if he—and every other alpha on the Senate—had leave to pass through ours. But as the rest of the votes came in, my stomach sank.

"The Snake Bend alpha votes in favor of this proposal." Shay was the last to vote. He smiled, a cat-eating-canary expression on his otherwise wolfish face. "Correct me if I'm wrong, gentlemen, but the proposal appears to have passed."

Even if I hadn't been concerned with what Shay and the other alphas might do if they caught the girl in question—*not Maddy, not Maddy, it couldn't be Maddy*—I couldn't run the risk of what might happen if they were given carte blanche to cut through my territory. Even if the other alphas stuck to the edges of my land and gave the Wayfarer a wide berth, I didn't trust the men in this room with the people closest to me.

With the kids in my pack. With the girls.

I locked eyes with Callum. If he'd seen this coming and hadn't told me, we were going to be having words. But either way, the two of us were aligned on one point: we needed to find this female before she became a real exposure risk.

Before the other alphas could invoke the vote that had just passed.

Before this Rabid— *not Maddy, not Maddy, please, God, don't let it be Maddy*—killed. Again.

CHAPTER ELEVEN

"WE HAVE NO WAY OF KNOWING IT'S MADDY."

Devon had been waiting to say those words since the moment I'd clued him in to Shay's big revelation, but he'd held off on even thinking them in my direction until we'd left the WELCOME TO NORTH DAKOTA! sign in our dust.

According to Senate Law, the rest of us could have remained in Shay's territory for another day, but I wasn't the only one who'd wanted to get out of there, fast. The Shadow Bluff alpha had left the second the meeting had ended. Several others followed on his heels—probably to make arrangements for my worst-case scenario and their best. Callum had lingered long enough to exchange words with the Luna Mesa alpha, but I hadn't been able to make out what they were saying or why it was important enough to delay what the two of us needed to be doing now.

Finding Maddy. Or Not-Maddy. Or whoever this female was.

It's not Maddy, Devon had told me, over and over again,

once we'd crossed state lines. *You know her, Bryn, and I know her.*

No matter how many times Devon said the words to me silently, I needed to hear him say it out loud. So when Callum stopped for gas, the two of us made our excuses and slipped out of earshot.

"We have no way of knowing it's Maddy." I repeated Devon's words, willing myself to believe them and unable to keep from saying the words that came out my mouth next. "But we have no way of knowing it's not."

The first time I'd ever seen Maddy, she was wearing a little-girl dress and speaking in a monotone. Her name was Madison, and she'd been the monster's favorite: his favorite punching bag, his favorite creation, his favorite little girl.

She was my age, and she'd already been through hell.

Of all the kids that Samuel Wilson had Changed, Maddy was the first one to throw off the mental bonds he'd used to control them. She was the first one to believe me when I told her that being Resilient meant that you could make your own choices about who to follow and who not to.

She was the one who'd chosen me. And after I'd killed Lucas, she'd chosen to leave.

If you force me to stay, she said, from somewhere in my memory, *I'll hate you.*

I tried not to think of the pain she'd been in, tried not to think about the way she'd looked at Lucas and seen herself.

79

Werewolves had a tendency to fall quickly, and Maddy had identified with Lucas, with the things he'd survived as a member of Shay's pack.

She'd loved him.

"Maddy's strong." Devon's voice broke into my thoughts. "She's a survivor, Bryn, and she would kill herself before hurting another human being."

I believed that, too. I did. But there was a problem with Devon's logic—Maddy *wasn't* a human being. She was a werewolf. A lone werewolf, broken down and beaten and alone.

Sooner or later, most lone wolves go Rabid. I kept a tight hold on the thought and didn't let it travel from my mind to Devon's.

When Maddy had left, I'd worried that another alpha might find her and try to claim her, but I hadn't thought about what it would be like for her, without the pack. I'd only thought of how horrible it was for us without her. She was a phantom limb, a missing piece, a yearning...

And she would have felt that—all of that tenfold.

"You two coming?" Sora called out, and I met Devon's eyes. If we could hear his mother, she could hear us. Good thing we'd been standing there for minutes in silence.

"Explain to me again why you granted that woman permission to step foot on Cedar Ridge land." Dev didn't raise his voice, but he didn't bother to lower it, either, and with werewolf hearing, there was no question that Sora would have heard it.

"Because Callum is our ride, and he asked."

Devon rolled his eyes. "Oh, really?" he said. "Callum *asked*?"

Actually, Callum had said it "might be a good idea" if Sora came with us. Personally, I'd thought it "might be a horrific idea," but then I'd noticed the way the other alphas and their seconds were looking at her and the way she was looking at them, and for the first time, I thought of what it must have been like to be Sora: the only woman among all these men, for years.

Then I said yes.

"Not only did Callum ask," I told Devon, "he said, 'pretty please.'"

Devon—and his nose—were unimpressed with that statement. "Liar."

"He said, 'pretty please with a cherry on top,'" I continued. "And now that I said yes, we're BFFs. He's going to make me a friendship bracelet and everything."

Devon tweaked the end of my ponytail. "You are a horrible liar."

Maybe—but I was very good at distracting people, including Devon, who didn't need to be ruminating on his relationship with Sora when we were all going to be stuck in the car together for another hour. Unfortunately, I wasn't nearly as good at distracting myself as I was at distracting other people. As Devon and I made our way back to the car, my mind went again to the dark place, to the thoughts I couldn't bear. If Jed had been there, he would have told me to let them in, so I did.

Human bodies, torn limb from limb.

Blood smeared against white walls.

Maddy.

Minutes went by, miles of travel, while I sat there, lost to images and possibilities and guilt.

"Did you know?" I said finally. My voice was quiet, but I was certain werewolf hearing would pick up on the words just fine, and confident that Callum would understand that the question was for him. "You said there was a Rabid. You never said she was female."

"I'm not omniscient, Bryn." Callum's voice was world-worn and weary, like he'd known the question was coming. "I can't see everything, and even if I could, I wouldn't be able to sort through it all."

"Did you know?" I repeated the question, because he hadn't answered it, not really.

In the front seat, there was silence, and then: "I knew there was a female involved. It honestly never occurred to me that she might be the Rabid."

For all the respect he afforded Sora—and me—Callum still thought like a Were. Females might not be sugar and spice, but they certainly weren't serial killers.

"Is she?" I forced the question out of my mouth. "The female you saw, is she rabid?"

Callum didn't give me an answer—though whether he was holding back or genuinely didn't know, I wasn't sure.

"Your other question," he said finally. "The one you haven't asked yet."

It was just like Callum to agree to answer a question I hadn't asked instead of the one I had, but at least this way, I didn't have to actually say the words.

Is it Maddy?

Callum met my eyes in the rearview mirror. "The answer is yes."

CHAPTER TWELVE

———

CALLUM PARKED THE CAR IN FRONT OF THE WAYFARER restaurant. I'd expected him to drop me off at the house, but given that Sora was with us, keeping our distance from Ali was probably a good idea.

I knew for a fact that my foster mother was an excellent shot.

"We have days, Bryn." Callum's voice was strained—just barely, but for him, that was the equivalent to cussing and screaming. "We have a week, if we're lucky. Every future I can find is coated in blood. I'll hold the other alphas off as long as I can, but you need to find her. Fast."

Her, as in *Maddy*.

Our Maddy. The Rabid.

"You're not going to look for her?" I asked, forcing myself to be calm, to not think about the pictures or the bodies or the way Maddy had looked—broken, but regal—last December, when she'd walked away. "You're just going to sit back and leave finding her to me?"

If the future was as dire as Callum was predicting, I

couldn't fathom why he wasn't going after Maddy himself.

"My staying out of it will give me more leverage with the others, and someone has to do damage control with the human authorities. Wherever the girl was before, she's gone now, and she won't want me to be the one to find her."

I was going to say that Maddy wouldn't want me to find her, either, that the whole point of her leaving was to get away from me, but Sora didn't give me a chance to speak.

"To catch a Rabid," she said, with a strange and quiet intensity in her voice, "you have to think like a Rabid. There's a dark logic to their thoughts. A hunger. If you can figure out what they're hungry for, you can find them."

Them, as in plural? Sora spoke like someone who'd spent a decent amount of time tracking down rabid werewolves. That shouldn't have surprised me, given that she had been there the day Callum had rescued me. Callum had been the one to pull me out from underneath the kitchen sink, but Sora was the one who'd fought Wilson.

Flashes of fur. White, gleaming fangs. Red eyes. Blood.

A warm hand on my shoulder brought me back to the present. Dev.

"Get inside her head, figure out what she's hungry for." Devon repeated his mother's words, pretending he didn't know what I'd been thinking, that the memories hadn't been written clearly on my face. "We can do that."

Sora glanced at Callum, then back at Devon. "She can do

that," Sora corrected, nodding her head at me. "Or I can. But, Devon, you'll be staying here."

I didn't remember taking a step forward, let alone four, but suddenly I was standing nose to nose with Sora, staring her down.

"That wasn't an order, Bryn-girl," Callum told me. "She's not telling your Devon what to do."

My Devon, my inner alpha echoed. *Mine*.

"The Senate meeting is over, and without the protections that provides, an alpha can't afford to leave his or her pack untended for long."

Callum's even words managed to penetrate the thud of possessiveness, protectiveness, rage in my brain.

I was the Cedar Ridge alpha. Dev was the most physically formidable person in our pack. If anything ever happened to me, he'd take over as alpha.

As much as I hated to admit it, Sora was right. Devon and I couldn't both go looking for Maddy—especially not when the other alphas might find reason to pass through our territory in a matter of days.

"I'll take Chase," I said, before Devon could object. "And Lake. You know they won't let anything happen to me, Dev, and if the other alphas end up passing through, Lake wouldn't want to be here anyway."

I wasn't going to say more than that—not to Dev, who knew Lake well enough to know that all the Senate Laws in the world didn't make her feel as safe as a loaded weapon did.

The last thing we needed was her shooting a foreign alpha.

"I should be there," Dev said, matching his mother's quiet intensity word for word. "With you. With Maddy. I should be there."

Hearing the way he said her name made me want to take him with me so badly that I could have screamed. Before Lucas, Maddy had been one of us. Not just one of the pack, but one of us. We'd been her family, her friends—

"The Cedar Ridge alpha would like to know if the Stone River alpha remembers that she applied no sanctions when he trespassed on her territory?" I felt like another person as those words slipped out of my mouth, like political Bryn was Dr. Jekyll—or possibly Mr. Hyde.

"I remember, Bryn."

Callum was resisting dealing with me on official terms, and I wasn't sure why. "If the Cedar Ridge alpha were to request sanctuary ..."

Callum put two fingers under my chin. He looked into my eyes, and I looked into his, unable to finish the sentence.

"I would give you sanctuary," he said. "I would take care of them as if they were my own. You know that."

I did. And if I could send the kids in my pack with Callum, back to Stone River, just for a little while, then Devon could come with me.

"But that cannot happen, Bryn-girl. Not with the other alphas coming through."

I took a step back, away from Callum's touch against my face.

"There's a reason you send Chase to run the perimeter of your territory, Bryn."

To check on the peripherals? Or because he would never be fully comfortable here? I wondered what Callum was getting at.

"Territory is only territory when it's occupied. Senate Law prevents trespassing, but if your pack abandons Cedar Ridge land, it won't be Cedar Ridge land anymore."

I thought of Chase running the border of our territory, of the peripherals spread out across the state, and then I thought of the way the pack gathered at the full moon, Shifting and running, overflowing with energy, at one with the woods and with each other.

The Wayfarer was *ours*. The land between Snake Bend and Stone River was *ours*. It smelled like us. It felt like home. But if the majority of the pack left, even for a little while, that could change.

Someone else could move in and take what was supposed to be ours, and we had less land than any other pack as it was.

So much for sending my pack with Callum and taking Devon with me.

Click.

The sound of bullets being chambered alerted me to the fact that we had an incoming visitor.

"You need to go." Caroline's eyes were locked on Sora's. How she'd gotten her body between Devon's mother's and mine without anyone hearing her approach, I did not know, but she had a gun in one hand and a crossbow in the other.

The gun was trained on Sora's temple, the crossbow on Callum's thigh.

"Caroline," I said, my voice dangerously pleasant. "Do you mind?"

"No," Caroline said, releasing the safety. "I don't."

"Caro, darling, as much of a Kodak moment as this absolutely is, pointing weapons at werewolves isn't something one does at close range." Devon was trying to be flippant, but neither one of us knew for sure how Callum or Sora would respond to the threat.

Neither one of us knew whether or not Caroline would pull the trigger.

"I take it you're Ali's sister?" Callum's look was measuring—but just cautious enough that I got the distinct impression even he couldn't be sure that Caroline wouldn't shoot.

"I don't know what you did to Ali," Caroline said, her voice barely more than a whisper, "but you're not going to do it again."

It took me a moment to realize that she was talking to Sora, not Callum. Sora and Ali had been friends once, before Sora had hurt me. Seeing her again would have affected Ali the same way it had affected me.

And Ali was the only family Caroline had left.

"Sora, get in the car."

That was the first time in a very long time that I'd heard

Callum give someone a direct order. A glimmer of surprise passed over Sora's face, but a second later, it was gone, and she turned to follow Callum's instruction.

Caroline tracked Sora's motion and took her eyes off Callum for half a second, but that was half a second too long. In a flash, both weapons were on the ground, and he was holding her very still, from behind.

"Devon's right," he said, a hint of an accent creeping into his words. "Shooting werewolves is a thing best done from a distance."

He leaned forward then, and whispered something into the back of Caroline's hair, something I couldn't hear that actually cracked the veneer of ice in the hunter's eyes. For a second, Caroline looked well and truly shaken. Vulnerable. Pissed.

Then Callum let her go. He turned and pressed a kiss to my forehead before beginning the walk back to his car. Halfway there, he paused and glanced out at the forest, at a large black wolf, keeping its distance, standing guard.

Chase.

I knew the moment I saw him standing there that the past day had been difficult for him. Shifted, his thoughts came to me as a mishmash of images and emotions, but I picked up on the fact that he'd stayed in wolf form the entire time I was gone. He hadn't said a word to any of the others, hadn't even seen them.

But now I was back, and so was he.

Callum glanced from Chase to me, taking in the way my body had oriented itself naturally toward the wolf in the distance, the way that even as Callum assessed us, Chase walked slowly toward me, pulled in like a planet orbiting the sun.

"I'm sorry," Callum said.

I couldn't tell which one of us he was talking to.

"Sorry for what?" I asked.

Callum gave me a look so tender, so familiar that I could feel tears burning in my eyes. "For something that might happen and might not."

I opened my mouth to ask another question, but the look on his face changed, his eyes narrowing and his eyebrows lifting in warning.

I knew Callum's This Subject Is Closed look better than anyone. I'd been raised on that look.

I'd never liked it.

"Find Maddy, Bryn." Callum turned back to his car, walking to join Sora in the front seat, continuing to talk as he did. "Before this is over, it's going to get bloody, and the longer she's out there alone, the worse it's going to be."

A few seconds later, he was gone, and Devon, Caroline, and I were standing in front of the restaurant in silence, Chase in wolf form at my side.

"Who *was* that?" Caroline said finally.

Devon glanced at the weapons on the ground and groaned. "Trust me, Caro. You don't want to know."

CHAPTER THIRTEEN

WORD TRAVELS FAST IN WEREWOLF PACKS. WITHIN THE hour, six of us sat around a circular table in the back room of the Wayfarer restaurant. Chase had Shifted back to human form; Devon had changed into a fresh and crisply ironed shirt. Lake was playing with empty bullet casings, rolling them around her fingertips in a motion halfway between juggling and twirling a baton. That just left Ali—who was sitting perfectly still, her hair pulled into a messy ponytail at the base of her neck and her hazel eyes unreadable—and Lake's dad, who was probably the only person at this table who had any personal experience in either Senate politics or tracking down Rabids.

"Here's what you need to know."

I laid the facts out for the others quickly and efficiently. I didn't stumble over Maddy's name, didn't let myself care or feel or hurt in any way.

Fact: there had been a murder near our territory that looked to be the work of a rabid werewolf.

Fact: a young girl fitting Maddy's description had been seen near the scene.

Fact: Callum had as good as said that she was involved in this up to her eyeballs.

Fact: if there was another attack, Shay and the rest of the alphas would use that as justification to come after Maddy themselves.

"We can't let that happen," I said. "I'll leave in the morning, head over to the site of the last murder. Lake and Chase are coming with me, but Devon's going to stay here." I flicked my eyes over to Lake's dad. "Mitch, I'd appreciate it if you did the same."

I could have made it an order, but Mitch had known me since I was a kid, and he and Ali were what I'd call *close*. If I was going to convince my foster mother that this was a good idea, I'd need his support, not just compliance.

"It might not be a bad idea to pull in the peripherals," Mitch commented, which I took to mean something along the lines of *why, yes, Bryn, I would be happy to stay here and help look after the pack in your absence.* "They'll be more at risk on the edges of the territory than they would be here."

"And," Devon added, "as feisty as the tween brigade is, it couldn't hurt to have a few more werewolves in residence who are at least close to full grown."

The majority of the members of our pack were between the ages of nine and thirteen. Despite the fact that I'd only been fifteen myself the first time I faced down the Senate, I couldn't help feeling the others were just kids, that they should get to stay that way as long as possible.

"They shouldn't know," I said, making eye contact with each person at the table, one after another. "You can tell the peripherals that we're going after Maddy, but the younger kids don't need to know where I'm going, or why."

They didn't need to know that a girl they'd looked up to and loved and missed like crazy might have become a monster.

I didn't need to know that.

Chase's hand worked its way into my palm, and he wove his fingers in between mine. I gripped his hand, pushing back the memory of the crime scene photos and the image my brain had conjured of Maddy in wolf form, tearing out the victim's throat.

"And if you get caught?" That was the first time Ali had actually spoken. "You can't exactly tell the local sheriff that he doesn't need to worry about tracking down this killer because you've got it under control. Three teenagers milling around a murder scene isn't exactly what I'd call inconspicuous, Bryn, and no matter what you are in the werewolf world, out there, you're just a kid."

I hated that Ali was playing the voice of reason and hated that she was right. Most of all, though, I hated that she acted like I didn't know the human world, like being part of the pack, heart and soul, had cost me my humanity already.

"We'll be careful," I said. I *did* know the meaning of the word *discretion*.

Sometimes.

"I'm good at not being seen," Chase told Ali quietly. "I always have been, and you know that I would never let anything happen to Bryn."

Lake looked on the verge of chiming in, but Ali didn't give her a chance.

"So we're just supposed to let you three go off on your own?" she asked.

I'd known this was coming. Mitch might have understood the rationale for my plan, but Ali didn't think like a werewolf. She thought like a mother. "Ali—"

I didn't get more than her name out of my mouth before she cut me off.

"I know, Bryn. Believe me, I know. Your life isn't normal. No matter how hard I try, it's never going to be normal, and I can't protect you from that. I can't protect you from anything, but you can't just expect me to be okay with the idea of you taking off for parts unknown to track down some kind of killer." She shoved her fingers roughly through her hair, a gesture of frustration I recognized all too well. "What if it's not Maddy?"

I'd spent so much effort trying not to obsess over the likelihood that Maddy had gone Rabid that I hadn't let myself really mull over the alternative, either.

"Callum said . . ."

"Callum," Ali said tersely, "never tells anyone more than half the story. You'll be lucky if you got a third, tops. He's not God, Bryn. He's fallible. He gets things wrong."

Right now we didn't have much else to go on.

Ali jabbed a finger at me. "All you know is that there's a killer who *might* be a werewolf, and there was a girl near the crime scene who *might* be Maddy. Even if the girl is Maddy and the killer is a werewolf, that doesn't mean they're one and the same, or that there's anything you can do about it if they are. So you'll have to forgive me if I don't like the idea of my daughter tromping through some crime scene like this is *CSI: Werewolf Nation*."

I waited a few seconds to make sure Ali was really done talking this time.

"I have to go," I said, softening the words as much as I could. "Callum said Maddy's involved, and he wouldn't lie to me, not about this. That means that either Maddy did this, in which case it's my responsibility to stop her, or somehow, it's all a big coincidence, in which case, we have no guarantee the killer won't turn around and start hunting Maddy next."

I willed Ali to understand.

"We can't just leave her out there alone. It's not right, Ali, and you know it."

She swore under her breath. Victory—but only a small one.

"I'm going with you."

Now it was my turn to glare at her. "What about Katie and Alex?" I asked. "You really want to leave them here alone?"

That was playing dirty, but I didn't care. Callum had said that things were going to get bloody, and there was a wolf out there hunting humans. I'd already lost one mother to a rabid werewolf. I wasn't going to lose Ali, too.

"Perhaps I can be of some assistance." Jed stepped into the room. I wondered how long he'd been listening.

Five minutes, Lake and Dev said at the exact same time.

"I'll go with them." Jed cut straight to the chase.

"You'll what?" Ali turned her mom glare from me to Jed.

"You don't want to send the kids off by themselves, but you're needed here." Jed leaned back against the wall, not coming any closer, as if he sensed he'd walked in on something so private it was almost sacrosanct.

"I've got experience with killers, and Caroline is the best tracker I've ever met. If anyone asks, I'll say they're all my grandkids and we're on summer vacation. People can't get too suspicious of four kids and an old man."

Caroline? Jed wanted us to take Caroline—who had been raised to kill werewolves—along on our hunt for the one Rabid we might *not* want to kill?

Didn't that sound like a fundamentally bad idea to anyone else?

Ali narrowed her eyes at Jed. "I don't like that Bryn has to do this, and I don't want to drag Caroline into it."

"Sitting here, doing nothing day after day, isn't any better for her. Caroline needs this, and you need me." Jed smiled, and for a second, I thought Ali might hit him. "If push comes to shove, I've got some contacts in law enforcement who might be able to get us out of a jam."

Ali's jaw twitched, but after a long moment, she nodded. "Fine," she said, "but you call me every night. Every single night."

It took me a second to realize that last statement was aimed at me.

"I'll call," I promised, and an instant later, she was beside me, hugging me so tightly, I couldn't breathe.

"If anything happens to you," Ali said, burying her face in my hair, "I'm never letting you out of the house again."

For a few seconds, I just let her hold me. I held on to her for dear life.

Then I straightened and pushed my hair roughly out of my eyes in a gesture I'd picked up from her. "You don't need to worry about me, Ali."

I might as well have been telling the wind not to blow. As I glanced around the table at the others, I was suddenly overcome with a horrible sense of premonition, one that told me that everything was changing, and that once we found Maddy, things might never be the same.

I'm sorry, Callum had told me.

You need to be human for this, he'd said.

But it was his other words that haunted me, as I looked from Ali to Devon to Lake to Chase.

Every future I can find is coated in blood.

CHAPTER FOURTEEN

~

THAT NIGHT, I COULDN'T SLEEP. WITH ALI IN MOM ON
the Rampage mode, I couldn't risk letting Chase sneak in the
window, and every time I closed my eyes, I saw bodies.

My parents.

The crime scene photos.

Lucas.

Fighting it, I listened for the sound of the twins sleeping
in the next room, and through the pack-bond, I felt the two of
them snuggled up together like pups in a litter. No matter how
many times Ali put them to sleep in separate beds, they always
ended up in one. Needing to see them, I crept out of my room
and into theirs.

Kaitlin's foot was resting lightly on Alex's cheek. His rump
was up in the air. When one of them moved, they both moved.
They were dreaming the same dream, *colors* and *sounds* and
running.

Ali's babies were safe and warm and happy, and I wanted
desperately to believe they could stay that way forever, that

Katie would never have to deal with the certainty Lake had lived with all her life, that she would never know what it was like to be looked at as a possession, a prize.

I wanted to believe that I would get to see them grow up. I wanted for their lives to be absolutely nothing like mine.

Giving in to the desire to be close to them, I climbed into their bed. Katie—in human form—yipped in her sleep, but didn't wake up. Alex snuggled in close to my right side. I let their thoughts override mine. I let their senses override mine.

I dreamed their dreams, and I slept.

I woke with the dawn to find two little faces curiously watching mine. Katie was sitting on my stomach. Alex was perched to one side.

"Whatcha doing?" Katie asked.

"Sleeping," I replied, closing my eyes.

Alex poked me in the side of my face with a damp and chubby hand. I half-expected him to say something, but no words accompanied the poke.

"You go 'way?" Katie asked, wriggling to get comfortable and elbowing me directly in the kidneys. "Mama's sad."

I gave up trying to sleep and opened my eyes.

"Big sister has to go away for a little while," I said. "You two have to take good care of Mama while I'm gone. Okay?"

Alex nodded solemnly. Katie screwed up her face until her little baby forehead was as wrinkled as a Shar Pei's. "Why?"

I wasn't sure if she was asking why I was leaving or why I wanted her to go easy on Ali while I was gone. Given that *why* was my sister's favorite question, it was probably both. I took the easy way out and didn't answer. Instead, I blew a stream of breath out onto her face, and she huffed back.

I was her alpha, and she was my girl.

Peeling myself out of bed, I managed to detach the little barnacles from my side. They ran ahead of me into the kitchen, where Ali was already making breakfast.

"Sit," she said.

I sat.

She placed a plate of food in front of me.

"Eat."

Ali couldn't protect me. She couldn't keep me here or give me the life she wanted for me, but she could feed me.

Wisely, I ate.

"You slept in the twins' room last night?" Asking questions she already knew the answers to was Ali's way of demonstrably *not* prying.

Yeah, right.

"I had a lot on my mind. They keep things simple."

As if to corroborate my statement, Katie knocked over her glass of milk and started screaming like an irate banshee.

Without missing a beat, Ali flipped into triage mode,

sopping up the milk and distracting Katie from her tantrum. "It's not your fault."

At first, I thought she was talking to Katie, but then I realized the comment was aimed at me.

"I know you, Bryn. I know what you're thinking, but what happened with Maddy wasn't your fault."

Ali and I had never talked about Maddy's leaving. We'd never openly acknowledged what Lucas had done, or the way I'd been forced to fight back.

"I killed him," I said, staring down at my plate. "I killed him, knowing what it would do to her."

For a long time, Ali didn't say anything. I wanted her to tell me that I hadn't had a choice, that if I'd let a challenge go unanswered, I would have been opening the pack up to more, but after all these years of living among werewolves, Ali still didn't think like one.

She wasn't thinking about the pack.

"You killed Lucas." Ali didn't sugarcoat it. She didn't hedge. "Just like I killed my mother before she could kill you." The weight of the things we'd done hung in the air between us. "It happened, it's done, and I'm not sorry that either one of us is alive. You can regret a lot of things, Bryn, but don't you ever feel sorry for that."

"Never," Katie chirped, like this was all a game—because at her age, everything was. *"Never ever ever ever!"*

So much for crying over spilled milk.

"Everybody decent?" Lake yelled those words from the front porch, and that was the only warning we got before she let herself in.

"Morning, Lake." Ali gestured toward the kitchen table, but Lake shook her head.

"I already ate. Twice. I just stopped by because I was packing and I thought I'd see if there was anything Bryn wanted me to bring."

When most girls said the word *packing*, they meant clothes. When Lake said *packing*, she meant heat.

"Fix me up with one of everything," I told her. "And make it silver."

Lake nodded. At any other time, weapons talk would have made her downright giddy, but this wasn't just any Rabid we were hunting.

There was a chance—maybe even a good one—that this was a friend.

"We'll need restraints," I said, thinking out loud. "And something to knock her out with if she's ..."

If she's out of control?

If she's a monster?

If she's insane?

Across the table, Alex peered curiously up at me.

"If she's *sleepy*," I said.

Lake glanced at the twins and nodded. "If she's *sleepy*," she repeated, "I reckon a Taser or two might help her *nap*."

Neither Katie nor Alex wanted anything to do with a conversation about naps. Ali set Katie back down, and the twins began babbling to each other, in words I couldn't make out or understand. They had their own language, their own gestures, their own little twin world that, even as their alpha, I could never truly enter. The older they got, the more intense that connection was. If I reached out for her mind, I felt his. If I reached out for his, I felt hers.

Beside me, Lake paused in the middle of a sentence in which she was referring to a tranq gun as a *pillow*. She trailed off, her gaze caught on the twins. Alex reached out and grabbed Katie's fist.

Griffin.

I didn't go looking for the thought through the bond, and Lake didn't send it to me, but in that moment, she was thinking her brother's name so intensely that I couldn't help overhearing.

Natural-born females, like Katie and Lake, were so rare because a cruel genetic quirk ensured that female werewolf pups were only carried to term if they were half of a set of twins. It had never occurred to me before that seeing Katie and Alex like this might be hard for Lake, whose own twin had died when we were only a few years older than my siblings were now.

I could barely remember the way Griffin looked and was suddenly struck by the realization that Lake would never forget. That what Katie and Alex had now was something Lake and

Griffin had once. Something they wouldn't ever have again. I reached out for Lake's mind and felt the ache, the emptiness, the space inside of her where her brother should have been.

How could I have missed this? She might as well have been missing a limb, and I'd never seen it, never noticed.

Stay out of my head, Bryn. Lake's voice was shaky in my mind, but I retreated, giving her space.

"So," I said, "about those *pillows* ..."

After a few more minutes of thinly veiled conversation, Lake went off to see about the weapons—and to get away from me. I hadn't meant to go nosing around in her head.

Just like I hadn't meant to send Maddy out into the big bad world to deal with a black hole of emotion alone.

Not wanting to prod Ali into another pep talk, I stood up from the table, restless and aching with everything I couldn't afford to let myself feel.

"We need to leave within the hour," I told Ali. "I'm going to check on Chase and Jed."

That much, I should be able to handle.

That much, I could do.

CHAPTER FIFTEEN

"SIT DOWN."

Checking on Jed wasn't exactly going as planned. He was already up when I got there, already packed and waiting for me when I showed up at the cabin he and Caroline shared. The Deadliest Little Psychic was nowhere to be seen, and Jed seemed to be under the impression that now was as good a time as any for lesson two.

"Jed, I don't think—"

He didn't let me finish that sentence. "Once upon a time, that might have been true, but I'd say that these days you're doing plenty of thinking. Not thinking doesn't keep a person up at night."

Jed's observation was mild, but it made me wonder just how tired I looked.

"Are you actually accusing me of thinking too much?" I raised one eyebrow in an imitation of an expression I'd seen on Devon's face one too many times. "Have you met me?"

I'd been guilty of a lot of things in my life, but an

overabundance of caution or logic had never been one of them. You didn't end up accidentally founding your own werewolf pack by thinking things through or making pro and con lists.

"I'm not going to pretend to know what it's like in your shoes, Bryn. You've got a lot on your mind, probably always will." Jed eased himself down on the ground next to me. "But if you want to control what you are and what you can do, you're going to have to learn when to think and when to give in and *feel*."

I couldn't help thinking that this would have been infinitely easier a year ago, or two, or three, back when I'd been nothing but feelings. Look Before You Leap Bryn could have mastered her Resilience in a heartbeat.

But I wasn't that girl anymore.

"Close your eyes. Breathe. And remember."

This time, Jed didn't have to tell me what to remember. I knew what he wanted me to do. Ultimately, the thing that prodded me into doing it wasn't that Callum had implied he wouldn't Change me until I'd learned. It was the realization that Maddy had survival instincts every bit as honed as I did.

She was Resilient, too.

If the worst turned out to be true and we couldn't get through to her, if she was caught up in a red haze of her own, too shattered on the inside to do anything but hurt, I'd need every advantage I could get just to keep the two of us alive.

So I forced myself to think of the look on Maddy's face—

broken, but regal and holding it together by a string—the day she'd left.

I'm going to go away, and I'm going to get better, because if I don't, the next time someone challenges you, it's going to be me.

Those were words Maddy had actually said to me. For once, I didn't fight the memories. I didn't fight back the darkness, the horror, the fear that she'd been closer to the edge than I'd realized.

You did this to me. You.

Now my mind was putting words in her mouth, things she'd never said.

You killed him. You left me to deal with it alone.

I heard the words in Maddy's voice. I allowed my imagination to conjure up the nightmares I hadn't let myself dream the night before. I saw Maddy covered in blood. I saw her Shifting to wolf form.

I saw Lucas—hopeless, hungry, and full of fury—leaping for my throat.

Blood, blood, everywhere there was blood.

Just like that, I was back under the sink at my parents' house, hiding from the Big Bad Wolf. Except this time, when I peeked out and saw the Rabid tearing through my father's skin and shredding it like a manic child opening a present, the Rabid wasn't the one from my memories, the one who'd haunted my dreams.

It was Maddy.

You did this to me.

The fear was overwhelming and absolute. I didn't want it to be true. I didn't want to be feeling it. I didn't want the world to be closing in around me as I watched blood splatter up against off-white walls.

All of a sudden, I was standing, yards away from where I'd been before. My back was to the wall of Jed's cabin, and I could feel my pulse throbbing in my stomach.

"Feel it?" Jed asked, over the sound of my breathing, the deafening beating of my heart.

I could feel the surge of energy, that whisper deep inside of me, the kind of power that let a panicked mother lift a car.

"Hold on to it."

My body was quickly realizing that there was no present danger. I could feel the power beginning to leak out of my limbs, but I pulled it back.

The smell of wet cardboard and rotting flesh. The heavy sound of breathing in the silence.

I lived and breathed the fear, and my senses heightened. I felt something—an odd kind of silence, not quite a noise—behind me. Hopped up on power, I whirled, and a second later, I slammed Caroline back against the exterior wall of the cabin, my hand around her neck.

I hadn't heard her coming, but I'd known she was there. After a moment, I let go of my Resilience, allowed it to slip away. I pried my hand away from Caroline's throat.

Unfathomably, she smiled. "I take it the lesson went well?"

CHAPTER SIXTEEN

$\sim$

Two psychics, two werewolves, and a psychic human alpha walk up to a crime scene...

It was like the beginning of a very bad joke, and I found myself wishing that Devon were there to share it with. Instead, our merry little band—Lake, Chase, Jed, Caroline, and me—stood in absolute silence, the wind cutting through the trees with a high-pitched whistle and carrying new scents to the Weres' noses.

"There's no one around for miles," Lake told us. "That it?"

She jerked her head toward a house in the distance, and I nodded, even though there was nothing about the way the house looked—from the outside, in the dark—that would have tipped off the average observer to the fact that days earlier, someone had been murdered there.

Unconsciously, I began running through everything we knew about the circumstances in which the death had been discovered.

The front door was closed when the police responded to a 911 call placed from the vicinity. They found the body—what was left of it—inside. The walls were dripping blood.

I forced myself to focus on the sights and sounds of the here and now. We were close enough to the mountains that even in the dead of summer it smelled like snow, and the moon overhead was a shade fuller than it had been the night before.

To my eyes, the world was shadowy and dark, quiet, still. I could barely make out the outlines of the people standing right next to me, but to the Weres, the scant moonlight would have been as good as a spotlight, illuminating the leaves on the trees, each blade of grass, and the house in the distance.

Beside me, Chase breathed in deeply through his nose. Through the bond, I could feel him sorting his way through layers and textures, scent upon scent upon scent.

"Anything?" I asked him, my voice quiet, but echoing through the silence nonetheless.

He closed his eyes and breathed in again. Even though I couldn't quite make out his features, I could picture the expression on his face almost exactly: long eyelashes lying still against pale skin, nostrils flared, and concentration playing around the edges of his lips.

"There was definitely a werewolf here," he said finally. "Female. Young."

He glanced at Lake, and she nodded, kneeling to the ground and bringing a handful of dirt up to her nose.

Was it Maddy? I asked her, not wanting to give life to the question by saying it out loud.

For the longest time, Lake didn't reply, but even through

the darkness, I could see her lowering her head toward the ground. Her blonde ponytail picked up the light of the moon, making her look like an angel caught midprayer, knees in the dirt, head bowed.

Chase joined her on the ground, crouching down with liquid grace, the whites of his eyes catching the moonlight the way Lake's hair had.

I translated their actions—and the things they weren't saying—for our human companions.

"Maddy was here." I paused, suddenly aware of how very much I'd hoped that Callum was wrong, just this once. "Was she in human form, or wolf?"

"In this exact spot?" Lake asked, sniffing again. "She was human, but there's no shortage of woods around here. If she'd decided to Shift, smart money says she would've gone farther in."

Chase stood, the motion fluid even in the darkness. "It'll be easier to track the scent if I Shift."

Lake said nothing, but when I nodded in response to Chase's unspoken query, she began stripping off her shirt.

Clearly, Chase wasn't the only one planning to Shift.

Turning my attention back to our human companions, I laid out a plan of attack. "Chase and Lake are going to check out the woods. We can get started inside."

If Lake said there wasn't anyone out here except us, I believed her, but that didn't mean it would stay that way for long. If we wanted to check out the inside of the house—the actual crime scene—sneaking in under the cover of darkness seemed like a good way to go.

"Police might have someone set up, watching the place," Jed said, "to see if the killer comes back."

Killer, my mind echoed. *Maddy*.

I didn't push the thought away, but didn't dwell on it, either. "There's no one here now. Chase and Lake would have smelled it if there were."

I spared a glance for Caroline, who was standing so silent and still that I couldn't be 100 percent sure I was glancing in the right spot. "You'll let us know if you hear a car coming?"

I didn't know the full extent of Caroline's knack, but I did know that she was a deadly hunter: impossible to track and good at tracking others. She also had perfect aim, no matter how impossible the shot. While her senses probably weren't as good as a Were's, I was going to go out on a limb and bet they were probably pretty darn close.

"No," she replied. "If I hear the police drive up, I'll keep that little gem to myself to spite you all."

Jed snorted, and I realized that Caroline was being sarcastic.

"If we're going to go," she said, impatience peppering her tone, "let's go."

Behind me, the sound of snapping bones and guttural, inhuman cries told me Chase and Lake had begun to Shift. A second later, a wave of power hit me, tantalizing and torture, all at once.

I wanted my pack. I wanted to run. I wanted to stay here with Chase and Lake, I wanted to Shift—

But I couldn't. Couldn't Shift. Couldn't stay here. Instead, I fought the call of the wild and took a step toward civilization.

The house.

We closed the distance between the woods and the front porch with quiet efficiency. Caroline circled the entire house, keen eyes looking for weaknesses and points of entry. She came to a stop beside us, unnaturally still and utterly sure of herself, and addressed her next words to Jed.

"Killer came through here."

I wasn't sure how she could be so certain, or so calm, but it was hard not to take Caroline's words at face value. When it came to games played between predator and prey, I had no doubt that she was as much of an expert as any Were.

All business, Jed took something out of his pocket and managed to jimmy open the front door.

"If you want to touch anything," he told me, glancing back over his shoulder, "you're going to need to put on gloves."

I hadn't brought any. In the course of my time as alpha, I hadn't had nearly as much practice breaking and entering as I had with breaking and reinstating psychic bonds. Clearly, I had not come prepared.

"Here." Caroline made no move to invade my personal space, but as Jed flipped on a hallway light, she held out a single white glove.

My eyes were drawn immediately to the skin she'd bared. Thick, sinewy scars—some white, some sickeningly pink, even after all these years—marred her flesh from the elbow down. Looking at it *hurt* and reminded me that Shay was the one who had given Caroline those scars—one more reason that we couldn't afford to let him be the one who found Maddy.

I took the proffered glove. Cold and detached, Caroline strode past me into the house. I followed, and in the dim light Jed had turned on, I could see dark blotches on the tan stone floor.

Drops of blood.

Someone had made an attempt at cleaning up since the crime scene photos were taken, but the after-effects of slaughter were still visible, tangible proof that what had happened here couldn't be exorcised with cleaner and bleach.

Drawn like a moth to the flame, I followed the trail of blood and watched as the dark spots got bigger and thicker the farther into the labyrinthine hallway we got.

"It started with a puncture wound." Caroline walked the path of blood, as light on her feet as a dancer, her head tilted slightly to one side. "A small one. A warning."

Caroline met Jed's eyes, but not mine. "Killer gave his target time to run."

The hallway dead-ended into a large, open living room. The stone fireplace on the far end was discolored, and Caroline stopped in front of it.

"Second and third puncture wounds. Then a long, deep cut." She gestured to the dark spots on the floor. Her words could have just as easily been describing a knife attack, but somehow, I doubted a rabid werewolf would have bothered with a blade.

No, our killer would have Shifted—in full or in part—and gouged the victim. Once. Twice. Three times.

"The target scrambled backward," Caroline said—and I realized for the first time exactly how different our mental vocabulary was. My *victim* was her *target*.

"Target was already bleeding. Here"—she touched her still-gloved hand to the ghostly remains of what had once been a pool of red on the ground—"he slipped and hit his head."

Caroline dragged her fingertips over the discolored area on the fireplace. Her face darkened. "And then it happened all at once."

I took those words to mean that her discomfiting expertise started and ended with the aspects of this kill that seemed almost human. What had happened after the victim had fallen on the fireplace wasn't human at all.

"The attacker Shifted," I said, carefully avoiding all use of the pronoun *she*—or anything else that might bring Maddy's face to my mind. "After a minute, maybe two, the smell of blood would have been too much for the wolf."

Based on the way the corpse had been positioned in the photos I'd seen, our Rabid must have dragged the victim—or possibly the *body* by that point—across the room. I followed the path, overcome with images that felt like memories, as my mind took what I knew and filled in the horrifying gaps.

Memorize the way it feels, I told myself. *Keep it under lock and key.*

In wolf form, a rabid werewolf would have been unable to keep from going for the throat, and that was probably responsible for most of the splatter on the baseboards and the walls.

I could smell it. I could hear the sound it made, that awful, ungodly sound of shredding flesh, interspersed with raindrops on a windshield.

"There should be footprints," Caroline said. Still caught up in a trance of my own making, I slipped on my borrowed glove and ran my right hand over the surface of the wall.

"With this much blood, the target shouldn't have been the only one slipping. If the killer didn't clean up afterward—and if this is what it looks like a week later, I doubt they did—then he or she should have left footprints. Paw prints. Whatever."

I thought back to the crime scene photos. There'd been evidence that someone had dipped human hands into the blood and smeared it along the walls, but Caroline was right—there'd only been one set of footprints.

The victim's.

There hadn't been any paw prints at all. How was that possible?

One of these days, I thought, *I'm going to excise that word from my vocabulary.*

Werewolves and psychics weren't exactly the height of *possibility*, either.

Beside me, Caroline snapped to attention, pulling her body back into the shadows, her eyes narrowed and her pupils wide. The sound of creaking wood on the front porch alerted me to the reason for her behavior. I reached out to keep her from flying into action.

"It's Chase," I told her. "Not the police."

Hearing his name, Chase ducked into the room, quiet and unobtrusive. "There's no evidence that Maddy ever Shifted in the woods," he said, by way of greeting. "If she was living there, she was living there as a human."

He paused and took in the sights and smells in this room. To his nose, the astringent smell of bleach would have washed away some of the blood scent, but not all of it.

Fresh off his own Shift, Chase was able to press down against his inner wolf, but I could feel the animal response bubbling beneath the surface of his mind. "Do you think she Shifted in here?" he asked, his voice throaty and low.

I turned the question right back around at him. "Do you think she did?"

Chase was silent, and for several seconds, none of us said a word. He breathed in and out. I watched the way his chest rose and fell, waiting for my answer.

The answer I didn't want to hear.

"Maddy was here," he said finally. "She Shifted—and I don't think she was alone."

Not alone?

"Was she with another werewolf?" I asked, my mind racing with the implications. If Maddy was with another Were, she might not have been the one to do the actual killing. Maybe she just stood there and watched.

Not that that's much better.

"I don't know." Chase's voice was intense with concentration. He took another deep breath, pushing his way past the overwhelming scent of blood. "The scent is different. It's faint. One second it's there and the next it's not, but I smell someone . . . some*thing* . . ."

A growl broke free from his throat as he tried to put what he was smelling into words. Even in the dim light, I could see the way Caroline responded to the sound. Her hands went automatically for the weapon strapped to her side. She turned her back to the wall.

Casually, I stepped in between Caroline and Chase, removing the glove I'd borrowed and handing it back to her, while he got control of his wolf.

"We should go." Jed had been so quiet while Caroline and I were walking through the killer's motions that I'd almost forgotten he was here. "We've seen what we came to see. No use pushing our luck."

I hesitated, not wanting to stay here any longer than I had to, but unable to banish the feeling that I was missing something. Maddy was here. Someone was with her. And Chase couldn't quite tell who—or what—that someone was. I'd assumed when Maddy left the pack that she wanted to be alone. But what if she'd met someone somewhere along the way?

With more questions than answers, the four of us left the way we came—softly, silently, disappearing back into the night.

"I lost Maddy's scent at the river." Lake, half-naked and utterly unapologetic about it, picked her discarded shirt up off the ground, skin glistening with sweat and hair streaming free down her back. "When she left, she left fast."

As Lake finished getting dressed, I took stock of what we knew. Maddy had lived in these woods as a human. She'd left quickly. The killer had somehow managed to avoid stepping in the rivulets of blood. The victim—whoever he was—had died bloody.

"Pain," Chase said. He brought the side of his face to rest on the top of my head. "Sora said that to track a Rabid, we needed to figure out what he was hungry for."

What she *was hungry for*, I corrected silently, unable to shake the image of Maddy in that house, Maddy's mouth covered in blood.

"Whoever killed that boy is hungry for pain." Chase closed his eyes for a moment, his forehead creased and a dark look falling over his face. "If it was Maddy, if she did that, if she's

looking for pain—I think I know where we should go next."
He opened his eyes and met mine. "Alpine Creek."

The town where Samuel Wilson had lived, where he'd kept
Maddy and the others like pets. The place where her pain had
started.

"Chase is right, Bryn." Caroline took a step toward us.
"This isn't just about killing. This is about hurting people."

I was fairly certain that was the first time Caroline had ever
referred to Chase by name. Of all the wolves in my pack, he was
the least human in appearance and behavior, and Caroline—
as much as she wouldn't have wanted to admit it—still wasn't
100 percent comfortable around Weres.

If the two of them agreed on something, chances were good
they were right.

"What happened in that house wasn't a clean kill." Caroline
shook her head. "It wasn't even an animal one."

"What was it?" Lake asked, her voice strained and high.

Caroline didn't answer, so I did, on her behalf.

"That," I said, shivering in the night and drawing what
little warmth I could from Chase's body, "was retribution."

CHAPTER SEVENTEEN

~~~

WE SET UP CAMP AN HOUR AWAY, JUST INSIDE THE
Cedar Ridge border. Tomorrow, we'd head back into No-Man's-
Land and swing down to Alpine Creek, a sleepy mountain
town where people didn't ask questions and the sheriff was
easy to bribe.

If Chase was right, Maddy might have gone back to the
place where this nightmare had started for her, a place where
she'd felt more pain than most people could ever imagine.

"Tent's up." Chase never used ten words when two words
would do. I looked up at the sky—cloud covered and seem-
ingly starless—and then back at our makeshift campground.

Jed had, at one point in his life, apparently been something
of a survivalist. He'd stated, in his quietly authoritative way,
that there was no reason for us to risk being seen checking
into a motel, no matter how far from the crime scene we'd traveled. I hadn't argued. The werewolves among us were just as
comfortable—maybe more so—sleeping outside, and I wasn't
holding out much hope that I would be able to sleep at all.

Chase sat down behind me and swept my hair off my neck. He laid his cheek against the skin he'd exposed, then pressed his lips gently to the place where my shoulder met my neck.

"Brought you something," he said. "To help you sleep."

I turned back, my face so close to his that I could barely tell where I ended and he began. "What?"

"Maps." With a crooked smile, he pulled back and began to spread them out between us.

It was easier out here, away from the rest of the pack, to believe that he understood me, my priorities, the things that made me tick. On the edges of the Cedar Ridge territory, I didn't feel quite so alpha, and Chase wasn't quite so self-contained.

"You brought me maps," I repeated. "To help me sleep."

"You'll sleep better once you have a long-term plan," he murmured, placing a hand on mine and dragging them both over the surface of the paper. "Maps. Plan."

I got up on my knees to get a better look. It was easy enough to see the lines of the maps by lamplight, though if Ali had been there, she almost certainly would have told me that reading in these conditions would ruin my eyes.

Had I thought there was even the slightest chance that I would stay human long enough for that to matter, I might have cared.

Instead, I turned my full attention to Chase's gift, sorting through the maps and arranging one next to the other until we had the whole of Wyoming, Montana, Idaho, and Utah spread out in front of us.

I drew an invisible circle with the tip of my finger. "We're here." I dragged my finger downward. "No-Man's-Land starts *here*, goes through Alpine Creek, and stretches up to the location of the last murder, here."

I quickly outlined the borders of No-Man's-Land.

"This side is Shadow Bluff territory."

Idaho.

"Cedar Ridge."

Montana.

"And Stone River starts here. There's another slice of No-Man's-Land between Stone River and Luna Mesa here."

Before Maddy had left, I'd advised her to stick to our territory, or Callum's. Whether or not she'd listened was another matter. From the moment she'd told me she was leaving, she'd seemed certain that she was fully capable of staying off the beaten path, that wherever she was going, no one else would or could follow.

"When I have to get away, I go for the mountains." Lake took a seat on the other side of the maps, stretching out her mile-long legs and eyeing our handiwork. "I usually turn around before I get there, but it's nice to have someplace to run to."

Mountains? Right now we were smack-dab in the center of the Rockies. Even if Maddy had headed for the mountains, we had no idea of knowing which ones.

"Why mountains?" I asked, hoping Lake's answer might jog something loose in my mind. I'd always wondered, but never asked about her tendency to Shift and run off into the night.

Like Griffin, Lake's occasional need for space wasn't exactly the kind of thing we discussed.

"It's quiet there." Until Lake actually said those words, I hadn't been sure she would answer, but once she started talking, she didn't seem inclined to stop. "You pick the right mountain, and you could get lost forever: just you and the rocks and the sky. The higher it is and the harder it is to get to, the less chance you have of running into other people. Or werewolves."

A glint of metal caught my eye, and I changed the subject to one I knew Lake would be more comfortable with.

"That Matilda?" I hadn't gotten a good look at the shot-gun Lake was currently cleaning, but her old standby had the status of a ratty old teddy bear or favorite pet.

"Nope," Lake said, not missing a beat. "This is Abigail. She's new."

The second Lake started naming weapons, Chase pressed another kiss to my temple and then made himself scarce. He seemed to sense that it had been a while since Lake and I had time for girl talk.

"Abigail, huh?" I said.

Lake grinned. "I named yours Greta."

Of course she did.

"Hey, Lake. Do you and Caroline ever talk weapons?" I don't know what possessed me to ask that question, except for the fact that as long as I'd known Lake, she'd been one hell of a shot, and most days, Caroline's knack seemed to be her single most defining feature.

Lake snorted. "Bryn, you might not have noticed this, but Caroline doesn't talk. Except to Devon, and that's only when she's trying to get him to shut up."

Actually, I hadn't noticed Caroline and Devon talking at all. It made me wonder what else I had missed, wrapped up in pack business and blind to anything else.

"It's not fair." The sudden fierceness in Lake's tone caught me off guard. If I hadn't known better, I might have thought her eyes were wet with unshed tears.

"The fact that Devon never shuts up?" I joked, knowing better than to act like I'd noticed the emotion on her face.

Lake shook her head. I waited.

"If Maddy was a guy, the worst they could do is kill her." Lake shoved her gun to the side. "Now, there's nowhere she can run that they won't find her, if we don't find her first. It's not right, and it's not fair, and *goddamn it*, we shouldn't have to do this."

Lake rubbed the heel of her hand roughly over her face, dashing away her tears. "She's our friend, and if it wasn't for Shay wanting her, wanting me—if it wasn't for that, he never would have pulled that crap with Lucas in the first place. He wouldn't have tried to kill you, and you wouldn't have had to kill Lucas, and Maddy wouldn't have lost her freaking mind. She wouldn't have lost control, and we wouldn't have to sit here, polishing our weapons and looking at this stupid map."

Lake slammed her elbow back into a tree trunk, hard enough to break her skin. I forgot sometimes that I wasn't the only one with things on her mind, that Maddy wasn't just *my* responsibility or *my* friend.

In fact, I had a sinking suspicion that parts of this outburst had been building up inside Lake for a very long time, and this was the first time she'd had someone to listen.

"It's not just me. Or Maddy. It's Phoebe, and it's Sage, and someday it's going to be Katie and Lily and Sloane—"

She stopped short of rattling off all of their names, one by one, but my mind completed the task, and I realized that if Lake had known I was planning on voluntarily becoming a Were—a female Were—she would have slapped me silly and shot me in the kneecap, just for good measure.

Lake never had a choice about what she was, and in the world we lived in, with the numbers the way they were, things would never, ever be fair.

"Shay's not getting within a hundred yards of Maddy," I said, because that was the only thing I could give her, the only promise I might be able to keep. "No one is getting to Maddy, because we're going to find her first."

Even if she'd gone Rabid.

Even if she was the monster who'd painted those white walls red with blood.

Even if the person she really wanted to tear limb from limb—the reason she wanted vengeance—was me.

CHAPTER EIGHTEEN

~

THAT NIGHT, I COULDN'T BREATHE INSIDE THE TENT.
Couldn't sleep. Couldn't think. We still didn't have a plan, and
when exhaustion finally beat back everything else competing
for space in my mind, I fell into a nightmare, the kind that
follows you seamlessly from one dream to the next.

I was running. Someone was chasing me.

Something.

Hands grabbed my shoulders. Nails that might have been
claws dug into my arms, but I couldn't feel the pain. I couldn't
feel anything.

Suddenly, the forest disappeared, and I was sitting at a
wrought-iron table that had been painted white. My hands
were folded neatly in my lap. My legs were crossed at the
ankles. Stiff, lacy fabric crinkled as I shifted in my seat.

The girl sitting across from me, dressed in a frilly frock
identical to my own, was Maddy. She reached forward, and
a tiny china teapot materialized. With dainty hands and an
expressionless face, she poured my tea and then her own.

The light all around us was bright, almost unbearable, but in the corners of the room, there were shadows, and in the shadows, there were eyes.

Unperturbed, Maddy lifted her teacup upward. With shaking hands, I reached for my own.

"It's not what you think," Maddy said.

For a second, I thought she was trying to tell me that I'd misconstrued everything that had happened in the past few days, that she wasn't the monster we were hunting, and relief washed over my body, pleasant and warm.

A smile cut across Maddy's features, sharp where they were round. Her teeth gleamed, the exact shade of porcelain as the teacups.

"It's not what I think," I said, in a singsong voice that didn't feel like my own.

"It's not what you think."

I brought the teacup to my lips, and that was when I realized—

We weren't drinking tea. The cup was filled with blood.

I woke with a start, no more capable of screaming than I had been when I was caught in the midst of the dream. This was what came of Jed's little lessons. Once you let yourself be scared, once you opened up the door to the darkest parts of your psyche—

There it was.

Not wanting to disturb the others, I glanced around the tent. Chase and Lake were missing—no surprise there. They didn't need shelter of any kind to feel at home in the woods. Jed was snoring on the far side of the tent, and in between us, Caroline was fast asleep.

Her eyes were open.

Somehow, it didn't surprise me that she was the only person I'd ever met who could bring that particular cliché to life. In sleep, she looked even more doll-like than usual: perfect and petite, with eyes so big and round that her eyelids only covered them halfway.

Given the dream I'd just had, the last thing I wanted to think about was dolls. Ignoring the chill crawling up my spine, I slipped out of my sleeping bag and tiptoed out into the night.

The sky had cleared enough that I could see the stars overhead, like fireflies trapped in glass. I wondered if Maddy could see them, wherever she was. I wondered if there was even a small part of her that was still Maddy, if there was anything left of the girl I'd known at all.

Where are you, Maddy?

I sent the words off into the night, knowing they'd never reach her. Our minds weren't connected anymore. The phantom I'd seen in my dream was just that—a phantom, the by-product of opening the floodgates and trying in vain to dam them back up, only succeeding halfway.

If I hadn't severed the pack-bond and withdrawn my mind

from Maddy's, we could have actually shared dreams. I could have seen her, talked to her. I could have asked her why. Instead, I was left with my own twisted subconscious and no way into Maddy's mind at all.

Lightning struck in the distance, so far away that it was nothing but a dull flash of light on the horizon. I waited for the sound of thunder, but it never came. Instead, a chain reaction went off in my brain, and I remembered the last time nightmares had kept me up at night.

Those nightmares had been real.

And the person who'd orchestrated them?

He'd had a knack for getting under people's skin and entering their dreams, the way I could sneak peeks at my pack's. *I* might not be able to connect with Maddy, but that didn't mean she was off the grid altogether.

This time, when I went back into the tent, I was able to close my eyes. I was able to sleep. Because the person who'd spent the better part of last fall haunting my nightmares, the one who might have stood a fighting chance at finding Maddy, or at the very least, her dreams—

He owed me. Big time.

CHAPTER NINETEEN

"CHANGE OF PLAN," I SAID TO LAKE, WHO HAD "weaponed up" in anticipation of the morning's adventures. "You, Caroline, and Chase are going to scout out the Rabid's old house in Alpine Creek."

I paused.

"*Wilson's* house," I corrected myself.

Samuel Wilson had been *the Rabid* in my mind for so long: the one, the only. Referring to him by name felt wrong, but with another killer on the loose, it seemed simpler—unless I wanted to give in and start referring to the current Rabid as *Maddy*.

She wasn't the only one there when that boy was killed. I clung to that thought, seesawing back and forth between believing that Maddy had lost it and hoping that, despite appearances, she had not.

Chase had smelled something else at that house. A partner? An intruder? A demon plaguing her mind?

There's no such thing as demons, I thought, but I could still see the Maddy of my dreams, sipping blood from a teacup. Six months ago, I would have sworn she wasn't capable of murder. Two years ago, I would have told you with a straight face that there was no such thing as someone who could see the future or a woman who could control other people's thoughts.

At this point, we really couldn't rule anything out.

"See what you can find at the old house," I told Lake, sticking to the task at hand and banishing the trip down memory lane until later. "Check the woods, too, but lie low."

The last thing we needed was anyone from Alpine Creek recognizing that two of my three scouts had been there before.

"If Maddy's there, call me. If you see anything, if you smell anything, if you even think you might remember something that could lead us to her, call me."

"Sir, yes, sir." Lake gave a lazy little salute, but the set of her jaw told me that she was glad to be *doing* something—and that she would have followed me straight to the ends of the earth if I'd asked her to.

"Where are you going?" Caroline announced her presence with a question. Unlike Lake, our human companion didn't trust me to hand out orders.

"Me?" I asked, figuring that it served her right for eavesdropping.

"No, not you. The other insomniac mutt-lover in the vicinity." The term *mutt-lover* should have made me angry, and it should have brought up bad memories, but instead, it sounded almost like a nickname. Caroline sounded almost human.

"Well, half-pint," I said, matching her nickname/slur for nickname/slur, "I'm hoping Jed will take me to see an old friend."

"And what old friend might that be?" Jed sounded only mildly put out that I'd already started breaking up the crew, when he'd been sent along specifically for adult supervision.

I took that as a good sign and turned around. "Do you keep in touch with the rest of the coven?" I asked him.

Jed mulled over the question, his stare telling me that there was only a fifty-fifty chance I'd get an answer. "Some, yes," he said finally. "Some, no."

Before Caroline's psychotic mother had come along, married the coven's leader, and had him killed, the group of psychics had lived together as a family. But under her influence, they'd done horrible things, and besides Caroline and Jed, who had stayed at the Wayfarer, the rest had scattered to the winds the moment Valerie's psychic influence had worn off.

"Who exactly are you wanting me to take you to see?"

I gave Jed a stare of my own, one that I hoped told him that if he didn't help me, I'd find some other way to do it on my own. And then I smiled in a way I hoped he would find at least a little bit endearing.

"Remember Archer?"

I didn't know Archer's last name. I wasn't sure how old he was, or what he'd been doing in the months since I'd seen him last.

Right now I didn't care.

He slid into the booth across from me. Jed had chosen our rendezvous point. The others had dropped us off, and calling this particular diner a dive would have been generous. Over in the corner, the old man dropped two quarters into an old-fashioned jukebox, leaving Archer and me some semblance of privacy.

I didn't beat around the bush. We'd spent enough time coming here to meet him—with the clock ticking, there was no time to waste.

"You stalked me." I opted for bluntness over charm. "You tormented me, you tried to burn me in my sleep, and unless my memory is mistaken, at one point when we were awake, you *actually* set me on fire."

The Archer I'd known—the one who'd dogged my dreams and played mind games with me, literally—was caustic. He was half seduction, half sadist, and he hadn't seen me as a person, because Valerie hadn't wanted him to.

Caroline's mother—*Ali*'s mother—had possessed a knack for manipulating other people's emotions. She'd tempered Archer's toward me with equal parts hatred, curiosity, and disgust.

But now he was just a guy—older than me, but younger than Ali—and I was the one playing with his emotions.

Specifically, his guilt.

"You didn't come all of this way just to yell at me," Archer said, though his tone suggested that he wouldn't have had a problem with it if I had. "And if you're trying to get me to say that I owe you, then you're right."

That was easier than I'd thought it would be.

"I need you to find someone for me," I said.

"I don't find people." Archer fiddled with a sugar packet, flicking it back and forth over his index finger and his thumb.

"But you can find their dreams." I didn't wait for a reply. "You can talk to them. You can manipulate what they see. You can, if memory serves correctly, *set them on fire—*"

"You're really not going to let that go, are you?" he asked. From the look on his face, I thought he might have been joking, but I wasn't sure.

"I need you to find a specific person's dreams," I said.

"And then what do you need me to do?" Archer leaned back against the booth, his eyes dull, and I realized that he thought I was going to ask for something else, that I was going to use him the way Valerie had.

As a weapon.

"That's it," I said. "I just need you to find her dreams and tell me what you see. Talk to her, see if she's okay, try to get her to tell you where she is."

"Consider it done." Archer looked like I'd challenged him to a game of chess. "Whose dreams am I finding?"

I told him and debated whether or not to mention the fact

that we had no guarantee Maddy was the same person she'd been when she'd left the pack, and had every reason in the world to think that she wasn't.

"If you can't give me a general idea of where her body is, I'm going to need something that belongs to her. Clothing is best, or maybe a piece of her hair?"

Did he seriously think that I carried around an inventory of hair for every person in my pack?

I was saved from asking that question out loud by the telltale buzz of my phone against my hip. Withdrawing it from the pocket of my jeans, I noticed that I had a text from an unknown number.

SHE WAS HERE.

For a split second, I thought the universe—or possibly Shay—was taunting me with vague declarations about Maddy's location, but then I realized that of the group I'd sent to Alpine Creek, Caroline was the only one not in danger of destroying a cell phone the moment she Shifted.

HOW LONG AGO DID SHE LEAVE? I typed back.

DON'T KNOW. The reply came almost immediately, and it was followed by an addendum, which set the phone to buzzing once more. LAKE SMELLS BLOOD.

Caroline and I were going to have to have a serious conversation about her texting habits. Seriously. "She was here"? "Lake smells blood"? These kinds of things merited a phone call.

Glancing back up at Archer, I noticed that he had a funny smile on his face. "I'm pretty sure this is the first time I've seen you actually look your age," he told me.

Right. Because texting was so very teen.

Unsure whether he'd find me making a phone call equally amusing, I dialed Caroline's number.

She answered on the third ring and cut right to the chase. "Maddy was here, but she's not anymore. Lake smells blood. I want to go inside, but Chase and Lake seemed to think we should ask you first."

Blood? Check.

Potentially rabid werewolf? Check.

Of course Caroline wanted to go inside.

"How far away from the house are you guys?" I asked, uncertain how close Lake would have had to get in order to pick up on the scent.

"We're about a hundred yards out."

My breath caught in my throat. At that distance, if Lake was smelling blood, it meant one of two things: either there was a lot of blood, or it was fresh.

"Archer," I said.

"Yes?" His amusement seemed to have dwindled, based on the content of my conversation.

"Three questions," I said, ticking them off on my fingers as I spoke. "One: do you have a car? Two: do you have plans tonight? And three: how fast can you drive?"

CHAPTER TWENTY

~

THE BLOOD WASN'T HUMAN AND IT WASN'T FRESH, but it was everywhere. The entire cabin smelled like copper and rotting meat. The floorboards—wooden and rotting themselves—had soaked up most of the actual liquid, but there was splatter on every wall in the house.

"You," Archer said, coming in on my heels and appraising the "decorations," "live a very strange life."

I couldn't exactly argue the point. Chase and Lake were waiting out in the forest. This much blood—even if it was animal blood, even if it was old—might have been too much for the predators inside them, and that wasn't a chance any of us could afford to take, so that left Jed, Caroline, and me to appraise the inside of the cabin—with Archer tagging along.

"*What* happened here?" I couldn't keep myself from asking the question. The pattern of gore made it look like something had been eviscerated.

Maybe multiple somethings.

"There aren't any bodies." Even Caroline sounded disturbed,

and that couldn't possibly have been a good thing. "There's nothing but blood."

As we walked from room to room, I noted the way Archer kept his distance from Caroline, and the way that Jed never took his eyes off Archer.

Four psychics walk into a rotting cabin . . .

I didn't let myself finish the joke. Instead, I tried to piece together what had happened here. Someone had been living in this cabin—most likely Maddy. How long ago had she left? What had she done while she was here? Was she the one who'd painted these walls red with blood?

In the corner of the back bedroom, I spotted a bundle of blankets. As I knelt down to investigate, I saw a small brown tuft of fur. For a split second, I froze, but after ascertaining that the tuft wasn't moving, I nudged it with the tip of my shoe, revealing the rest.

A teddy bear.

It was old, worn, and missing both eyes, and I was fairly certain someone had made a regular habit of gnawing on its ear.

"Who lives here?" Archer asked.

I picked up the teddy bear, running my thumb over the edge of its worn fur and wondering if it had belonged to one of my kids.

"No one lives here," I said. "Not anymore."

I grabbed the blankets, too, and headed back out to the woods. I'd seen enough. Remembered enough.

This place had been steeped in blood long before someone had taken to slaughtering animals here. Wilson had seen to that, and the last thing I wanted to do was spend any more time than I had to imagining what life would have been like for the kids in my pack growing up under a psychopath's thumb.

The last thing I wanted to think about was Maddy coming here because she couldn't come home.

Wordlessly, Chase took the blankets from me. Lake took the teddy bear. Without my even having to ask, they lifted their respective targets to their faces and inhaled. My mind was flooded with their impressions.

Running water. Fresh-cut grass. Maddy.

She didn't smell like us anymore, but she didn't smell like a killer, either. If anything, she smelled a little bit like—

"Shampoo," Lake declared out loud. "Drugstore shampoo—the cheap kind. Smells like she used the whole bottle."

"How long ago was she here?" I asked. "Can you tell?"

Lake looked at Chase.

"It's hard to be sure," Chase said. "She slept on these blankets every night, so her scent would be strong, regardless."

I digested that piece of information. There was no shortage of beds and cots in Wilson's cabin, but Maddy—who'd come back here for reasons I couldn't quite wrap my mind around—had slept on the floor.

"Are we talking days? Weeks? Months?" Caroline was all business.

"Months," Chase said, looking up from the blankets. "I'd say she left three, maybe four months ago."

That left three months unaccounted for after Maddy had left the Wayfarer, and at least as much time between when she left here and the Wyoming murder. I wouldn't have been surprised if she'd hunted in the woods, but couldn't figure out why she would have gone to the trouble of killing so many animals in the house. Why had she come here in the first place? Why had she left?

"Did she sleep with this, too?" I turned back to the battered teddy, the one that had probably once belonged to Lily or Sophie or one of the younger kids.

Lake nodded, and I wondered if she could picture Maddy the way I could, curled up on a blanket, holding on to the only piece of the pack she had left.

My heart hurt.

The day was almost over, and Callum had told me we'd have at most a week. We weren't any closer to finding Maddy than we had been when we left, and the state of Wilson's cabin didn't do much to assuage my doubts about Maddy's mental state.

Time to bring out the big gun.

"Here," I said, taking the teddy bear from Lake and handing it to Archer. "You said you needed something that belonged to Maddy. It's not clothing or hair, but hopefully, it'll do."

CHAPTER TWENTY-ONE

NIGHTFALL—AND SLEEP—COULDN'T COME FAST enough. We set up camp again, on our side of the border, but Archer opted for sleeping in his car—either because he didn't like people watching him work, or because the idea of sleeping in close proximity to two werewolves, a girl he'd tried to kill, and a girl he'd been conditioned to think of only as a killer probably fell under the classification of "let's not and say we did."

Or maybe a little of both.

Rather than sleeping myself, I practiced. I practiced taking everything I'd seen the past few days—every horror, every drop of blood—and locking it away, so deep in my mind that I could pretend that nothing had happened.

And then I practiced letting it out.

This time, I didn't start with a specific memory. I didn't walk myself step by step through a scene. Instead, I built a room inside my head—a tiny room with white walls and no windows and no doors. No way out.

In that room, I put the sound of screams, tearing flesh, and heavy breathing, the smell of rancid blood. Everything I'd been holding back, everything threatening to devour me whole was there—in the ceiling of that room, the corners, the floor.

In a way, I'd been building rooms just like this one in my mind my entire life—for fear and sadness and everything I couldn't let myself want. But this time, it was different, because even though there were no windows or doors, no way out— there was a way in.

I just pictured myself there, surrounded on all sides until I could taste it, smell it, feel it in my pounding pulse. *Fear.* It was endless, infinite and overwhelming.

Copper on the tip of my tongue.

Chills on my skin.

A breath caught like sandpaper in my throat.

Can't stay here, I thought desperately. *Can't. It's too much, it's all too much. Have to—*

Escape. That wasn't a thought. It was a feeling, familiar, but ancient.

Escape. Escape. Escape.

My eyelids fluttered.

Survive.

"Bryn?"

Archer made the mistake of placing a hand on my shoulder, and suddenly, it was like I was watching myself from outside my body. The world around me settled into slow motion, silence—

And the next thing I knew, he was down.

Realizing, on some level, that Archer wasn't actually a threat, I jerked myself out of the room I'd built for my fears, slamming an extra set of mental walls up all around it.

Safe. The feeling—the instinct—the adrenaline subsided.

"I'm sorry," Archer said. Coming from someone I'd just tossed through the air like I was training for the shot put, that was the last thing I'd expected to hear.

"Sorry for what?"

Archer tilted his head forward and rolled his eyes up to meet mine, his brows slightly arched. "Not entirely sure what the right answer is here, so I'm going to hedge my bets and go with *everything*."

His tone was sardonic enough that I wasn't sure whether he meant the words or not. If Devon had been there, he probably would have started crooning apology songs, just to break the tension.

"Well, *I'm* sorry—for kicking your butt," I said finally.

He snorted.

"Did you find anything?" I asked, then amended my question. "Maddy." I made myself say her name. "Did you talk to her?"

Archer shook his head. "She wouldn't talk to me. She ran."

I was fairly certain that when Archer had entered my dreams, I hadn't been able to run. He'd been able to freeze me in place, or beckon me forward.

"I could force her," Archer said lightly. "I don't want to."

My first instinct was to tell him to do it anyway, but the part of me that was still human couldn't form the words.

Archer saved me the trouble. "I'm hoping that if you come with me, I might not have to get rough."

"Come with you?" I asked. I hadn't known that kind of thing was even possible. "How am I supposed to come with you?"

He shrugged. "I enter your dream. I enter hers. We hope I can splice the two together, and voilà."

That seemed like the kind of thing he should have mentioned in the first place. He must have seen the irritation on my face, because a matching expression flickered across his features, and I remembered that, technically, he was the one doing me the favor.

"Do you need a piece of my clothing?" I asked, deciding this wasn't worth arguing over.

Archer gave me a look. "You're right here," he said slowly, as if I were very dull. "Why would I need your clothes?"

Well, excuse me for not knowing exactly how his knack worked—I was just learning the ins and outs of my own.

"You sleep," Archer said, in a voice that reminded me he could be a dangerous person. "I'll do the rest."

I might have balked at the idea of letting him inside my head again, but he was still holding that ratty old teddy bear that smelled like Maddy and had probably belonged to one of the younger kids, once upon a time.

It's hard to hold anything against a guy with a teddy.

"Okay." I didn't say any more than that. I just made my way back inside the tent and lay down, ignoring the open-eyed Caroline sleeping six inches away.

I closed my eyes, I opened my mind, and I slept.

My dream started off the way my dreams always seemed to these days—in the forest. I didn't remember, at first, that this wasn't real, but then I came to an opening at the edge of the woods and saw a cartoon mouse the size of a man. He was wearing overalls and sitting on a motorcycle, and although that didn't strike me as particularly unlikely or strange, I began to get that nagging feeling that said, "Something isn't right."

"Bryn." A voice called my name softly. The moment I saw Archer, I remembered—why we were here, what he was trying to do.

"Maddy?" I asked.

He reached out to take my hand. I didn't hesitate as I slipped my fingers into his. He caught sight of the mouse on the motorcycle and shook his head.

"I'm not even going to ask."

The scene around us changed slowly. The sky overhead went from night to day. The leaves on the trees thinned to needles; the grass underfoot turned a bright, spring-sheen green.

And then I saw her.

Maddy.

I wasn't sure whether I thought her name, or said it out loud. Either way, she heard me.

She ran.

I ran after her, and for the first time in days, I wasn't scared of her, of what we would find. I just wanted to be there, to see her, to put my arms around her and know that she was real.

Or at least, as real as anything in a dream could be.

"Maddy, wait!" This time, I called after her out loud, and she turned to glance at me, just for a second.

Something isn't right.

I didn't know what it was, so I kept running—through forest after forest, with changing scenery, changing leaves. Abruptly, Maddy stopped running. I stopped running, too. I walked toward her, weightless and light on my toes. Her brown hair was straight and neat, not a strand out of place. Her clothes were dirty and torn, but there was grace to Maddy's stance, the tilt of her head.

I reached out to touch her shoulder, and my hand passed right through.

"It's my fault," Maddy said, without turning around. "Everywhere I go, it never stops." She turned her head to the side, until I could see her profile in the shadows. "You shouldn't touch me."

I *couldn't* touch her. Whether that was the work of her subconscious or mine, I wasn't sure.

"Everything I touch dies," Maddy said, the words quiet, but distinct.

Suddenly, the two of us weren't in the forest anymore. We were in a cabin. Samuel Wilson's cabin, in Alpine Creek.

There was blood everywhere—fresh blood.

"I didn't do it," Maddy said. "I didn't mean to."

"Maddy." I tried to touch her arm again and failed. "Where are you?"

She didn't answer, but a jolt of images crossed from her mind to mine: sharp stone, dark walls, a little river.

A tiny slat of light.

"Maddy, look at me."

She looked at me, and I was struck by the fact that she didn't look different. She looked like Maddy, *our* Maddy, not the specter from my dream the night before.

She didn't look like a killer.

"The Senate knows about Wyoming."

She weathered those words like a blow.

"Callum's stalling them, but if I can't find you, if something happens again—"

I couldn't put what had been done in that house in Wyoming into words. I couldn't even think the word *monster*.

"The other alphas will come for you. First come, first served. I need to find you, Maddy. You need to let me help you."

"Help me?" Maddy said, and this time, she didn't sound

like herself, not at all. "You can't help me, Bryn. The only person who can help me is dead."

Lucas.

She was talking about Lucas.

"You don't know," Maddy said. "You just don't know."

She didn't cry, but the intensity in her voice made me want to. A physical change came over her body—the way she stood, the arch to her back, the lines of her threadbare clothes.

"You just don't know," she said again.

I touched her arm, really touched it this time, and she turned all the way around to face me. I watched as she brought her right hand to rest on her stomach.

Her very pregnant stomach.

And then I woke up.

CHAPTER TWENTY-TWO

I HAD NO IDEA IF ARCHER HAD SEEN WHAT I'D SEEN, but as soon as he opened his eyes, I was right there in his face.

"Tell me that was just a dream," I said.

You don't know. Maddy's voice echoed in my head. *You just don't know.*

The only person who can help me is dead.

"The life-size mouse was a dream," Archer said, his tone almost comically serious. "The forest, the cabin, the way she looked when you first saw her—that was all a dream."

But her stomach…

"It wasn't a dream, Bryn." Archer's voice was very soft, very gentle. "I knew there was something when I went into her dreams on my own. I couldn't tell what it was, exactly, but—"

"Maddy's pregnant." My voice was even softer than Archer's. He didn't reply, and I didn't wait for him to. I just walked away—away from Archer, away from our camp, away from everyone and everything.

Maddy had left the Wayfarer in December, two weeks after

Lucas had died. She'd been holding it together by a string, and she'd said she was leaving because she couldn't get better with me in her head.

She'd said that she needed to be somewhere that I wasn't.

Now, seven months later, she was pregnant—and judging by the size of her stomach, pretty far along.

The only person who can help me is dead.

I'd known objectively that Maddy had loved Lucas. I'd known that the time I'd spent fighting Valerie's coven, she'd spent with him. But I hadn't realized—

I'd never even thought—

She was pregnant when she left. I couldn't hide from that realization, couldn't deny it. *And that means Lucas is the father.*

Just like that, I was right there again, in the woods outside the Wayfarer, kneeling next to him, running my hand over the fur on his neck, telling him to go to sleep.

To die.

And now Maddy was out there broken and alone and *pregnant*. A wave of nausea crashed into my body, and I bent over at the waist, afraid that I might actually throw up.

The Senate didn't know. Shay didn't know. Because if they had, if they'd known that not only was there a female up for grabs, but also a *baby*, not even Callum could have kept them away.

There was nothing more important to Weres than children. *Nothing.* The idea that I'd let a pregnant teenager carrying a werewolf pup go off into the big, bad world alone would have seemed more monstrous to the other alphas than the Wyoming murder.

Was that why Maddy went Rabid? I wondered. Werewolves were wired for pack living. Lone wolves were under enough strain going it alone in normal circumstances, but werewolf pregnancies were notoriously difficult, notoriously painful. Most human women didn't survive, but even for female Weres, it was far from a walk in the park.

It wasn't the kind of thing anyone should have to go through alone.

With sudden clarity, I saw Maddy's life stretched out before me, from the day she'd been Changed until now.

Viciously attacked by a Rabid, her human life torn away.

Forced to live under the thumb of the monster who'd done that to her—a sadist just as psychopathic in human form as he was as a wolf.

Then, finally, she'd gotten a break. Finally, things had gotten better. She'd had friends, a family. She'd been safe. She'd met a boy and fallen in love.

She'd gotten pregnant.

And then the one person she'd trusted—more than anyone—that person had killed the boy she loved, the father of her baby.

Pregnant, alone, heartbroken, in pain of every conceivable kind—was it any wonder she might have broken? Was it that unthinkable that a splintered part of her might have started craving other people's pain?

Everything I touch dies, she'd told me. *I didn't mean to.*

"Bryn."

I was still bent over at the waist, but now I was actually on the ground, rocks and dirt digging into my kneecaps. Chase wrapped his arms around me, pulled my body back against his.

"It's okay," he said. "I've got you. It's okay."

But it wasn't okay. How could anything be okay? How could it ever be okay again?

I pulled back from Chase's grip, but he held tight, and I didn't fight him. "Maddy," I said, croaking her name. I didn't have to finish.

"I know," he said. "Archer told us."

Now all of them knew—what had happened to Maddy. What I'd been a part of. What I'd done.

"Stop it." This time, Chase's voice wasn't soft, and it wasn't gentle. "Just stop it."

"Stop what?" I said, jerking backward and out of his arms for real. I stumbled to my feet, my hair falling into my face and covering my eyes, my cheeks hot with tears I could no longer hold back.

"Stop doing this to yourself," Chase said, his voice throaty and low. "Stop telling yourself that this is your fault."

"This is my fault."

He was on his feet now, coming toward me, but I took a step

back. I didn't want him to touch me, not when Maddy would never touch Lucas again.

"*He's* the one who challenged *you*." The fury in Chase's voice was undeniable. "Lucas did this, Bryn. He challenged you, and you did what you had to do."

"Did I?" That was the question, the one I hadn't let myself think for seven long months. "What if there was another way, and I just couldn't find it? And even if I didn't have any other choice, I should have known. I should have seen what was happening. I shouldn't have accepted him into the pack. I shouldn't have given him the opportunity to challenge me. I should have found a way—"

"A way to what?" Chase didn't move any closer to me physically, but he kept pushing. He didn't back down, not even when I stood straighter and met his gaze, head-on, everything I was and everything I was feeling palpable in my stare.

"You should have found a way to what?" he asked again.

I didn't answer. I didn't know.

"You can't keep doing this to yourself, Bryn. I've sat back and watched for months. I've given you space, but this is tearing you apart, and I can't just keep sitting here, watching you, doing nothing—"

I hadn't known—that he'd seen what I'd kept hidden, that not being able to make it better hurt him the same way that it would have hurt me if our positions were reversed.

"You don't understand, Chase." The words burst out of my

mouth. I couldn't stop them, even though I wanted to. "You won't ever understand. You *can't*."

"You think you're the only one who's ever made a mistake?" This time, he did take a step toward me. Just one. "Do you think you're the only person who's had to make horrible decisions, or who's felt like everything they do lets someone down?"

He took another step forward.

"Do you think you're the only person who can't let themselves feel things, because you feel them too damn much?"

There was something dark in his eyes, something powerful and raw. The edges of his mind blurred against the edges of mine, and I knew that, somehow, in his human life, he'd been where I was now.

"You're not perfect." Those were the last words I'd ever expected to hear him say—because from the first moment we'd met, I'd been his everything. "You don't have to be. You can't be—no one can—and you need to *let it go*."

Maddy, Lucas, the murder in Wyoming—how could I let any of that go?

"You did what you had to do, Bryn, and even if there was another way, if there was something that none of us thought of then and none of us have been able to think of since, if there was some mythical answer that would have made things turn out differently, made them better—you'd still have to let it go."

We were right next to each other now, his cheek very nearly touching mine.

"People make mistakes, Bryn. It's what we do."

I felt the fight drain out of me, and with it, some fraction of the emotion that had been pent up inside of me for months. He put his hands under my chin, angled my head toward his.

My lips met his, and I closed my eyes, my hands reaching around his body and grabbing on to the back of his shirt, like I was holding on for dear life.

That was the most I'd ever heard him say at once, the most of the person he'd been before the Change that I had ever seen. I wanted this, wanted him, but there was still a part of me that couldn't do what he wanted me to, couldn't entirely forgive myself, couldn't let it go.

Because, yes, everyone made mistakes—but when I made them, people died. Chase had lifted some portion of the burden off my shoulders, but there was still a weight there.

There always would be.

His thumbs traced the lines of my jaw. I leaned into his touch, opening my eyes and staring into his, so blue that I could have lost myself in them, if only for a moment.

"Ahem."

Chase broke away from the kiss, and the two of us turned to our left to see Caroline and Lake standing side by side. Lake had a good nine inches on Caroline, and though they were both blonde, they looked nothing alike—but the expressions on their faces were almost identical.

This wasn't awkward or anything.

Lake, who'd known me longer and was less capable of keeping her smart mouth shut, broke the silence. "Sorry to interrupt, but we weren't sure if or when you two crazy kids were going to come up for air."

I wondered how much, if any, of our fight they had overheard.

"I mean, really, B., you and lover boy here ought to look into careers in deep-sea diving."

Sometimes, having friends who were like family was a good thing, and sometimes, it was like having an endless supply of very nosy, very irritating siblings.

For a second, it looked like Caroline was considering chiming in as well, but ultimately, she exercised that trademarked restraint. "You have a phone call," she said instead. "On your cell."

I glanced back at Lake and saw that, all teasing aside, there was tension in her body and a sharpness to her eyes.

"Who is it?" I asked.

Lake gave me an apologetic smile. "It's Callum."

CHAPTER
TWENTY-THREE

I DEBATED WHETHER OR NOT TO TELL CALLUM WHAT, exactly, had sent Maddy over the edge, and then I debated what the likelihood was that he already knew about the baby. The second I came on the line, though, he spoke, and I immediately had other concerns.

Bigger ones.

"She's going to kill again. Tomorrow."

"Are you sure?" It was a stupid question, one that came out as a reflex.

"I'm sure someone dies," Callum replied. "And I'm sure that we'll have thirty-six hours after the body is discovered before Shay learns there's been another attack and moves to enact the Senate's vote."

Thirty-six hours? We'd been looking for Maddy for longer than that already, and while the picture of how she'd spent these past few months was becoming clearer and clearer, I still didn't know where she was now.

Thinking back to the dream we'd shared, I grasped for clues. I'd seen images in her mind: sharp stones, the dark walls of a hollow place, some kind of stream. The mountains, maybe? Was she holed up in some kind of cave?

That didn't exactly narrow things down.

"Is there any way to stop this?" I wasn't sure whether I was asking if there was a way to prevent another attack, or to keep the other alphas from racing to find Maddy on their own.

Both, probably, but I would have settled for either.

Callum did not oblige. "The future's been uncertain, Bryn, but in the past hour, certain outcomes have become more and more likely." He didn't pause, didn't give me time to process. "Someone else *is* going to die."

I thought of blood-streaked walls, of Maddy's haunted eyes and broken words.

Everything I touch dies.

"And the Senate?" I asked. There was no use dwelling on the things I couldn't change, not if this was something that I could. "Is there anything we can do to keep that from happening?"

"There might be. There might not."

Well, that was less than helpful.

"Either way, Bryn, you need to find her first."

A year ago, I might have snapped at him for telling me the obvious. Instead, I relayed what I'd seen in the dream, the images that I'd pulled from Maddy's mind of the place she'd been staying.

"If we could get an idea of the general area she's in," I concluded, "I might be able to find her, but there's too much No-Man's-Land, and we don't even know for sure that she hasn't crossed a border somewhere."

She could just as easily be holed up in the remotest areas of our territory—or someone else's. If she was careful to stay far enough away from the other wolves, they might not even know she was there.

"There's a third-rate ski resort near your western border in a town called Winchester. It falls between Shadow Bluff territory and Cedar Ridge, but the northern packs could reach it through the mountains."

"And that's where Maddy is?" I asked, wondering why, if he knew that, he hadn't just sent me straight there, before the countdown to confrontation had gotten so tight.

"That's where the next attack happens," Callum said. "You won't get there in time to stop it."

"But if we move quickly," I said, "she might still be in the area when we get there."

Maddy wouldn't stay in the immediate area—she was too smart for that, but if she was hiding out in the mountains, she might retreat to the place I'd seen in the dream. Assuming it was close by, we might be able to put two and two together and find it.

Find her.

"Be careful, Bryn. Things could get bad, and I'd not have you dying, not for this, not now."

"Don't worry," I said reflexively. "Rumor has it I'm hard to kill."

For the first time in memory, I hung up the phone on him first. There was something Callum wasn't telling me—probably lots of somethings. That was nothing new, but this time, I couldn't tell whether this was just another stage of the Let Her Make Her Own Mistakes plan in which he seemed to revel, or if there was another reason for keeping me in the dark.

If my knowing something would cause me to act differently than I otherwise would have, and if that difference led to an undesirable future, Callum wouldn't bat an eye at keeping things to himself—even if those were things I wanted—and maybe even needed—to know.

Then again, I hadn't exactly told him that Maddy was pregnant.

"This is my cue to leave." Archer kept his distance and very wisely did not put a hand on my shoulder this time. "I was happy to help, but I gave up danger for Lent."

"It's August," I told him.

"Global warming," he replied, without missing a beat.

"Fine," I said. "Go." I didn't even watch him leave. Instead, I turned my attention back to the others.

"We're going north," I said. "Weapon up."

CHAPTER
TWENTY-FOUR

WINCHESTER, IDAHO, WAS A TWO-BIT TOWN COVERED in dirt. Winchester, Montana, wasn't much better. The two sat nestled beside each other in the middle of a pile of rocks that looked less like a mountain than an environmental death trap.

"Ski resort?" I muttered. "Yeah, right. And I'm Molly Ringwald."

In the silence that followed my words, I felt Devon's absence like a missing piece of my own body. I wasn't sure how he would have replied to my sarcastic statement, but I was almost certain it would have involved some variation on the phrase *pretty in pink*.

Getting to Winchester hadn't been easy—especially since we didn't have the option of entering from the west. The Montana side of Winchester wasn't exactly accessible by car—not if you didn't want to risk blowing a couple of tires, at least. Since we couldn't risk trespassing on Shadow Bluff territory, that left us traversing the last few miles by foot.

Chase and Lake could have made the distance in short time,

but Caroline, Jed, and I were stuck with "slow and steady," and when we finally made our way to the edges of "town," it was already abuzz with news of the body that had been found, right outside the Bait & Tackle. They were calling it an animal attack, but I knew better.

Most animals didn't play with a corpse and then leave it in the middle of Main Street, like a present for the masses. Then again, most werewolves didn't, either.

"Victim's a teenage girl, and she wasn't killed here." Caroline's voice was quiet enough that if she hadn't been standing right next to me, I wouldn't have heard it. Still, talking about this in the light of day, out where anyone could hear us, didn't seem like the best idea in the world. "The blood's not right," she murmured, "and the body . . ."

We were standing far enough away that my eyes couldn't make out the details, but Caroline had incredible long-distance vision. The same thing that let her hit a target a football field away meant that even from our vantage point, a block away, she could still make out the details of the scene.

Unlike in bigger cities, there was no police tape here. Just a sheriff, a couple of deputies, and an off-white sheet that someone used to cover the body.

Badly.

"I'm starting to think our killer wants to get caught." Jed's voice was just as low as Caroline's. "You all got any reason to believe that's true?"

I thought back to the dream Maddy and I had shared. She'd been quiet, self-contained, maybe a little unhinged, with the way she'd insisted that she hadn't done anything and immediately gone on to qualify that she hadn't *meant* to.

"I don't know," I said. "I don't know if she's the one who did this, or why she'd choose to do it like this."

The one thing I was sure about was that if Maddy was killing, it wasn't because she *wanted* to. It was because she couldn't stop.

"It's like a hound," Lake said, "dropping a dead bird on your front porch and expecting you to be pleased."

From the way they were talking, you would have thought that Maddy did this—all of this—for me.

That thought never left my mind—not as we made our way to the lone Winchester gas station and not as Jed gave our cover story, which involved fly-fishing, family bonding, a very bad sense of direction, and a car running out of gas. The possibility that Maddy had killed to get my attention was there as I listened to the loud whispers of the town folk, fascination warring with horror in their tones.

"I reckon it was a bear. Strange that it would come this far into town, but the Sutton boys have been at their old tricks again—probably led it straight to us."

"Those Suttons are a menace. And that poor Johnson girl. First, her daddy kills her mama, and now this. Earl and Betsy must be taking it hard."

I didn't get to find out who Earl and Betsy were, because at that exact moment, I noticed a change in the pack-bond. Across the room, Chase stiffened, his nostrils flaring outward, his fingertips curling slightly inward, like claws.

"—just coming home from work, and now she's gone. Funeral won't be open casket, that's for sure—"

Beside Chase, Lake paused, too. They smelled something.

Someone.

Making my way out to the front of the gas station, I scanned the streets for Maddy. Surely, she wouldn't have come back here. Surely, she wouldn't have stayed so close to a kill.

I smell . . . I smell . . . Chase whispered the words straight into my mind.

What? What did he smell?

The answer came to me as nothing more than a vague sense that Chase was smelling something he'd smelled before—at the Wyoming murder site, at Wilson's cabin in Alpine Creek.

It was faint. Different. It smelled like a werewolf, and it didn't.

It smelled the way things did in dreams—a fraction off, a shade too, too . . . *something*.

For the first time, I really and truly let myself believe that Maddy might not be the one behind the murders. But that meant someone—or some*thing*—else was. Something that Lake and Chase couldn't quite scent.

Something that was close.

Caroline and Jed must have noticed something was wrong, because they paid and followed us quickly out of the store.

Watching Caroline sparked a memory, and I sent a question silently to Chase and Lake. *You guys can't smell Caroline,* I said. *You can't track her. It's part of her knack. Do you think what you're smelling—not smelling—now could be something similar?*

Based on the crime scene, I'd been certain that our killer was a werewolf, but like Callum and the Resilient wolves in my pack, some werewolves had knacks, too.

In Wyoming, the killer hadn't left any footprints in the victim's blood.

What if this thing wasn't a werewolf? What if it was something else? Something that made as much sense to me as psychics and werewolves would have to anyone else?

Without warning, Chase took off, as quick as a serpent's strike. Lake followed, holding back on her speed enough to appear human. Jed, Caroline, and I slipped out of town, following them to the edge of the mountain and then into the forest.

We stopped at a densely wooded area where the smell of blood was so thick in the air that, even with human senses, I wanted to gag.

Fresh blood this time—and it didn't belong to an animal. It was human blood, and odds were good that it belonged to the girl whose remains had been found on Main Street.

This was where she was killed.

Through the pack-bond, I could hear Chase's racing thoughts, and Lake's, and I realized that beneath the pungent scent of iron and human flesh, they could smell something else.

The kind of something that smelled like a werewolf, but not. A dream smell, a memory, a scent they couldn't quite make out.

I heard a noise then—a rustling in the brush to my left. Caroline whirled, her blonde hair fanning out around her baby-doll face. She had a crossbow in her left hand and a pistol in her right, and she was halfway to pulling the triggers before my eyes even locked in on her prey.

It was a boy, about my age, standing only a few feet away—a pale and almost see-through boy, standing in a field of blood. He had golden hair, halfway between honey and a light, sun-kissed brown. There was a smattering of freckles across the bridge of his nose. His cheekbones were sharp, and his eyes were green, the exact same shade as Lake's.

Caroline fired, and I watched as a bullet passed straight through the boy. A bolt came within a foot of his body, but he waved his hand, and it fell to the ground.

This was what Chase had smelled at the crime scene.

This was the kind of monster who could kill without leaving a trail.

This was a nightmare, dressed up like a boy.

It started walking toward us, and a sense of déjà vu washed over my body. There was something familiar about this thing, this boy. Something more than the way he smelled—or didn't smell—and the serious expression on his face.

"Lake," he said.

For a split second, there was silence all around us, and then Lake replied, her voice barely more than a whisper, but filled with a whole host of emotions, each as sharp as glass.

One word.

She just said one word.

"Griff."

CHAPTER TWENTY-FIVE

GRIFF? AS IN *GRIFFIN*? AS IN . . .

"Lake," he said again. "Lakie."

I hadn't heard anyone call her that, not since the first summer she and Mitch came to visit the Stone River Pack alone. We were six years old, and she was wild—wild with grief, with anger, with an emptiness that slowly, over time, Devon and I had seemed to fill.

An emptiness that, looking at Lake now, I knew we never had.

"This isn't happening," Lake said. "You aren't real. You're never real."

The depth of anguish in her voice told me how much I'd never known about one of my closest friends. She made a point of being strong and fearless and bulletproof in every way that mattered. She was the one who'd pulled me out of the dark place after Callum had ordered me beaten, and I'd never fully realized—she'd never let me realize—that she had a dark place of her own.

Every time I'd come close to it, she'd pulled back.

But now all of that darkness was bleeding off her, like radio waves of pain—and her brother, her *dead* brother, was standing there in front of us, with a body that bullets passed straight through and a scent the others couldn't quite grasp.

A scent present at the Wyoming murder.

"Lake—" I was going to tell her to back away from him, but realized that she wouldn't hear me if I did. It was like she and this boy—this creature with her dead brother's face—were the only two people in the world.

She walked toward him, her body shaking with every step, her head thrown back, like if she could just face this head-on, everything would be fine.

She would be fine.

Watching her, I thought of Katie and Alex, the bond between them growing stronger by the day. I felt something building up inside of Lake, fire where she once was frozen, numbness giving way to pain.

"I told you once," the boy who couldn't have been Griffin said, "that I was never going to let anything get you, and I never have. Every fight you fought, I fought. Every tree you climbed, I climbed. And when you ran, Lake, I ran with you. Always."

I could hear Griffin in this thing's words. I could see the boy I barely remembered in the lines of his face. But this couldn't be Griffin. Griffin was dead, and we had every reason to believe that this thing in front of us was a killer.

"You weren't there." Lake's voice was uneven and shrill.

She sounded like a little kid on the verge of a meltdown. "You weren't there, and every time I thought I felt you, every shadow I saw out of the corner of my eye—on our birthday—"

"I was there. I was always there." His voice was an echo of hers, quiet and intense and so full of emotion that I thought he might choke on the words, trying not to cry. "And now I'm here."

The thing I felt building up inside of Lake—the fire, the pain, the *hope*—filled her. It overcame her. Something deep in her soul reached out for something deep in his. The bond between them surged, electric and undeniable, and I felt it the way Lake did, like a phantom limb brought suddenly back to life.

I knew then, beyond a shadow of a doubt, that whatever else this thing in front of us was, whatever it had done, Griffin's face wasn't just some mask it had chosen to wear. This *was* Griffin, as surely as Lake was Lake.

"What are you?" Caroline took a step forward, her eyes narrowed into slits, her tone lethal. She may have revised her opinion of werewolves in the past six months, but the Griffin standing before us wasn't a werewolf.

Not anymore.

"I'm dead," Griffin said, then he nodded toward Lake. "But she's not."

To Caroline, who couldn't feel the bond between them, those words probably weren't very illuminating, but to me, they sounded like an explanation, intuitive and complete.

Griffin was dead.

Lake was not.

Female werewolves were always half of a set of twins, the girl's survival in the womb dependent on the boy's. Katie and Alex were two halves of the same whole. That was what Griffin was to Lake, what she was to him.

"You're dead," Lake said, bitter and trying not to sound broken. "You're dead, and I'm not, and you're telling me that you just hung around? And you didn't say anything, didn't tell me—"

"I *couldn't*," Griffin said, the words cutting through the air like a whip. "Don't you think I tried, Lake?" His voice got very soft, and I felt like I was eavesdropping, even though I wasn't. "Sometimes, late at night, there were moments when you could see me, right before you fell asleep. And on our birthday, every year, when hurt was tearing through your insides and you were smiling on the surface, I tried even harder. That one time, when we turned sixteen …"

He trailed off, and I realized that maybe Lake had seen him—in her dreams, on her birthday. Maybe she'd seen him, or thought she'd seen him, or imagined seeing him and hadn't told me. I wanted to believe that, to believe that this was some kind of miracle and not a nightmare, but Griffin's scent—as faint and hard to define as it was—had been all over the Wyoming murder site.

We'd found him here, where another victim had just been killed.

No. Lake's voice was firm in my mind. She must have known by the look on my face what I was thinking, but she didn't want me to go there. *Just no, Bryn.*

"Why now?" she asked Griffin, but I knew she wasn't asking for my benefit or because she had any lingering suspicions herself. She was asking because she had spent years broken and incomplete, missing him, and she needed to know.

"I couldn't make you see me before." The quieter Griffin's voice got, the harder it was to hear anything in it but truth. "But now I can. Everything's changed, Lake. *Everything.*"

Lake nodded, her lips pulled into a thin and colorless line. Through the pack-bond, I could feel a nauseating ball of fear unfurling in the pit of her stomach—not because she was afraid of her brother, but because she was scared to believe that things had really changed. Scared to close her eyes, for fear that she might open them and discover that all of this had been a dream.

"You're dead, but you're here." Caroline sounded calm, but her eyes were locked on to Griffin's, like a snake's as it swayed gently in front of a mouse. "What exactly does that make you?"

"I'm a dead werewolf with a twin who's still alive," Griffin replied, giving the hunter a look I remembered well from my youth—one that said she was really very slow. "If you want to get technical, I'm pretty sure the word you're looking for is *ghost.*"

Werewolves. Psychics. And now ghosts. It made a sick

kind of sense—especially given the things we'd seen—and not seen—smelled—and not smelled—at the murder scene in Wyoming. What kind of predator smelled like a memory, a dream? What kind of werewolf could drag a body to Main Street without being seen? The same kind that could dance in blood without ever leaving footprints.

A dead werewolf, brought back as a ghost.

"You killed that girl." Chase said the words that I couldn't force myself to speak. Griffin didn't bat an eye, didn't seem surprised at the accusation.

Lake reared back like Chase had punched her. "Griffin didn't do this," she said, her lips peeling back into a snarl. "He gets sick just looking at human blood. Dad always said he had no stomach." Her voice wavered, and for a moment, she looked less like she was about to shoot someone and more like she might cry. "If one of us so much as skinned a knee..."

Lake believed what she was saying. She did. But Griffin wasn't a kid anymore. He wasn't even a werewolf. He was a ghost, and we didn't know what that meant, what dying and lingering and existing in some kind of limbo without contact, without touch for years could do to a person.

Everything's changed. Griffin's words echoed in my mind, and I couldn't help thinking that if *everything* had changed, we had no idea what Lake's brother was capable of—what he had done to get back here, what he might do to stay.

"Back away from him, Lake." I didn't realize I'd said the

words as an order until her feet started moving backward, against her will.

"Bryn," she bit out, "you go alpha on me now, and there's no going back."

I came to stand beside her, reaching out to touch her arm. "Sorry." I reined in the power building up inside of me and broke off the command. That wasn't the way to get through to her, not about this.

"We don't know for sure, Lake—what he's doing here, what he is."

She didn't want to listen to me, but she couldn't entirely shut out my words, either.

The target of our discussion cleared his throat. "You could always ask, Bryn," he said quietly.

That was the first time Griffin had said my name, and I couldn't steel myself against the sound of his voice, couldn't help remembering that for a while—a short little while—he'd been my friend, too.

"You were there," Chase said, stepping in between Griffin and me. "First in Wyoming, and then here."

That wasn't a question, but Griffin responded as if it was. "I was there, but I was too late."

"Too late for what?" Caroline asked. I didn't need any kind of special access to her mind to see that she didn't trust anyone—or anything—she couldn't shoot.

"I was too late to stop what happened in Wyoming." Griffin

closed his eyes, his head bowed, his entire body tense. "I was too late to stop this." He forced his eyes open and spread his arms out, gesturing toward the blood-splattered grass beneath our feet. "Not that we know how to stop it, exactly."

We? I'd been so focused on Griffin—what he was, what he might be capable of—that I hadn't thought even for a second about the person we'd come here expecting to find.

Maddy.

In the dream we'd shared, she'd told me that the only person who could help her was dead. I'd assumed she was talking about Lucas—but what if she wasn't?

"We," I repeated, watching Griffin's reaction and searching his eyes for some hint of what was going on inside his head. "As in you and Maddy."

I should have put it together earlier, but when your friend's twin brother comes back from the dead and lands smack-dab in the middle of a murder spree, it has a way of short-circuiting the part of your brain responsible for logic.

"I spent years watching you all," Griffin said finally, "watching out for Lake. But after that last fight, after the challenge—"

For the first time, the word *challenge* didn't take me right back to the forest, to standing over Lucas's dead body. I was too busy trying to diagnose the expression marring the boyish innocence of Griffin's face. Guilt? Sorrow?

Hunger?

"You didn't need me, Lake." Griffin said the words like he

was making a confession, like Lake was his priest. "But Maddy did."

"You went with her." Lake reached out to touch the side of his face and pulled back at the last second, as if she'd only just remembered that her hand might pass straight through. "When Maddy left the Wayfarer, you left me and went with her. You watched out for her."

It was a beguiling thought, that even once Maddy had lost us, she'd never really been alone. But whether or not I could afford to believe it—that was another story. A drop of water landed on my forehead—rain. I looked up. This was thunderstorm season, and by the looks of the sky, things were only going to get worse.

"We need to go," Griff said. "The weather's getting bad, and Maddy shouldn't be alone." An alien intensity fell over his face, his eyes glowing in a way that made me wonder how anyone could ever mistake him for a human or a Were. "When I'm not there," he said, his voice low and hoarse and nothing like the boy I'd once known, "when I have to go somewhere— that's when it finds her."

The words sent a light chill over the back of my neck. I could feel my palms sweating, clammy.

"When what finds her?" Caroline asked.

Griff glanced at the scene around us—the signs of the struggle, the blood. "The thing that did *this*," he said. "The other ghost."

CHAPTER TWENTY-SIX

GRIFFIN HAD JUST GIVEN ME EXACTLY WHAT I WANTED: a reason to believe that he wasn't our killer, an alternative explanation that fit the evidence just as well. Chase could barely grasp Griffin's scent. If there was another ghost, it made sense to think it might have that same not-quite-there smell.

But the Griffin I'd known had been a very smart little boy. Smart enough to know exactly what to say to make us follow him. Smart enough to throw suspicion onto someone—some*thing*—else.

"Here." Griffin—who hadn't said a word the entire time we'd been following him—spoke in the low voice of an adult trying not to wake up a napping child. He tilted his head toward a small opening in the brush.

Maybe he was leading us to Maddy. Maybe he was leading us off the side of the cliff. Right now that was a risk I had to take. Finding Maddy, making sure the rest of the Senate *didn't* find her—that had to be my top priority.

Glancing back at Griffin, I thought of the room I'd built for my fears. I readied myself. Then I ducked through the brush.

The cave I'd seen in Maddy's dream was smaller than I thought it would be, and darker. My head scraped the ceiling as I stepped over the threshold; Lake and Chase had to duck. Behind us, Jed and Caroline lingered near the mouth of the cave, either to cover our backs or because they knew that what was about to happen was private.

Griffin wasn't lying. Not about Maddy. She's here.

Knowing Maddy was close, knowing what she had gone through—already, it cut me to the bone. Beside me, Chase's mind was flooded with scents: damp stone, fresh dirt, sweat, and something sour.

Outside, the storm was raging. Inside, it was quiet.

Too quiet.

An unreadable expression on his too-pale face, Griffin pushed past me and made his way farther back into the darkness. When my eyes adjusted, I saw a small form huddled against the wall of the cave. She was lying on one side, her arms curved protectively around her middle. Her clothes were worn, her face dirty, and the slant of light from the entrance caught her eyes just so, giving her the look of a person caught in the throes of fever.

But she was Maddy, unmistakably *Maddy*, and a breath I hadn't realized I was holding whooshed out of my chest when I felt that spark of recognition deep inside me. Even after listening to the story Griffin had spun, I hadn't been certain what we would find here.

Who we would find here.

But she still looked like our Maddy. She still felt like Maddy. She wasn't the killer, and she was alive. That was more than I'd hoped for, more than I had a right to ask for, when I'd believed she was capable of the things we'd seen.

The other ghost. Griffin's words lingered in my mind. He'd brought us here, to her, but what was the likelihood that there were two ghosts following Maddy around?

Then again, what had the likelihood been that there was even one?

"Bryn?" Maddy didn't sound sure of herself, like she thought I might have been a dream—which was probably a fair assumption, all things considered.

"Maddy." Everything in me wanted to go to her, to kneel beside her, but I couldn't bring my feet to move—not until I knew that she wanted me there, wanted me close. "Mads."

"You came," Maddy whispered. For a moment, all I could think was that the first time I'd seen Chase, locked in a cage in Callum's basement and half out of his mind with the Change, he'd said the same thing.

"Of course I came."

Maddy closed her eyes, and as Chase inhaled beside me, he caught a scent, too faint for my human nose to pick up.

Tears.

She hadn't shed them yet, and I didn't know whether I should go to her or just go. But we'd come here for a reason, and Callum's warning was still fresh in my mind.

"The other alphas will be looking for you," I told Maddy, matching her whisper with one of my own. "Soon."

I wanted to be saying something else—that we loved her, that we missed her, that if I could have taken her pain and made it mine, I would have, in a heartbeat.

"The Senate doesn't know about the baby, Maddy, but if they find out, you won't be safe here." I paused, and my eyes traveled to her stomach, round against her rail-thin frame. "Neither one of you will be."

This wasn't how I'd imagined our reunion with Maddy going, but I didn't know how to say anything else. Hesitantly, I crouched where I was, my knees pulled tight to my chest. I forced my own guard down, so she would know that I wasn't trying to scare her or threaten her or imply that she'd made a mistake. Instead, I let my face show my feelings, let my own tears come.

"I was scared, Maddy, so scared that something had happened to you, and that we wouldn't get here in time."

She looked at Griffin and nodded, and he shot me a warning look and then backed up to stand next to Lake, leaving nothing but a few feet of space separating Maddy and me.

"I left to get better," the girl who'd been one of us said simply. "And everything got worse."

I ached for the bond missing between us, for the ability to take on her thoughts as my own, to feel them with and for her and protect her from those who would see her harmed.

But every instinct I had was screaming at me that I wasn't Maddy's alpha anymore.

I wasn't even sure we were friends.

"I knew," she said, her hand rubbing small circles over her bulging stomach and leaving no question what she was referring to. "When I left, I knew, Bryn, and I didn't tell you. I didn't tell anyone. I thought I could do it—just go away and get better and stop missing Lucas, who I thought he was, what I thought we had. "

She eased toward me. Or maybe I eased toward her. I couldn't be sure.

"I didn't know how much it would hurt."

I wasn't sure if she was talking about the pregnancy, or leaving the rest of us behind.

"I didn't know that having someone inside of you could make you a hundred times more lonely on the surface. But I was doing it. I was." She nodded, as if to convince herself of that fact, even as the tears she'd been holding back spilled over and carved tracks into the grime on her face. "We were doing fine, but then there was a full moon. It wasn't the first one, but the baby..."

"He Shifted, too," I said.

Maddy met my eyes. "She," the pregnant girl corrected softly. "She Shifted, too."

It wasn't uncommon for werewolf pups to Shift in the womb—that was part of the reason so few human women survived giving birth to werewolf kids. Combined with Maddy's own body morphing and breaking, the effect must have been excruciating, so much so that I could almost overlook the other thing she'd just said.

Behind me, Lake could not. "She?"

"It's a girl," Maddy said. "Don't ask me how I know, but I do, and that full moon, when she was Shifting, and I was Shifting, I thought—"

She'd thought she was having a miscarriage. Because female pups only made it to full term if there were twins.

"But nothing bad happened, Bryn. I was fine, and she was fine, but my body—it was like being split in two, cut up from the inside out. It was like dying, and then, suddenly, I wasn't alone."

Her eyes landed on Griffin's, and he smiled, a tragic smile that looked out of place with the freckles on his face.

"You brought Griffin back?" Lake's voice was very small. Through the bond, I could feel the slight tightening of her throat, the aching knowledge that, for years, she hadn't been able to do what Maddy had that night. "There was a full moon, and you Shifted, and you just brought him back? That doesn't even make any sense."

Maddy looked down at her hands—away from Lake and her question. Griffin picked up where Maddy left off, speaking the words she couldn't bring herself to say.

"It wasn't like that, Lake. One second, I was there, watching, invisible, and the next, I could feel Maddy's Shift, feel the baby Shifting, feel the moon pulling me closer, turning me inside out. Maddy was screaming, Lake, and it hurt me. I started to Shift, too, and then it was like a nuclear reactor went off inside my body."

His eyes shone just describing it, even now.

"Being dead is like being under anesthetic." Griffin struggled to put the feeling into words. "Your emotions are there—the important ones—but everything else is numb. Nothing is the way it used to be. Nothing is right, but that night—" His eyes went back to Maddy. "I could *feel*. I was *there*."

For one second, maybe two, Maddy smiled. Then she looked down at her hands, and I knew that whatever she said next wouldn't be good. "The corpses started showing up a week later."

There was a full moon. Griffin came back. And a week later, things started to die. Maddy had to realize how that sounded—but it was clear from the way she looked at him that she did not.

"Corpses?" Jed prompted, his voice so gentle it surprised me.

"They were animals," Maddy said. "At first."

I thought back to the blood in the cabin in Alpine Creek. "Something killed them?" I asked, forcing my gaze to stay on Maddy and not dart over to Griffin.

Maddy continued on as if I hadn't said a word. "I woke up that morning, and Griffin was gone. He just disappeared, and the moment he left, I felt it." Maddy shivered. I was close enough to her now that I could have reached out and wrapped my arm around her—but I didn't.

"I didn't see anything, not at first, but I heard the door open. Then I heard bones snapping and skin stretching, and even though I couldn't smell anything, I knew someone was Shifting. At first, I thought it was Griffin, so I walked out into the hallway." Maddy stopped blinking, her eyes far away and glassy, as if she could see it happening, all over again. "The front door was open, and there was a dog standing on the porch. You could tell it was someone's pet, because it was wearing a little red collar."

I could see where this was going—well enough that she didn't need to relive it by putting the experience into words, but when I opened my mouth to tell her that, her voice grew louder, more decisive.

"I didn't know what the dog was doing there, and I thought that maybe I'd imagined the sound of Shifting. But then I saw the tag on the dog's collar moving, and I realized he was shaking." Maddy swallowed, but forced herself to continue. "The dog was a mutt, maybe a year old, and he was shaking so hard that I knew whatever I'd heard, whatever I was feeling, he could feel it, too."

Now *I* could see it: Maddy and the mutt and a villain neither one of them could see.

"The puppy saw me. It came right up to me. It nuzzled my hand. And then something cut it in two."

Blood on the floor and walls of the cabin. I couldn't see through Maddy's eyes, but I didn't need to. I'd smelled the cabin, I'd seen the blood.

"It just kept going and going, claws digging into it, teeth ripping out chunks, and I just *stood* there."

"You couldn't have stopped it," Griffin murmured. "You couldn't even see it."

Maddy continued on, as if she hadn't heard him. "And then it stopped, and I thought whatever had killed the dog might come for me, but it didn't. Griffin came back." Maddy blinked, and I could see her coming back into the present. "We buried the dog—what was left of it—out back."

It was an odd thing for a werewolf to do, to bury an animal that should have smelled like prey, but the horror of what had been done to the little dog in the red collar had left a mark on Maddy that was visible on her face even now.

This wasn't just hunting.

This was torture.

And she'd been helpless to stop it. There was nothing a person like us hated more.

The rest of the story made its way out of her mouth in halting, staccato bits. She'd showered, scrubbing her hands raw, using an entire bottle of shampoo, but never feeling clean. Griffin had come back, and whenever he was near, things weren't so bad, but the second he disappeared . . .

It happened again. And again. And again. Sometimes it was

strays. Sometimes it was someone's pet, but always, it was brutal. She and Griffin left Alpine Creek, but wherever they went, whatever Maddy did, the monster followed. It always knew where to find her, and Griffin was the only thing that kept it away.

"What happened during that full moon, Maddy?" Jed spoke before I had a chance to, and I wondered if he knew something on the subject of ghosts that the rest of us didn't. "The night you saw Griffin for the first time—I need you to tell me exactly what you did to bring him back."

I saw the logic in the question—if we could figure out how Maddy had brought Griffin back, we might be able to figure out the likelihood that she'd brought something else back, too.

Let it be something else, I thought. *Not someone she cares about. Not someone Lake cares about, too. Just this once, let it be something else. Let it be easy.*

For a long time, Maddy didn't answer Jed's question. When she did speak, the words came out in a whisper. "We don't think it's anything I did," she said, each word hard-won. "We don't think it's *me* at all."

She looked down, but not at her hands this time—at her stomach.

It hadn't just been Maddy Shifting that night. According to what they'd told us, the baby had, too.

The baby Maddy said was a girl.

The baby who—based on everything we knew about werewolf biology—shouldn't have lived past that night.

"You think She did this somehow?" Lake said the word *she* like it was capitalized, like it was a name.

Maddy didn't answer.

"You have a knack, Maddy," I said, trying to get her to look at me. "You're Resilient, but maybe the baby is something else. Maybe her knack isn't just surviving."

"It's not her fault." Maddy's eyes flashed. "If having her means this monster following us—I won't let you touch her. I won't let anyone touch her."

"Maddy." I held my hand out, palm up, and then slowly placed it on her stomach. I didn't say a word, but as Maddy put her hand over mine, I hoped that every assurance I couldn't put into words would flow between us, with the exchange of body heat.

Even when I'd thought she was the killer, I'd been determined to keep the other alphas away from Maddy. I wasn't about to let anyone—or anything—hurt her baby now.

Not even if the baby was somehow responsible for raising the dead.

"What happened last week?" Chase turned the conversation back to the event that had brought us here in the first place. If anyone else had asked, Maddy might have winced, but this was Chase, and for whatever reason, she seemed to trust him.

"We stayed away from people." In Maddy's mouth, the word *we* took on new meaning—whatever else she'd thought or done, she was a mother now, would never just be *I* again. "I swear, we stayed away from people, but we were outside for months, and then there was this house, and it was empty. The people who lived there had moved, but they hadn't sold it yet, and we thought—I was hungry, and I was tired, and I just wanted to sleep for one night, just one night, Bryn."

"Hey." I caught her chin in my hand. "It's okay."

She looked at me, incredulous. "It's not okay," she said. "There was a boy. A runaway, and I guess he thought the house looked pretty good, too."

Blood in the foyer.

Blood on the fireplace.

Blood on the walls.

"He came too close to me, and then Griffin disappeared. I tried to get out of the house. I tried to run, but it was too late."

"And today?" Caroline asked, her voice decidedly less gentle than it had been before.

"Today, I was hungry." Maddy met Caroline's gaze head-on, and for a second, I saw a flicker of the inner steel she'd always hidden beneath that quiet surface. "The baby needs meat."

"So you went hunting," Lake said, like it was the most natural thing in the world. For a werewolf, it was.

"I went hunting," Maddy replied.

Not for humans. Not for pets. For a rabbit or deer, a clean kill that wouldn't have felt any unnecessary pain or fear.

"And you?" Caroline turned her piercing gaze to Griffin. "If you knew she had to go closer to town to hunt, why weren't you with her? If this *invisible* killer only shows up when you're not around, then why in God's name would you leave her alone? Why *disappear*?"

The emphasis Caroline put on those words was unmistakable. She didn't trust Griffin, and to her, all Maddy's story had confirmed was that he didn't have an alibi for the murders.

"I don't have a choice," Griffin shot back, his voice rising, his jaw clenched. "I'm new at this. I don't know how it works. Most of the time, I'm here, and I can control it, but sometimes, I lose my grip, and it's like there's something else out there, just waiting to push me away. I fight it. I fight to stay, to keep Maddy safe, but if my attention wavers, even for a second—"

He looked at Lake. No matter who asked the questions, he always ended up talking straight to her. "It might be easier to stick around now that you're here, Lakie." He tried to smile, but couldn't coax his lips into doing anything more than baring his teeth. "The baby might have brought me back, but she's not the reason I lingered in the first place. Having you here makes everything feel more solid. It makes me feel real."

None of this made sense to me. It wasn't an alibi for the murders. It wasn't an explanation. It was vague and wishy-washy and—

I believe him, Bryn. Lake's voice cut off all other thoughts in my mind. *We're connected. I don't need to be able to smell him to know if he's lying. He's not. If he says there's another ghost, there's another ghost. If he says he's been trying to fight it, he's been trying to fight. And if he says that having me here will help, then I'm damn well going to do whatever he needs me to do.*

She meant it, more than she'd ever meant anything in her life, and she was sure. I could feel that certainty bleeding over into my own mind, so overpowering I thought my head might explode.

She was in his mind, and I was in hers. She was asking me—begging me—to let that be enough.

"Okay," I said, but even as the word left my mouth, I thought about Lucas, about the way Maddy had loved him and believed in him and asked me to let him in. What if I was making the same mistake again? What if being alpha meant that I could never really trust anyone, not even the people I loved the most?

He could kill you, my instincts whispered, from somewhere deep inside my mind. *He could kill you all.*

"We need a plan in case this thing shows up again," I said, pushing down my doubts, keeping them from Lake, who would never understand. "Right now we're defenseless. Caroline tried to shoot Griffin, and the bullet went straight through. We have to assume that weapons wouldn't have an effect on the other ghost, either."

If there *was* another ghost.

Caroline didn't seem to appreciate being reminded that she'd tried to shoot Griffin and failed, but after a few seconds, she transferred her glare from me to him. "Powers and weaknesses. Yours. What are they?"

Griff answered the question without hesitation. He swiped his left arm at the wall of the cave, and it passed straight through. "Walls aren't a problem. Neither are doors."

A look of concentration fell over his face, and he placed a hand on my shoulder. I jumped.

"Solidifying is hard," he said. His touch was ice-cold on my shoulder. The place where his skin met mine felt numb. "But staying solid is easier if I'm not trying to stay visible at the same time."

He disappeared halfway through that sentence, and the weight of his touch intensified. Beside me, I could feel Lake pushing down a stab of unwanted panic.

A second later, when her brother reappeared, Lake bit her lip.

"Don't do that," she said, her voice small. "Don't ever do that, Griff."

"Hey." He caught her eyes. "Lakie, I'm here. I always was."

"As touching as this reunion is," Caroline bit in, "can we concentrate on the part where weapons go straight through ghosts? I hate to be the one to point this out, but it's not exactly a handicap for a killer to be *more* capable of violence when he's also invisible."

Lake gave Caroline a disgruntled look, but the latter was clearly immune.

Jed cleared his throat—about as close to diplomatic as the old man could come. "There's not a thing alive that can't be killed, Caro. Dead things included."

If Jed saw the contradiction inherent in those words, he gave no indication of it. "You just have to know where to hit it."

Caroline's hunter eyes appraised Griffin. Lake's lip curled upward, her incisors gleaming in the scant light of the cave.

"No, Lake," Griffin interceded. "She's right. This thing isn't going to stop until someone stops it."

It was getting easier to believe that he was on our side, that we really could trust him. But what if that was the point?

"There's only one thing that hurts me." This time, Griffin directed his words at me, like he knew what I was thinking.

"What is it?" Lake didn't give her brother a chance to reply, before fixing him with a look. "I recommend you open that mouth of yours and start talking, Griffin."

Caroline might have wanted to know a ghost's weaknesses so she could hunt one, but I was fairly certain Lake wanted to know what could hurt Griffin so that she could make 100 percent certain that nothing did.

"There's only one thing that hurts me," Griffin repeated.

Lake didn't seem to appreciate his stalling. "What?"

He gave her a weak smile. "When something hurts you."

CHAPTER
TWENTY-SEVEN

HOURS LATER, WITH THE STORM RAGING OUT ON THE mountain, the seven of us were still crowded into the tiny cave. We'd settled into a loaded silence, the heat of our bodies fighting back the wind and brutal rain, neither of which showed any signs of stopping.

Our cell phones—not shockingly—had no reception, which meant that I hadn't been able to get in touch with Callum. I was hoping that once I did, he'd be able to call off the Senate and keep Shay and the others from coming after Maddy. That was the one good thing to come from this.

One way or another, our killer wasn't a female werewolf.

The killer wasn't even alive.

If that wasn't enough to stay the Senate vote, I wasn't sure what would be. Glancing at Maddy out of the corner of my eye, I wondered what her response would be if Shay and the others really did start making their way here.

The only way to prevent them from trying to claim her by force would be for me to reinstate our pack-bond, but I wasn't sure she'd want that, either. The reasons she'd had for leaving were still reasons. Lucas was the elephant in the room, even now, one that made the already crowded quarters that much more claustrophobic.

If Callum could call off the rest of the Senate, I wouldn't have to press the issue. But if he couldn't—

I tried not to think about it, tried not to ask myself what the right thing to do would be, if she didn't want me in her mind, but giving her what she wanted put her—and her baby—at the mercy of men none of us could trust.

And if the baby really was female . . .

That wasn't supposed to be possible. It wasn't possible for human mothers carrying a werewolf child, and it wasn't possible for female Weres. Girl pups never made it to term. Not on their own.

But Maddy was different. The same way that I was different, the same way that Lily and Phoebe and Sage were different. They were werewolves, but they'd been born human. They were Resilient. Maybe Maddy's baby wasn't a girl. Maybe she was wrong. But if she wasn't, and the other alphas found out about it, my pack would be even more in their sights than it was now. Having a surplus of female werewolves was bad enough. Having girls in my pack who might be able to give birth to female pups—whatever alliances were brewing in the Senate, whatever plans Shay was cultivating, the second they got wind of it, the onslaught and machinations would increase tenfold.

For most of the Senate, there probably weren't many things that would be worth risking Callum's wrath—but that might be one.

Borrowing trouble? Chase's voice was calm in my mind, and I wondered how he could just look at me and know.

Am I that obvious? I asked.

There was a sound halfway between a snuff and a snort, more animal in my mind than it would have sounded out loud. *You* are *trouble,* he said. *It's part of your charm.*

Maybe, but I had to admit that he was right: at the moment, we had enough on our plates already. The future—as tenuous and terrifying as it might be—would have to wait.

Okay, I thought, as much to myself as to Chase. *Griffin says his weakness is Lake.*

If Griffin was telling the truth—about everything—what did that mean for our killer? What was his weakness? Or, more to the point, *who?*

Assuming the killer was a werewolf—and based on Maddy's descriptions and the crime scenes we'd seen, I was betting he was—did that mean that this monster had a twin, too? Or was Griffin a special case? Maybe this ghost wasn't tethered to a person. It could be a place, or an object.

It could be anything.

Or anyone.

I didn't want to look at Maddy, and I didn't want to look at her stomach. I didn't want to think about the child inside— the one who'd somehow brought these specters to life.

I'd done things that dogged my dreams and chipped away at whatever humanity I had left. I made the hard choices so that other people didn't have to, but I had a line, and this was it.

Nothing was going to happen to that baby. Not if Griffin was telling the truth and not if he wasn't. Not by my hand, and not by anyone else's.

"Rain's clearing up." Jed's tone was mild, but all of us snapped to attention like he'd barked out some kind of command.

First order of business was getting off this mountain and back to the real world. With cell phone service, I could call Callum. If we were lucky, maybe in addition to putting out political fires, he'd be able to tell us something about ghosts.

Something that gave me more than Lake's assurances and Maddy's blind faith in Griffin to know that he was on our side.

"We should go," I said.

"No." Maddy's voice was loud, borderline hysterical. It cut through me, like a knife to the gut. The Maddy I'd known was quiet, self-contained, controlled. This Maddy was just as strong, but on edge.

So on edge that if we weren't careful, she might fall.

"I can't leave. I can't go anywhere." She ran a hand through her hair, and her voice settled down into a steadier pitch, low and even, sure. "If I go somewhere, that thing is going to follow me. I have to stay here."

"No." I was surprised by how calm I felt, how naturally I could just step back into the role of giving orders, without questioning for one second that they would be obeyed.

"You don't get to decide," Maddy told me, the tone in her voice closer to heartbreak than defiance, like there was a part of her that wished I could.

"Maddy, if you don't leave, I *can't*." In my mind, it was as simple as that. Until I got word from Callum that the others weren't coming for her, I couldn't take the chance of leaving Maddy here alone. "If I can't leave, I can't call Callum. If he can't tell the rest of the Senate that he's heard from me personally, he might not be able to stop them."

Maddy's eyes narrowed in a way that reminded me that I wasn't the only one who'd gotten through the dark parts of life by sheer force of will. I could outstubborn most people, but not her, not once she made her mind up about something.

"I think it might be okay." Griffin inserted himself into the conversation, walking *through* me to stand by her side. "Lake's here now, Maddy, and I feel ..." He searched for the right word and seemed to find it in the expression on Lake's face. "Solid. I feel solid."

Griffin had a way about him that made it easy to believe what he was saying. I could see his words weakening Maddy's resolve. Was he comforting her—or trying to lull her into a false sense of security, so she'd go closer to town?

Stop it, I told myself. Like Chase had implied, there was a fine line between planning for all eventualities and borrowing trouble. I'd told Lake I believed her. I'd decided to trust Griffin—for now. And that meant assuming that everything he'd told us was true: the killer only came around to torture Maddy when Griffin was gone, and if Lake could keep him grounded in the here and now, at least until we figured out a plan, Maddy could go back to civilization.

Or at least to a crappy motel.

"You don't know that it will work," Maddy said, turning her stubbornness on Griff.

"Mads, if you think I'm going to let Ugly here go *anywhere*—" Lake's lips pulled back into a terrifying smile— "you've got another think coming."

Ugly wasn't a word I would have used to describe Griffin, but I knew better than to argue with Lake in sister mode.

"It's settled, then." Caroline—who hadn't said a word since Griffin had told us the only time he felt pain was when Lake did—was all business. "We all go. Bryn calls Callum. And if this thing does show up . . ."

Her baby blues glowed with predatory hunger.

"Somehow, some way, we damn well make it wish it hadn't."

Those were big words from such a little girl, but eminently effective, because within moments, we were headed down the mountain, Maddy, baby, and all.

CHAPTER TWENTY-EIGHT

"GRIFFIN?" CALLUM SAID THE NAME THE SAME WAY I would have said Lucas's, like Lake's twin was the one he thought about—his regret—staring up at his ceiling at night. "Mitch's son."

"Yes." I didn't say much more than that. I waited for Callum to answer my unasked questions, to tell me that I was right to trust Griffin or vaguely hint that the choices I was making were wrong. But for once, Callum sounded like he hadn't seen this coming. It was a novel enough experience that I figured he might need a moment.

After a few seconds of heavy silence, I decided he'd had enough time to adjust. "We don't know how or why we can see him now, but whatever happened went down on a full moon three months ago. Maddy was Shifting at the time."

Another silence fell. This time, it was Callum who broke it. "You think her baby had something to do with it."

I hadn't actually told Callum Maddy was pregnant, but I wasn't surprised he knew. In fact, the only thing surprising about this was that he'd thought Maddy might be the Rabid in the first place.

He hadn't seen this turn of events coming at all.

"We don't know for sure that it's the baby," I told him. "But Maddy's never had a problem with ghosts before."

That was an understatement—like the rest of us, she'd had no idea that ghosts even existed. The question was, had Callum?

"Griffin says that he never left, that he was always here, and we just couldn't see him." I waited to see if Callum would take the bait.

He did.

"He stayed for Lake." This time, there was no question in Callum's voice.

"He stayed for Lake," I repeated, and then, because I couldn't help myself, I asked the question never far from my mind where Callum was concerned. "Did you know?"

Did he know that Griffin's spirit hadn't ever really left Lake? Did he know what kind of person Lake's brother was now?

"There are stories, Bryn. Old stories, about what happens when a female werewolf outlives her twin—but if you're asking if I knew that there was a way, any way, to bring a Shadow back, the answer is no."

"Old stories," I parroted. With Callum, there was no telling how "old" the stories in question might be. "About Shadows."

The word felt funny on the tip of my tongue, but given that Griffin claimed to have been watching Lake for years, going where she went, aging as she did, it seemed somehow appropriate.

He'd been her Shadow, in more ways than one.

"I didn't know it was more than a story, Bryn." On the other end of the phone line, the man I'd come to see as omniscient expelled a breath. "This explains some things."

I waited for him to elaborate. Given proper motivation, I could use patience like a weapon. He'd taught me that.

"I've never seen a future that included Griffin," Callum said finally. "And when I foresaw the murders, I only saw Maddy."

There'd been a kind of cold comfort in knowing, these past couple of years, that Callum could see the future. No matter how awful the situation I got into was, the fact that he'd probably seen it coming had helped me believe that there might be a way out of it.

Experience had taught me that Callum might willingly step back and let me go through hell. He would let me, maybe even *make* me fight my own battles. But I didn't believe he'd let me die.

"You can't see ghosts." I said the words out loud.

"Shadows," Callum corrected. "*Ghost* is a human word, and Shadows aren't human. They never were."

"Fine," I amended. "You can't see Shadows."

"No." That admission seemed to cost him something. "I can't."

"And you're just *now* figuring this out?" Maybe I shouldn't have sounded so shocked, but Callum had been alive long enough to see entire empires rise and fall. There wasn't much he didn't know.

"Werewolf twins are relatively rare, Bryn. One twin dying a violent death while the other lives on is even rarer—and besides, this is the first instance I've heard of where anyone except the living twin has been able to see, feel, or interact with a Shadow in any way."

Violent death? I couldn't help looking toward Lake—and Griffin. *I thought he drowned.*

Since those weren't words I could say out loud—or even *think* to anyone else in the room—I turned my attention to a topic that Callum might actually be able to shed some light on.

"Think this will stop them from coming after Maddy?" I didn't specify who *they* were. I didn't have to.

"Do you recall what, precisely, the proposition was that the Senate passed?"

I got the distinct impression that Callum wasn't asking because *he* didn't remember.

I wasn't exactly in the mood for a test. "They voted to intervene if the Rabid became an exposure risk," I said.

"No," Callum corrected, "they voted to intervene if *the girl* became an exposure risk."

I'd spent my formative years skirting Callum's orders and

looking for loopholes. I knew how to speak the truth without really telling it better than anyone I knew.

"The girl," I said slowly, "isn't a risk."

"No," Callum agreed. "She's not."

"So the Senate can't use the Winchester attack to justify coming here," I continued. "And since neither you nor I will give them access to our lands . . ."

Maddy was safe—at least from them, which meant one less thing to worry about for me. I just wished Callum had known something more about Shadows—how much of their original personalities they retained, how likely it was that Maddy had raised two, how exactly one might go about fighting a Shadow, besides trying to get at it through its living twin.

For a moment, I let myself consider the implications. If Griffin wasn't telling the truth, if Lake was wrong about him . . .

"How many female Weres are there besides Lake who have a dead twin?" I needed to know. There were so few natural-born females that if the number was bigger than zero, it wouldn't be bigger by much.

Callum didn't get the chance to answer my question. The line went suddenly dead. I tried to redial, but three things stopped me dead in my tracks.

The lights started flickering.

The door to the cheap motel room we'd rented slammed shut.

And Griffin disappeared.

CHAPTER TWENTY-NINE

IN AN INSTANT, CHASE WAS BY MY SIDE AND LAKE WAS at Maddy's. Caroline slipped effortlessly into the shadows, her back pressed up against the corner of the room, her eagle eyes sharp.

Something dark and primal crept over Jed's eyes.

For a second, there was silence, and then I heard laughter— a deep, throaty chuckle that sounded absolutely nothing like Griffin.

Not Griffin.

Caroline went to draw a weapon, but I met her eyes, and she read the order in mine. Blades and bullets might pass straight through this predator, but the rest of us in this room weren't immune. The last thing we needed was someone going down to friendly fire.

Lake, try to find Griffin. I kept my words short and to the point. *Wherever he went, whatever just happened, get him back.*

I stepped sideways, appraising the room, feeling the air on my skin and trying to pinpoint the origin of the laughter.

Nowhere. Everywhere.

To my left, cracks spread along the surface of the mirror, giving it the gossamer appearance of a spiderweb.

Then it shattered.

Jed lunged to his left. A blade of glass flew into the wall behind him, grazing his back.

There were too many of us in this room. Too many targets, too much glass.

Run, my instincts whispered, from the most ancient part of my brain. *Run, and it will chase you.*

The thought came out of nowhere. I'd spent enough time worrying—and trying not to worry—about Griffin that I hadn't thought much about the alternative, yet now I knew beyond knowing that if I ran, this thing would follow.

A hand clamped over my arm. Chase. He didn't want me going anywhere. Our eyes locked, and we stood there, staring at each other, neither one of us willing to give.

On the far side of the room, cracks began spreading along the surface of the window. They spiraled outward, and then there was a *whoosh* of air, and glass exploded inward. The shards rained down, embedding themselves in skin—mine, the others'—tiny, razor-sharp, incessant.

If we stayed here, this thing might pick us off one by one. We couldn't see it, couldn't touch it, couldn't fight back. Short of decapitation, Lake and Chase would survive, but Caroline and Jed were a different story.

Maddy's baby was a different story.

Griff's close, Bryn, but he can't break through. Lake's words were punctuated by the rumbling sound of the dresser, vibrating against the floor. *Whoever or whatever this is, it's shutting him out.*

Griffin had been telling the truth—about everything. I'd doubted him, doubted Lake—

The top drawer of the dresser flew outward, crashing against the opposite wall with enough force that it splintered into pieces.

Another drawer. Then another. Shards of glass from the mirror. The nightstand.

In the middle of the room, Jed straightened suddenly, and his eyes narrowed, his pupils pulsing. There was something almost reptilian about his stare, but as the Shadow tore the room to pieces, debris biting into my skin, Maddy's, *Caroline's*—Jed's posture changed from defensive to offensive.

Our assailant might not have been solid, but his makeshift weapons were. Bleeding adrenaline and power, Jed lashed out with a roundhouse kick, shattering one of the dresser drawers. A piece of debris became a staff in his hands, and then he was nothing but a blur of motion, deflecting projectiles with agility and speed that were beyond that, even, of a Were.

Run. Run, and it will chase me. I couldn't shake the idea. What was happening in this room wasn't our killer's MO. It hadn't Shifted yet. It hadn't laid a ghostly hand on any of us directly.

Maybe it wasn't used to facing off against groups.

That thought unlocked another one in my mind, a memory: the victim in Winchester was a girl. A teenage girl. Human. Before she had been reduced to blood and bones, she might have looked something a little like me: brown hair, tan skin . . .

The Wyoming victim had been a boy. A teenager. A human.

Most killers had a type. If this ghost—*Shadow*, whatever— was thirsting for prey, of all the people in this room, Caroline and I were the only two who might suffice.

Human. Teenagers.

Run, and it will chase me.

I ran. I jumped through the empty frame of a shattered glass door into air so humid it clung like sweat to my skin. I ran harder, ran faster, ran like something was on my heels.

Come and get me, I thought. This was what our killer wanted, wasn't it? One human, alone? At his mercy? Defenseless?

If I'd miscalculated, I'd just left the others to face the Shadow down alone. And if I was right, I might have just traded my life for theirs. I had no way of fighting this thing, no plan.

I could only hope that if I drew the monster out, Lake might be able to help Griffin break through, and together, they might be able to do to this Shadow whatever it had done to Griffin, send it wherever he was now.

Red, red, red.

I stopped fighting my racing pulse, the acid in my throat. I let it come. I beckoned my Resilience. I lost myself in—

Fear. The way it smells. The way it tastes. A small white room. No windows. No doors.

The change was instant and unmistakable. The sound of my own heart beating was drowned out by things a normal girl wouldn't have been able to hear: the slight wind working its way through each blade of grass; gravel and rocks under my feet; heavy breathing, all around me.

It was here.

I'd run. The Shadow had followed. Had I not already been in Resilient mode, that would have flipped the switch, but this time, I felt the rush of power like a current instead of a wave. Each limb, each muscle, each cell of my body felt it separately.

It's coming.

I ducked, falling into a roll and landing in a crouch. I couldn't see the Shadow, couldn't make out its form, but I knew where it was. I could hear its silence, feel the bloodlust.

I lunged to my left. It charged right. I dove forward. It came at me from behind. In a world of our own making, we danced, the monster and me.

Fight. Fight. Fight.

Harder, faster, farther, more. I couldn't keep going like this indefinitely. Eventually, the Shadow would land a blow. Eventually, my knack would drain my body of everything it had.

Fight. Fight. Fight.

Without warning, the onslaught stopped. I felt nothing, heard nothing, saw nothing. A week ago, I might have lost hold of the state I was in—no immediate danger, no power—but I didn't let myself.

Couldn't let myself.

Flashing out—as Jed called it—took energy. If I fell back into an ordinary state, getting here again would cost me. Maybe this thing really was gone.

But maybe it was waiting.

So I stayed right where I was, my mind in a room with nothing but the sound of heavy breathing, the smell of rancid blood. Endless, infinite, overwhelming.

Fear.

I stood perfectly still, caught up in a nightmare I'd made for myself, playing possum and waiting.

Come and get me, I thought.

The Shadow obliged, but this time its form felt nothing like a person. This time, it felt like a wolf.

It hadn't wanted me to hear it Shifting, so I hadn't—but if I'd been outclassed before, I was completely screwed now. I couldn't keep running. Couldn't keep dodging. The world settled into slow motion around me, but it didn't matter.

Paws caught my shoulder, knocked me down. Nails as sharp as knives dug into my shoulder, tearing through fabric and into skin. I felt its breath on my face and twisted viciously to one side.

Teeth tore into my shoulder, instead of my throat.

Survive. Survive. Have to—

I was still fighting, still scrambling, still holding out and holding on, but I lost track of the details—of time and space and everything but the incredible need.

To get out of there.

To get away.

To *live*.

I couldn't see anything but red, couldn't feel anything but fear and power and red, red, red—

And then I was lying on the ground, and people were yelling my name, and the thing I'd been fighting—the thing that had sunk its teeth into me—was gone.

Vision came first, then exhaustion, then pain—a strange, numb pain, halfway between frostbite and a phantom limb.

"Bryn." The last thing I heard before losing consciousness was Chase saying my name—his voice aching and angry, equal parts boy and wolf.

The last thing I saw was Griffin standing over my body.

And then I was gone.

CHAPTER THIRTY

~

I DREAMED ABOUT NOTHING. NOTHING BUT THE SKY overhead and the dirt under my feet. Nothing but rain that hung in the air without falling.

Nothing but the moon.

"If you're dead, Miss Ali is going to be really, truly, *exceptionally* pissed."

I turned sideways and found Dev standing beside me. For a second, I thought he was like the raindrops and the dirt and the moon, but then he took a step toward me.

"Bronwyn." His voice was dangerously pleasant.

"Yes?"

"Picture, if you will, my feelings about Pierce Brosnan's performance in the *Mamma Mia* movie, circa 2008."

I winced.

"Now," he continued, "picture someone forcing me to grow a mini-mustache and setting my entire summer wardrobe aflame."

Uh-oh.

"Dev," I started to say, but he didn't give me the chance to finish.

"And now," he said, closing the space between us, "tell me what the hell is going on here."

This was Devon in full-on alpha mode—a hint to the person he'd someday be.

"It's not that bad," I told him.

He gave me a look.

"Okay," I said, "maybe it is that bad. But I'm at least sixty percent sure that I'm unconscious and that we're sharing a dream. I really don't think I'm dead."

Dev buried his head in his hands and then ran them through his artfully mussed hair. "Start at the beginning?"

A rush of emotion—his, not mine—hit me all at once.

I nodded. My teeth worried at my bottom lip. Then I told him everything.

About Griffin.

About Maddy.

About Shadows and the one that had just done its best to kill me.

Devon was silent right up until the point when I finished talking, and then he let loose. "Lake's brother is alive and up until a few minutes ago, you thought he might be evil; Maddy's pregnant; Callum's knack is on hiatus; and the Rabid you're supposed to be hunting is capable of tearing a person to pieces without ever assuming physical form?"

Well, when you put it that way, it did sound really bad.

Rather than acknowledge that fact, I concentrated on the last bit. "Shadows are hard to describe," I said. "It was like, one second, he was almost solid, and the next, he was everywhere. When he was on top of me, I could touch him, I could feel him, but I couldn't hurt him."

The word *hurt* was a reminder of all of the pain that awaited me on the other side of this dream.

"How bad is it?" Devon asked.

I tried to avoid the question, with little success.

"How bad, Bronwyn?"

I could have lied. In a dream, he might not have smelled it—but I couldn't do that, not when we had no guarantee that this was an expedition I'd make it back from alive.

"Two inches to the right, and this thing would have had my throat."

If I'd been any slower, any weaker, if my senses had been any less sharp, if even a bit of exhaustion had managed to beat its way through my altered state, I wouldn't be here.

Not in this dream.

Not on this planet.

I'd be splatter—like the boy in Wyoming, the girl in Winchester.

Like my parents.

My parents. I don't know if it was the dream, or the fact that Dev was there, the way he had been the day Callum had brought me home, but the universe realigned itself, suddenly and without warning.

I'd known that if I ran, the Shadow would chase me.

To catch a Rabid, you have to think like a Rabid, Sora had said. *There's a dark logic . . . a hunger . . .*

This thing was following Maddy. Torturing Maddy. And when I had run, it had come after *me*.

"Devon," I said, feeling like the earth itself had been jerked out from under my feet. "I need you to talk to Mitch and find out something for me."

I'd asked Callum how many female Weres had a dead twin—but that wasn't the right question. Not now, after feeling that thing's breath on me.

Now that it had tasted my blood.

"What do you need?" Devon didn't hesitate, wouldn't, no matter what I asked of him.

I thought of the cabin in Alpine Creek. The dead animals. The Shadow's human victims, teenagers all.

"I need you," I said slowly, "to find out if Samuel Wilson had a twin."

I came to on a bed in a different motel. Apparently, we'd become personae non gratae at the old one.

Go figure.

Chase was lying beside me, his body curled around my smaller frame. On my other side, Jed was calmly and efficiently digging a needle into my flesh: quick, clean strokes.

Stitches.

If the Shadow bite had been numb before, my shoulder was on fire now. Lovely.

"How long was I out?" I ground out. Jed eyed Caroline, and she tossed me a rolled up pillowcase.

"Little over an hour," she said. "Bite down on that."

I wanted to refuse, just on principle, but as the needle dug deep into my skin, I stuffed the pillowcase into my mouth and bit down as hard as I could, muffling the scream that wanted to make its way out of my mouth.

I could do this. I could handle this. I hadn't faced off against a ghostly opponent to be undone by a few measly stitches.

"Is poor wittle Bryn going to cry?" I could see worry playing at the edges of Lake's mouth, but her tone was an exact match for the time I'd broken my arm, when we were nine. "Don't be such a bawling little crybaby. You'll be fine."

Chase gave her a disgruntled look, but I found myself appreciating the distraction. It was easier to deal with Jed sewing me back together like a patchwork quilt when I had something else to concentrate on.

To that end, I turned my attention to Lake and said something that does not bear repeating into the pillowcase bunched up in my mouth.

She grinned, but the expression didn't go all the way up to

her eyes. I may have only been out for an hour, but that was an hour too long. She'd worried.

They all had.

"Almost done here, Bryn." Jed made good on his words, and thirty-five excruciating seconds later, he tied off the last stitch. He smoothed something that looked like mud and smelled like booze over the wound and then bandaged it.

I spat out the pillowcase.

"Guess I can scratch 'get eaten by an immaterial being' off my to-do list," I groused, trying—and failing—to find some humor in the situation. Beside me, Chase swallowed a noise halfway between a snort and a cry and ran his hand up and down my good arm.

I could almost feel the pain flowing from my body to his. If he could have borne this for me, he would have, in a heartbeat.

"I wouldn't recommend trying to move that arm," Jed told me—no muss, no fuss, no pity. "Unless you're looking to repeat this particular experience."

More stitches? No, thank you. The throb of pain was constant—burning, aching, incessant assaults against each and every nerve ending in my shoulder.

"I'll take it easy," I said.

The rest of the room scoffed audibly. In unison.

I took the high road and ignored their obvious skepticism. Instead, I focused on the real issue here. "The Shadow's gone, but he could come back."

Griffin caught my gaze and lifted his eyebrows slightly. I thought I'd done a good job hiding my doubts about him, but the look on his face was enough to tell me that he'd known. He may as well have written *do you believe me now?* across the sky in large block letters.

I nodded—as close to an apology as I could come when there was something much, much bigger at stake. The very possibility that the Shadow might be Wilson had changed everything, even though I had no way of knowing if my instincts were on point. Maybe the specter that had been following Maddy *wasn't* the same monster who'd turned her into a werewolf when she was six years old—but maybe it was.

That same monster had killed my parents, Changed Chase. The kids in my pack had once been his, until they'd turned on him and literally torn him to pieces.

Female twin. Violent death. Those were the ingredients Callum had said went into making a Shadow. I hoped I was wrong, but we knew for a fact that Samuel Wilson fit at least one of those requirements.

As soon as Devon got back to me, we'd know if he fit the other one, too.

"I'm sorry."

It took me a second or two to figure out who was apologizing and another stretch of time to work my mind around why.

"I thought having Lake here would keep me grounded—and

it did, to an extent. I think our killer got tired of waiting. When he realized I wasn't going anywhere . . ." Griffin trailed off.

I thought back to what he had said earlier, about sometimes losing his grip on this reality. I hadn't understood until I'd seen it myself, but now I had to wonder—what if the other Shadow didn't *choose* to wait until Griffin was gone until it attacked? What if they *couldn't* be in the same place at the same time?

Without even realizing I was doing it, I let that thought bleed over onto Lake's and Chase's minds. With absolutely no ceremony whatsoever, Lake turned immediately to Griffin and proceeded to show him the exact same amount of sympathy she'd shown me.

"Stop your caterwauling," she said, though I could hear the undercurrent of sadness, worry, and fear in her voice. "That thing came here, and you left. We could all do with a few less sorrys and a little more figuring of the hows and the whys."

"Caterwauling?" Griffin repeated dryly. "You think I'm *cater-wauling*?"

Lake nodded and then made an imperious shooing motion, which Griff must have interpreted as encouragement to stay on task and start talking. With an aggravated look at his sister, he did.

"The second before I blinked out, I could feel a presence trying to get in. There was this pressure, inside my head, outside it." He paused. "Then it was here. For a split second, we both were. And then . . ."

He stopped talking, and the moment he did, memories passed from Lake's mind to mine. I didn't know how she'd picked them up from Griffin, or how he'd known that she would be able to pick up where he left off. If the bond between them was that strong, why hadn't I picked up on Griffin's innocence sooner? Why hadn't I believed what Lake was telling me? Why hadn't I seen?

Because you didn't want to. I answered my own question. *Because you couldn't let yourself let him in—not after Lucas. Not again.*

I shook myself free of the thought like a dog shaking off the rain. Through my bond with Lake, I let myself feel what Griffin had in the second before the other Shadow began the attack—the incredible pressure, the chill, and finally, the pull of a vacuum.

Pulling Griffin apart.

Pulling him to pieces.

"Two Shadows can't be in the same place at the same time," I said, mulling it over and wondering if there was any way we could use that little tidbit to our advantage. Besides an attack against the Shadow's twin, that was the only thing we'd found that even approximated weakness.

Facing off against Wilson had been bad enough when he was a corporeal Rabid. Taking him down in this form would be much, much harder.

Maybe even impossible.

"What are you thinking?" Chase was the one who asked the question, but I could see reflections of it on the others' faces—all except for Maddy, whose pale face was carefully, curiously blank.

"I asked Devon to look into something." That wasn't exactly an answer, but it was true. "When he gets back to me, I'll let you guys know."

I wasn't going to dig up the past we'd tried so hard to bury, not until I was sure. At this point, all I had were a string of coincidences and a gut feeling, like lead in my stomach.

I wasn't going to rip open Chase's wounds—or Maddy's—for that.

"I'll go." Maddy whispered the words, but there was a certain strength to them nonetheless. A finality.

"Go?" Lake and I repeated, our voices combining to make the question sound more like an exclamation.

"This is my fault," Maddy said, enunciating each word with almost maniacal precision. "This thing is following me. The animals and the girl and that boy in Wyoming—it's all me."

"Maddy." There was something in the way Griffin said her name that reminded me of the way Chase said mine. "None of this is your—"

"*All* of this is my fault." Maddy wasn't whispering anymore. Her vocal cords tensed with the weight of the words. "I did this. *Me.*"

She had her hand on her stomach again, and I wondered what exactly she was blaming herself for.

"You could have died, Bryn." Maddy swung her gaze toward mine, but made no move to come closer to the bed. I struggled to stand, moved closer to her.

Maddy didn't bat an eye. It was like she was trapped in her own little world, her own nightmare. "This monster went after *you*. It hurt *you*, and the last thing I wanted to do—"

She stopped talking and bit her lip. I could see her trying not to cry, trying not to remember.

"It was my fault," she said again, but this time, it felt like the two of us were the only people in this room. "Last time, it was my fault."

She wasn't talking about the Shadow. Not anymore.

"You got hurt. You could have died, and I should have seen it."

"Maddy—"

"No!" She didn't let me finish, didn't even let me start. "You took him in for *me*. You made him Pack for *me*. I loved him, and he would have killed you! He was always planning on killing you, and I didn't see it. What kind of monster does that make me?"

All this time, I hadn't realized that Maddy had been carrying the weight of guilt around, too—that she blamed herself for Lucas, more than she blamed me.

"I loved him, Bryn. I would have died for him, and he—" She took in a sharp breath, her grip on her stomach tightening. "I still loved him." Those words held the weight of a confession. "Even afterward. Even after he—"

She couldn't say the words.

I knew then with haunting prescience that the moment when Lucas had challenged me and I'd faced down the challenge would always be between the two of us. We would never get past it. I would always think of it when I looked at Maddy, and she would always think of it when she looked at me.

It wasn't anger, it wasn't betrayal, it wasn't even hurt—but that unnameable emotion, that burden, might lighten in time, but it would never really go away. Not because we couldn't forgive each other—we had.

Things would never be simple with Maddy and me because neither one of us would ever fully forgive ourselves.

"This isn't your fault." I brought the conversation back to the present, back to a place where I might be able to make a difference and chip away at her guilt. "This Shadow is playing with you. It's torturing you."

"I let it do this," Maddy said. "Somehow, being near me—"

"No." I wracked my mind for something I could say, something that would smell true to her nose. "There was another murder, in Missouri, just north of the Arkansas state line. The Senate thought it was the work of the same Rabid."

Or at least, some of them had.

"You're not making this thing kill, Maddy. It's following you because it can." I could feel myself coming close to something I didn't want to say out loud. "It wants you to feel like this is your fault. It wants your pain."

Maddy's eyes flickered with uncertainty, then horror, then the barest hint of recognition. She knew firsthand what it was like to live with someone who got pleasure out of other people's pain.

"Don't give this thing what it wants." There was an alien depth to the emotion in those words—one I heard, even as I was saying them. Maddy heard it, too, and she heard the wealth of things I wasn't saying.

Understanding shone in her eyes, then hardened into something else.

She knew.

Beside me, I could feel Chase's mulling over the fact that something had passed between Maddy and me—something unspeakable. Across the room, Lake looked severely tempted to beat the answer out of me with the butt of her gun.

My cell phone rang, breaking the tension in the room. I knew before I answered it that it was Devon. The ring tone—the theme song from *Moulin Rouge!*—was a big tip-off.

"Remind me never to leave you alone with my cell phone again," I said, answering on the second ring.

"Hello to you, too."

"What have you got?" I asked. It would have been better if we'd been able to have this conversation silently, but the farther away the two of us got from each other, the fainter the connection. We'd been able to connect in our dreams, but it would be more difficult now that we were both awake, and this was one of those times when I needed to hear every single word—even if that meant that Lake, Chase, and Maddy would hear them, too.

"As soon as I woke up—and assured Ali that you would be fine, for which you owe me a day at the spa, at the very least—I went to find Mitch."

I wasn't sure how old Mitch was, but he was by far the oldest person in our pack—and the only one likely to have the answers I'd asked Devon to find.

"I caught him near Keely."

"Devious," I commented. Keely was the bartender at the Wayfarer. Like me, she had a psychic knack, but hers was for making people spill their secrets. If Mitch knew the answer to Devon's questions, Devon would have gotten it out of him, just by virtue of Keely being in the room.

"You were right. Mitch says Samuel Wilson did have a twin."

Chase didn't respond in any visible way to Devon's bombshell. Maddy looked down. Lake reared back. Of the three Weres in this room, she was the only one who seemed truly surprised.

The rest of us knew too much about the monster, firsthand. Even in death, he'd never let us go.

Later, I told myself. Later, I could process this. Later, I could think about what it meant, but right now I needed one more piece of information.

"I need to know what pack Wilson was born in."

While male Weres sometimes transferred packs, females usually stayed in their natal pack until they died. If we knew which pack Wilson was born in, there was a good chance we'd be able to find his living twin. If Griffin was right, if his only real weakness was Lake, finding this monster's twin was the first step toward identifying his Achilles heel.

"I suspected you might need that information." Devon's voice was too light, too calm. He was playing a part, and I had no idea why. "I asked Mitch that very question."

"And?"

Devon cleared his throat. "Samuel Wilson," he said, in that same, unnatural tone, "was born a member of the Stone River Pack."

I had to remind myself to keep breathing. I fought the urge to gasp.

The Rabid who'd killed my parents had been born as one of Callum's wolves. That revelation alone would have been a bombshell, but the implications were far, far worse.

At one point in time, Callum's pack had counted among its numbers three female Weres, but now that Katie and Lake were in my pack, Stone River only had one.

"Devon." I said my friend's name and then swallowed hard.

No wonder he sounded so off.

The only female in Callum's pack old enough to be Wilson's twin was Sora.

Devon's mother.

CHAPTER THIRTY-ONE

I HUNG UP THE PHONE WITH DEVON AND SUNK BACK onto the stiff motel bed. Callum had to have known, back when we were hunting Wilson, that he was Sora's twin.

Sora had to have known.

To catch a Rabid, you have to think like a Rabid.

Had she been talking about her brother?

Unwittingly, my mind flashed back to the day Callum had found me hiding under the kitchen sink in an old house I barely remembered—the day I'd seen a rabid werewolf kill my parents like they were nothing more than meat. Sora had been part of the cavalry that had come with Callum to rescue me. She'd been the one who Shifted, the one who leapt for the monster's throat.

The two had grappled.

Flashes of fur. White, gleaming fangs.

My memory was piecemeal, at best, but the images were there, and they were hard to shake. The Rabid had gone out the window, and Sora had followed. The monster should have died that night. We'd attributed the fact that he hadn't to his knack—a perfect match for my own. But maybe Wilson's survival hadn't just been a combination of Resilience and luck.

Maybe Sora had let him go.

Not because she wanted to, but because she couldn't stick around to watch him die, knowing that she'd been the cause.

Now, he was back, and the only thing we knew of that might hurt a Shadow was attacking its twin. I hadn't wanted to think about the implication of that when I'd believed Griffin might be the killer, and I certainly didn't want to think about it now. For better or worse, after everything we'd been through, Sora was still Devon's mother.

My Devon's.

Hurting Lake hurts Griffin. I didn't want to take that line of reasoning one step further.

To kill a Shadow . . .

No.

I couldn't go there. I couldn't let the thought form in my head. I couldn't let it be true.

There had to be another way.

Numb, except for the constant throb of my shoulder, I looked back down at my phone. Slowly, painfully, I dialed Callum's number.

He answered on the first ring.

"Bryn?"

I could tell by the way he'd said my name that until I'd

called, he hadn't been sure that I'd made it. If Shadows really did interfere with his knack, he might not have seen the outcome of the last attack, or the way Jed had stitched me back together. For all I knew, maybe my future was so intertwined with this monster's that Callum couldn't see anything at all.

"I'm fine," I said. Chase made a snuffing sound under his breath, and I amended my statement. "Mostly fine."

"What happened?"

I don't know what possessed me to reply the way I did, but the only words I could seem to manage were: "I got bit."

A manageable bite, like this one, wasn't enough to Change a person. Even if it had been, there was no way of knowing if a Shadow could do that kind of thing at all—and still, the only response I could muster was the same phrase Chase had said to me when I'd learned it was possible for someone to be born human and Changed into a Were.

"You got bit," Callum repeated, using a tone that I recognized well as the calm before the storm.

"I'm fine," I said, cutting his temper off at the pass. He rarely lost it, but right now none of us had the time to deal with the fallout if he did. "Jed stitched me back together. Pain sucks, but it's manageable." I let out a half laugh, short and harsh. "Just call it practice."

The change in the room around me was immediate, and I realized I'd said that last bit out loud.

Practice? Lake said. *Practice for what?*

Chase didn't ask, and I realized that he knew the answer—maybe he had always known the answer.

"Why didn't you tell me that Samuel Wilson had a twin?" I turned my focus back to Callum, hoping that it would provide sufficient distraction for Lake. "That it was Sora?"

I wanted him to tell me that I was mistaken, that Sora wasn't this monster's twin, that I had it all wrong. I *willed* him to say that. I prayed.

"When?" Callum asked. "When would you have had me tell you? When we rescued you? When you latched on to Devon and he on to you? When Samuel resurfaced, and we realized he'd never stopped killing? When the kids in your pack killed him?"

Would I have wanted to know? I couldn't help asking myself the question. If it hadn't been for whatever happened that full moon, with Maddy and the baby, if the Shadows hadn't come back—would I have wanted to know that the Big Bad Wolf was Devon's uncle? That my second family in Callum's pack had been his family, too?

"Once you realized we were dealing with a Shadow," I said, neatly cutting those questions out of the equation. "Two hours ago, when we were on the phone, and you knew that a Shadow was stalking Maddy, why didn't you tell me *then*?"

"Had we not gotten cut off, I would have."

I believed him—not because he wouldn't hide key information from me, but because we were dealing with an enemy whose actions he couldn't foresee. If he'd had a line on the future, Callum would have had no qualms about withholding information, but I didn't think he'd play fast and loose with my life, not when he had no way of knowing how that might turn out.

This particular Rabid had died obsessed with the idea of Changing me.

"He and Griffin can't be at the same place at the same time." I leaned back against the wall, wincing as my shoulder protested the movement. "If Griffin hadn't broken back through when he did, I'd be dead. And if Wilson isn't tied to Maddy, if he's playing with her because he can and not because he has to, there's no limit on where or who he might have killed."

I could see the victims in my mind, their corpses lined up like paper dolls. The boy in the cabin. The girl in Winchester. The unidentifiable mass of skin and blood and bones in Missouri.

How many victims had we'd missed? How many more would there be if we didn't find a way to stop this thing? In life, Samuel Wilson had been the worst kind of monster. He hadn't just attacked teenagers. He'd killed *children*.

And now he was bullet proof.

"This is just the beginning." I tried to stay calm. I tried to be rational. "Sooner or later, he'll find a way to push Griffin out. He'll come to finish the job, and then—"

The corpses in my mind multiplied, stacks upon stacks of

bodies. Little bodies. The Shadow would kill me, and then he'd move on—to Caroline and Jed, Chase and Lake. To humans who never stood a chance. To children.

There was nothing we could do to fight back. *Nothing.*

To kill a Shadow . . .

I couldn't afford to follow that thought to completion. In my mind, I saw Devon's face. I saw his smile, the way he could look utterly ridiculous one minute and like a lethal fighter the next. I saw Sora, who had his eyes, but none of his humor.

No.

It wasn't fair. It wasn't fair that Sora was this monster's twin. It wasn't fair that stopping him should fall to us. But most of all, it wasn't fair that being alpha had turned me into the kind of person who *could* think the unthinkable.

I didn't want to be that person.

"We don't know how to kill him, Callum." I swallowed, hard. "All we have is a theory."

What we had wasn't a *theory*. It was unspeakable. And there I was, saying the words.

"Now that he's tasted my blood, he'll be hungry for more. He'll kill me, but it won't stop there." I paused, wishing that my life was the only one on the line, that this was my sacrifice to make. "It won't ever stop."

"No." Callum wasn't telling me I was wrong about this monster. He was saying what the voice in my head kept saying, over and over again.

No. No. No.

"Tell me there's another way," I pleaded. "Tell me there's something I can do, somewhere I can go to look for answers. Tell me I'm wrong."

Callum didn't say a word.

"Tell me."

Nothing.

"We have no way of fighting back," I whispered. "Once he gets done with us, who's next? Ali? The twins? Human children who don't understand that monsters are real, any more than I did, cowering underneath that sink?"

Even if there were another option, another way of fighting back, there was no guarantee that we would find it in time— and while we looked, more people would die.

No matter what I did, people always died.

"You do not know what you are asking, Bronwyn."

For the first time, Callum's use of my full first name didn't affect me at all. I knew exactly what I was saying, and he was the one who'd raised me to be the kind of person who could say it.

"Sora's his twin, Callum. He's a Shadow because he's shadowing her. She's his link to this world."

Get rid of the link, get rid of the Shadow. I wanted him to tell me there was a flaw in my logic. I wanted to be wrong.

"You'll hold the knife, then?" Callum asked. "You'll look into Sora's eyes and cut out her heart?"

Devon had his mother's eyes.

The temperature in the room around me seemed to drop ten degrees. My face felt clammy and flushed. The brutality of what I was suggesting hit me full force.

To kill the Shadow, we might have to kill Sora. Sora, who'd bandaged my cuts and fed me cookies when I was a kid. Sora, who'd taught me to use a slingshot. Sora, who for better or worse, was one of Callum's most trusted soldiers.

Devon's mom.

"I'll have no part of this," Callum said. "If you're certain it's the only way, you'll do it yourself."

I hadn't expected this from him, hadn't imagined he would put this decision in my hands. Sora was his wolf. At one point in time, our killer had been, too. Everything Callum had done in the past few years had been aimed at protecting me, shaping me. But this?

This wasn't a choice the Callum I knew would ever have put in my hands. I still dreamed about Lucas, still thought about him, still felt the weight of snuffing out his life, and that had been self-defense. He'd been a danger to the pack, a loose cannon, and he was the one who'd challenged me.

But Sora wasn't a danger. She wasn't evil. This wasn't self-defense. This was me, sitting on a ratty bed in a motel room, thinking about sacrificing her life for the greater good.

This was me, talking about murder like it was an option.

"I don't know what else to do," I said.

There was a long silence on the other end of the phone, and I waited for him to say something to make this—any of it—better.

"What would you do if it were Lake?" Callum asked finally. Something in his tone made me feel like, this time, he was looking for something from me—absolution, understanding? I wasn't sure which.

"If it were Griffin that was the killer, and the only way to kill him was to kill Lake, what would you do?"

I'd thought that Griffin might be the killer, but I'd never let myself follow that thought to completion, because the idea of hurting Lake, sacrificing Lake—I couldn't have done it.

Could I?

That was the position I'd put Callum in. He was so old, so powerful that it was easy to forget that he had emotions, that his pack mattered to him, that there were people—other than me—who he loved.

"Three hundred years," Callum said softly. "She's fought by my side for three hundred years, Bryn. I wouldn't see her dead on a theory, and neither would you."

Three hundred years? Sora had been a part of Callum's life longer than the United States had been a country, longer than any human would ever live.

And still, if it wasn't just a theory, if he were *sure* that this would work and there was no other way—he would have done it. That was what it meant to be alpha.

That was what I was becoming, even now.

"You wouldn't have to." Lake came to stand next to the bed, and I realized she was talking to Callum as much as to me. "If it were Griff doing the killing, if we thought me dying might make a whit of difference, Bryn, you wouldn't have to kill me."

I read between the lines to what Lake wasn't saying.

If it had been her, if her death was the way to stop the monster, she would have killed herself.

"This isn't your choice," Lake told me. "It's not his," she continued, jerking her head toward the phone. "You two don't just get to sit there and talk it out and decide that she lives, no matter how many other people have to die. You don't get to keep this from her."

I realized suddenly how Callum and I must have sounded, talking about Sora like she had no stake in this. I wondered if this was what being alpha would ultimately turn me into—a person who was so used to making hard decisions that she assumed every one that came along was hers to make.

"Bryn." The voice on the other side of the line wasn't Callum's, not anymore.

"Sora." For the first time, saying her name didn't take me back to the night when she'd beaten me. I didn't see her driving her fist into my rib cage. I saw her the million times before that, taking care of me like I was her own.

I saw Devon—the way she looked at him, the way that, once upon a time, he'd looked at her.

"You're sure the killer is my brother?" Sora sounded younger than I'd ever heard her—like Lake when she'd realized that Griffin was here, that he was real.

I thought of the bodies, the blood, the breath on my neck. "I'm sure," I told her.

Sora didn't hesitate. She didn't stutter, she didn't even breathe. "If the only way to stop him is to kill me, then you kill me." She paused, and I could picture her sharp features settling into a mask, every bit as unreadable as Callum's. "I'd prefer not to have to kill myself."

But she would—that was what she was telling me. If one of us didn't kill her, Sora would kill herself. She'd die to stop her brother.

"I'll meet you at the border," she said. "Three hours."

That didn't give her much time to say good-bye—to Callum, to her husband, to Dev.

"Sora—" I wasn't sure what to say, but it didn't matter. The line was dead.

She'd already hung up.

CHAPTER THIRTY-TWO

THE WEREWOLVES IN THE ROOM WERE SILENT—
they'd heard every word Sora, Callum and I had said. They
knew what was coming. Jed and Caroline were another story.

Chase told them, so I didn't have to. He was brief, to the
point, and calm, but inside, I could hear him howling—not for
Sora or Devon or all the things that might never be.

For me.

I could feel him thinking about what this would do to me.
On the other side of the pack-bond, he was thinking about the
future: about years and years of being alpha chipping away at
everything else I was. About everything I would have to give up
and everything I'd already given up.

If it wasn't one thing, it would be another, year after year,
for as long as I lived—Lucas had just been the beginning.
Lucas had been the *easy* part, and that had almost killed me.

This was Devon's mother.

I stopped listening to Chase's thoughts, because I didn't
want to know where they would lead. This was hard enough

without knowing that Devon, Callum, and I weren't the only ones who would pay the cost—that as long as Chase was with me, whatever hurt me would hurt him, too.

"She wants you to kill her." Caroline's voice was as calm as Chase's, but there was an edge to it, brittle and sharp.

"She doesn't want to kill herself," I corrected, easing myself off the bed and ignoring the constant throbbing in my shoulder. "She shouldn't have to."

Neither should you. Chase's words bled their way into my mind despite the barrier I'd thrown up. I met his eyes and then shook my head.

Not now.

I couldn't do this with him now.

"Griff?" Lake's voice broke into our silent exchange, and I whipped my gaze around to Griffin. His jaw was clenched, his eyes glittering with equal parts concentration and rage. Of the duo, Lake was taller. She was the one with a temper, but in that moment, Griffin looked dangerous—freckles, light lashes, and all.

"He's here," he said. "I can feel him. He's trying—"

Griff's eyes narrowed. His mouth settled into a thin line, then his upper lip pulled backward to reveal gleaming white canines.

"Not gonna happen," he said through clenched teeth, sounding so much like Lake that I would have known they were twins, even if I were a total stranger.

Griffin glimmered—there was no other word for it. His

skin became paler, almost incandescent. His hands curled into fists. His eyes gleamed with unnatural light—and then, just as suddenly as the change had fallen over him, it was gone.

"I take it you won?" Lake asked, arching one eyebrow.

Griffin nodded. "For now."

"He'll keep trying." Maddy had been silent since I got off the phone, but when she spoke, it was with utter certainty. "It's all about control with him. He hates losing, but he's patient. He'll try again and again and again, and you have no guarantee that you'll get to Sora before he gets to you."

I saw where this was going, even if the others did not. Maddy and I were too much alike, and in her shoes, I knew exactly what I would have done.

"You have a plan," I said.

She nodded. "You only need a few hours. Maybe Griffin can hold him off that long, and maybe he can't, but I know I can."

"You can what?" Chase said, his brow furrowed, his blue eyes dark.

"I can keep him busy," Maddy said. "Distract him."

The others were slowly realizing what I'd known from the moment Maddy had spoken up—she wanted to do what I'd done earlier: run and entice the monster into chasing her.

Play bait.

"He's spent months following me around, playing with me, killing for me. If I leave, if I'm alone, there's a good chance he'll follow."

The predator in Wilson might get bored with Maddy eventually, but we didn't need her to distract him forever—just until Sora was dead.

Just until I killed her.

"I'll go back to the mountain," Maddy promised, "back to the cave. Griffin will go with you, in case Wilson tries to manifest, but with any luck, he'll take the easy way out."

Take the easy target, I corrected silently. Maddy was deaf to my thoughts, but they must have been painted on my face, because she nodded anyway.

"You can't go out there alone." Griffin was the one who said it, but we were all thinking it.

"I *have* to go alone," Maddy corrected. "If anyone goes with me, that's who he'll go after. He'd kill you—any of you—just to make me watch."

I didn't want to let Maddy do this. Every instinct in my body rebelled against the idea of letting her go off by herself again.

"You didn't let me," Maddy said, as if I'd said the words out loud. "You didn't *let* me go. You didn't *let* me do anything, Bryn. It wasn't your decision then, and it's not now."

You can't make me stay.

I felt the words in the set of her chin, the spark in her eyes. Part of being Resilient was being resistant to the kinds of mental bonds that normal Weres were helpless against. If it had been Lake who was dead set on a suicide mission, I could

242

have used the pack-bond to stop her. I could have forced the issue. If she'd left the pack, I could have bound her to me, against her will. I could have *made* her obey.

But I wouldn't have—just like I couldn't fight Maddy on this, if this was what she wanted.

Sometimes, being willing to die for those you loved wasn't enough—it was harder, tenfold, to let them make that kind of sacrifice for you.

"What about the baby?" Lake, apparently, wasn't above fighting dirty—not that this was news to anyone in the room. "If Wilson follows you and there's no one else there to attack, if you're alone, what's going to keep him from going after you? Or her?"

Maddy wavered, but a moment later, her jaw was set, her gray eyes clear. "He won't hurt me, because he won't risk something happening to her."

We didn't know exactly what had happened during that full moon three months ago, but neither did our ghostly opponent. The one sure bet was that it had something to do with Maddy's unborn child. If the baby had brought the Shadows back, Wilson wouldn't risk hurting her—not if there was even a slight chance it might undo what had been done.

It's just a theory, I thought dully, Callum's objection echoing in my mind. It was just a theory that Sora's death would ensure the Shadow's. It was just a theory that Maddy's baby's death might do the same.

But what else—other than theories—did we have?

"I'll be careful," Maddy said. "I'll stay away from people. I'll be fine."

It seemed wrong that we'd spent so much time looking for her and now she was walking away. It seemed wrong to stand by and watch it happen, but there were some battles that even I couldn't fight.

"If something happens to you," I said—and didn't get any further than that.

"The other alphas won't be looking for me," Maddy replied. "Callum said they won't be able to enact the vote. I'll stay off the grid. I can handle the Shadow. I'll be fine."

"Will you come back?" The question came from Jed, his voice worn and ragged, and I realized that none of the rest of us had wanted to ask it, because we were scared to know the answer.

We'd gone into this with the goal of bringing Maddy home. The fact that she wasn't rabid—and *was* pregnant—made the desire to do so a million times stronger, a million times worse.

Maddy looked at each of us in turn. "I don't know," she said, giving us what honesty she could.

She didn't know if she was coming back—now or ever. She didn't know if she was ready, didn't know if things could ever be the same.

This might be good-bye, then, I realized. Maddy might leave here and disappear, the way she had before. Her plan could backfire. She could die. Even if she didn't, we might never see each other again.

And there was nothing I could do about it—nothing any of us could do about it.

I walked forward and wrapped my good arm around her. She wrapped both hers around me, and for a moment, I could hear her heartbeat, feel the baby shifting position restlessly in her womb.

Good-bye.

CHAPTER THIRTY-THREE

WE GOT TO THE BORDER BETWEEN CEDAR RIDGE AND Stone River with twenty minutes to spare on Sora's timetable. Griffin was still holding strong, and I could tell by the worry lines that had taken up residence around the corner of his mouth that the constant onslaught had subsided.

The killer had taken the bait.

I said a quick and silent prayer that wherever Maddy was, she was well, and then turned my attention to what we'd come here to do.

What *I* was going to have to do.

Werewolves were difficult to kill. Purebreds, like Devon and Shay, could survive anything short of decapitation, having their hearts ripped out, or being literally torn to pieces. I wasn't sure whether Sora's mother had been a werewolf or not, but even if she hadn't been, killing Sora wouldn't just be a matter of pulling a trigger.

Not if we wanted to make sure she stayed dead.

Dead.

Don't, I told myself. *Don't think it. Don't picture it. Don't picture Dev.*

"Silver," Lake said, nodding toward the weapons she'd packed us. "And you have your knife."

Since the challenge, I hadn't gone anywhere without it.

"I'll do it." Caroline crossed the border to stand on the Wyoming side—something that neither Lake nor I could do, without invitation.

"You'll do what?" I asked, jarred by the sudden reminder that Caroline wasn't one of us and wondering how I'd gotten to the point where any part of me thought that she was.

"I'll kill her." Caroline was holding a knife in her own hand, and she ran her thumb over the tip of the blade, so lightly that it didn't draw blood. "That's what I am. A killer."

I could tell by the tone in her voice that those were someone else's words, ones she'd heard often enough to believe them.

"It's what I do, Bryn. It's what I am. You know that."

At one point, I would have believed what she was saying, but now?

"You have a knack for hunting," I said. "That doesn't make you a killer."

"I shot Eric. The others killed him, but I shot him, and now he's dead."

If you'd told me a week ago that I would be arguing with her about this, I never would have believed it, but she'd weathered the events of the past three days with me. She'd fought by my side.

If she was a killer, so was I.

"You know Sora," Caroline said finally. "I don't. It will hurt you. It won't hurt me. Nothing hurts me."

"Liar." Lake beat me to the punch. "Just breathing hurts you so bad, you want to beat the snot out of something."

Eloquent was Lake.

"I can do it," Caroline insisted.

I nodded. "You could," I said, "but I'm not asking you to."

I owed it to Sora to see this through. To do what she'd asked of me—what Callum couldn't do.

There has to be another way. I couldn't push down the part of my brain that was desperate for that to be true. I wished I could believe that wanting a solution, wanting it so badly it hurt, was enough to make it so that one could be found.

But it wasn't enough, and there wasn't another solution—and even if there were, we didn't have the luxury of time to find it.

I don't want to Change. That thought came fast and vicious, and this time, I didn't have the mental wherewithal to fight it back. *I don't want to be a werewolf. I don't want to live forever, having to make these decisions over and over again. I don't want to stay young and watch Ali and Keely and Caroline grow old and die.*

I don't want to kill my best friend's mom.

I didn't want this.

I didn't want any of it.

I'd already lost Maddy. I couldn't take losing Devon, too. He was my rock, my friend, my constant from the time I was four years old, and this—this unspeakable thing I had to do—it would always be there between us.

I'd lose him and lose that much more of myself.

I felt Sora approach before I saw her. Her dark hair was pulled into a low, loose ponytail. She was wearing a black tank top and jeans. Her feet were bare.

Without my having to ask it of them, Lake and Caroline fell back. I was standing on one side of the border, Sora was standing on the other. For the longest time, we looked at each other, neither one of us speaking.

"Tell Devon," Sora said finally, "that he's the only thing I ever did right."

I fought the urge to hunch over, to weather the words like an actual blow, because Devon would never get to hear them for himself; because one of the last things his mother would ever hear him say was a complaint that they'd even had to ride in the same car.

"He's strong, and he's smart, and I know that he is going to do great things." A soft, sad smile worked its way onto Sora's thin lips. "He'll do what has to be done in a way that I never could."

I wondered if she was talking about her failure to kill her

twin, or about Shay. I wondered if it even mattered, when death was just around the bend.

"I'll tell him," I said, my own voice shaking. Sora reached across the border and caught me by the chin. She angled my face upward, my eyes toward hers.

"You're it for him," she told me. "You always have been."

I didn't pull out of her grasp. I felt it, all the way to my toes.

"Hurting you," she said, after a moment's pause, "hurt me."

Those words nearly undid me—because she'd never acknowledged what had passed between us, never given any hint that ripping my world apart had been anything more than a chore.

"I want you to promise me something." Sora reached back and pulled her ponytail over to one side, baring her neck on the other. The knife in my hand felt heavy.

Too heavy.

"What?" I asked, my mouth cotton dry, my palms sweating.

"Don't let things end between you and Callum the way they're ending for Devon and me. Whatever Callum does, whatever he sees or doesn't see, says or doesn't say, however the next year plays out"—she took a deep breath, her chest rising and falling with the effort—"trust that he has his reasons, and that you matter."

She looked over my shoulder, at the setting sun.

"You've always mattered."

To Callum? To her? To Devon? She didn't elaborate. Instead,

she reached down and took the knife from my right hand and placed it in my left.

"Start with a gun."

A moment later, I had one in my hand. Was it hers? Mine? I wasn't sure. I felt like I was moving through a fog. Sora wrapped her hand around mine and brought the gun to rest on the side of her head, where neck met skull. She angled the barrel upward.

"Put a bullet here," she said, and then she nodded to the knife. "Then cut out my heart."

My hand shook. My eyes stung with tears. I tried to blink them away, but they built behind my eyelids until I couldn't see—I couldn't see her face, couldn't see her waiting, ready and willing to die.

"You can do this," Sora whispered. "You have to."

I hurt for Dev. I hurt for me. I hurt, and I hurt, and I hurt—and I had to kill her.

"Bryn." The voice came from behind me, but I didn't recognize it. Chase? Griffin? Jed?

I didn't know. I didn't care, because I was standing there with a gun, and Sora was waiting. The trigger was cool against my finger. My injured shoulder was screaming with the effort it took to hold the gun.

Do it, I thought.

"He's back, Bryn. He's coming."

So the voice was Griffin's, then. There was tension in it, and exhaustion. The monster was here and ready to play. Maddy's distraction had only worked so long.

Do it.

"Bryn." Sora's voice was gentle, but unwavering. If I didn't kill her, she'd take care of the job herself, and I owed her more than that.

I owed her this.

"Okay," I said, a sob catching in my throat. "Okay."

Beside me, Griff stepped into view, a visual reminder that we were running out of time, a ghostly countdown clock to the next attack. He trembled. His eyes took on an odd, otherworldly light.

"I'm losing it," he said. "The pressure—it's pulling me— he's pushing me—"

Lake stepped into my peripheral vision, right next to Griff. I began counting down in my head.

Three, I thought, training my eyes back on Sora's.

"You're not going anywhere," Lake said from beside me, her words aimed at Griffin, not me.

Two, I thought.

"Lakie, I'm so sorry—"

One. I took a deep breath. The muscles in my arms tensed. I went to pull the trigger.

"Ow!"

I stopped.

"Bryn, please." Sora's voice was more insistent this time, less gentle, but I turned to look at Griffin.

"What did you say?" I asked, my voice catching in my throat. "You said *ow*," I continued, my voice rising—high-pitched, desperate, loud. "You said *ow*. Why?"

Griffin stared at me like I had lost my mind. Maybe I had. My fingers tightened around the barrel of the gun.

"Tell. Me. Why."

"Lake hit me," Griffin said.

"Of course I hit you! You think you can just blink out of existence, and I won't even hit you?"

Lake had punched him, and he'd felt it. It had *hurt*.

I lowered the gun, my body shaking like it might never stop, my arm weak, my shoulder useless.

"She hit you," I said dumbly, "and it hurt." I didn't wait to see the words register on their faces. Instead, I turned back to Sora.

Her eyes were sharp.

"You don't know that it will work," she told me.

"We don't know that anything will," I countered. "All we know is that up until five seconds ago, the only thing that had ever hurt Griffin was someone hurting Lake, and now it looks like *she* might be able to hurt him, too."

Two Shadows couldn't exist in the same place.

A Shadow was injured when you injured his living twin.

And—if Lake and Griffin were any kind of test case—the twin in question could fight the Shadow.

"Let him come," I told Griffin, before turning back to Sora.

There was no room for questions here, no room for doubt. I took the gun from my hand and transferred it to hers.

"You can fight him. You can win."

Sora handed the gun back. Without a word, she began to strip off her shirt, and that was when I knew—she'd fight the Shadow, the way she'd fought her brother when he was alive.

As a wolf.

Her face was impossible to read. Her hands hung loose by her sides. The last thing she said to me, before she started to Shift, was five little words.

"Permission to enter your territory?"

Beside me, Lake dropped her hand from Griffin's shoulder. She took a step back, masking her anguish with a broad and predatory smile. Griff closed his eyes, spread his hands out to the side, and stopped fighting.

The moment before he disappeared and everything went to hell in a handbasket, I gave Sora her response.

"Permission granted."

CHAPTER THIRTY-FOUR

THE SECOND GRIFFIN DISAPPEARED, THE REST OF us scattered like shrapnel. Behind me, I heard Sora Shifting: *snap-snap-crunch-scream-snap.* The sound was an unholy rhythm, a grossly melodic call to arms. My skin itched with the sound of it; my bones ached with the desire to shed my human flesh like unwanted clothes.

Opposite me, Chase tilted his head slightly sideways, the muscles in his neck straining against his human form.

Shift. Shift. Shift.

The call was there, in the air—but it wasn't alone. There was another presence, just as feral, just as hard to deny.

He was here.

The humid summer air was thick with violence, thick with rage—everywhere, all around us.

Small room. No windows. No doors.

I called up the image, and power rose in my body, heat radiating outward from my stomach. The constant pain in my shoulder faded to mere memory, taking with it my limitations, my awareness of anything except my opponent.

I felt his presence like an actual shadow, blocking light from my eyes. I whirled around and stepped sideways, caught in an unthinking waltz.

I just had to survive until Sora finished Shifting.

I just had to keep him here until she could take him out.

Ghostly fingers stroked the back of my neck—human fingers. For now. I ducked out of their ice-cold grasp, exploding forward and away, adrenaline pumping through my body, my limbs tingling with an almost electric charge.

And then I saw him.

He must have wanted me to, must have chosen that moment to let me see his face. His hair was dark brown, a shade or two lighter than Sora's. His eyes were darker than they'd been in life—so dark that the pupil bled into the iris, a single, inky orb.

He smiled.

"Hello, little Bryn." He didn't sound like a monster. He never had. "Still so beautiful. Still so strong." He breathed in deeply through his nose and stepped forward. "Still *mine*."

Seeing him made it easier to track his movements, but I held to my Resilient state, let it flow through my body, like water through a dam.

Fight. Fight. Fight.

"What do you think will happen," the Shadow with Wilson's face said slowly, "if I Change you now?"

The question sent a chill down the back of my neck, like

a spider crawling down my spine. The chunk this thing had already taken out of my shoulder had numbed me, before it had hurt. This wasn't a normal Were we were dealing with. If Wilson brought me to the brink of death and Changed me—the way Callum hadn't, not yet—what manner of beast would I be?

No. I wouldn't think about that. I wouldn't think about anything, except the smell of death and clammy palms and the claustrophobic room in my head, where my nightmares lived.

Fear.

The Shadow stepped forward and then blurred. One second, he was ten feet away from me, the next, he was rubbing his cheek over mine. In a flash of black fur, Chase leapt for me, leapt for him, but Wilson disappeared.

"Nuh-uh-uh," the monster said, his voice coming from all around us. "Can't run, can't hide."

I felt him, felt his breath on my skin, felt him closing in.

"I should thank you," he whispered, in stereo. "For killing me."

I flew backward and hit a tree trunk. I absorbed the blow and rolled to my feet. I heard the sound of paws on the ground. I felt him leaping—

Thud.

A large wolf—tan fur, white markings, lethal—collided with the invisible predator midair. A high-pitched yelp turned into a growl as the two of them hit the ground, each grappling for control.

Sora was brutal, efficient. Fighting an invisible opponent, she was nothing but fangs and claws, beautiful, deadly grace. Blood, so dark it was nearly black, marked the white fur around her muzzle. Phantom teeth sunk into her flank, but she shook her assailant off violently and whirled around, jaws snapping, fur on end.

The air quivered, like the surface of a pond under an onslaught of skipping stones, and then Wilson appeared again.

This time, I doubted it was on purpose.

In wolf form, he was the creature I remembered from my nightmares. There was a white star on his forehead. His eyes were intelligent, his fur matted with blood. Suddenly, I didn't have to work to hold on to the red haze.

It threatened to overwhelm me.

Escape. Have to—run—have to—

I reined it in, pulling the power inward, feeling it as a ball of fire in my chest. I wasn't four years old anymore.

I wasn't running.

Sora flew through the air again, mouth full of blood-marked teeth, death in her eyes. She grabbed him by the throat.

She pinned him.

His legs scrambled for purchase, but she slammed her body sideways, crushing his limbs under her weight. She met his eyes, his blood filling her mouth.

And then he Shifted—silently, effortlessly, as only a dead

werewolf could. She let go of his neck, just for a second. Blood dripped off his body, disappearing the moment it hit the ground.

He gargled.

For a second, they stared at each other—wolf and human, twins. I knew, beyond all rationale or reason, that she'd held him at this point before.

That she'd let him go.

I stopped breathing. She nudged his face with her nose. Licked his chin. And then, without warning, she lunged. Her teeth closed around his human neck. She bit down, until she hit bone, and then she jerked her head sideways.

His spine snapped.

His eyes lolled backward.

His head hung on by a thread.

I felt Sora begin to Shift before I heard it. In human form—naked, her body smeared with blood—she knelt next to him.

"Give me a knife." Her voice was rough, her words short and sharp. I walked to her, knelt next to her, placed my knife in her hands.

She leaned forward, whispered something in his ear. Then, dark hair running free down her back, her lips ruby red with her brother's blood, she drove the knife into his chest and cut out his heart.

His legs turned gray, then his torso, his arms, his face, until we were looking at a corpse. His eyes sank back in his skull;

his body decomposed. The earth rumbled under our feet, and in an explosion of light—fireworks at midnight, the sun just after an eclipse—he was gone.

Sora collapsed backward on her knees, her body folding in on itself. The curve of her spine caught the last bit of twilight, and I could see heavy breaths wracking her body.

Fifteen, twenty seconds later, she rose. She walked calmly to her discarded clothes. She got dressed, and then she turned back to me.

"The message I gave you?" she said. "For Devon?"

I nodded.

She closed her eyes. "I'll tell him myself."

Belatedly, I remembered to let go of the little room, the panic, the fear—and the fight drained out of my body with it. I was so tired, exhausted—and I hadn't even done anything.

"That's the danger," Jed said gruffly. "You stay there too long, you hold on too tight—it can kill you."

Because what I really needed was to add more to the list of things that could kill me.

One by one, I surveyed our little group. We'd survived. All of us. But as I met Lake's eyes, I realized something was wrong.

"Where's Griffin?" I asked.

She didn't respond, and I realized that he hadn't come back. Wherever he went when he wasn't here, wherever Wilson had sent him—he hadn't come back.

"Bryn." Sora—a clothed Sora—called my name from the

Stone River side of the Montana–Wyoming border. I forced myself to tear my attention away from Lake, even as I felt her fighting a silent battle with herself—

Not to care.

Not to let it hurt this time.

Not to think about burying him again.

I staggered toward the border, turning my eyes and mind away from Lake, giving her what little privacy I could.

"Thank you," I told Sora quietly, wondering if taking her twin's heart had provoked in her some measure of what Lake was feeling now.

The bond between them had outlasted even death—and now he was gone. Really gone.

Sora inclined her head slightly, but didn't otherwise acknowledge my thanks in any way. I waited for her to speak and wondered if there was something I was supposed to be saying.

Hallmark didn't exactly make cards for occasions like this.

"You promised me," Sora said finally, her voice dry and hoarse, "that when this was over, you would give Callum a chance to make things right."

Apparently, the fact that she hadn't died didn't void that promise in her eyes, and that made me think—

"Make what right?"

There was another long silence.

"Make *what* right, Sora?"

She may not have been part of my pack, but I was an alpha, and that dominance was audible in every single syllable as it exited my mouth.

"Griff!" Lake's voice broke into our standoff, and reluctantly, I tore my eyes from Sora's in time to see Lake launch herself at newly reappeared Griffin. In a flurry of overly long limbs, her body collided with his, nearly bringing them both down. She wrapped her arms around his body and squeezed, hard enough to leave marks.

Anyone else's hands would have passed through him, but not hers.

Never hers.

Griffin ran a hand through Lake's hair and tweaked the end of her ponytail, a calming gesture and a familiar one. Then he pulled back. He untangled himself from Lake's arms, extracted himself from her steely grip, and turned his attention to me—and by extension, to Sora.

"It's Maddy," he said.

The second I heard her name, my insides twisted—a portent of things to come.

"She's in labor," Griffin continued, sounding calmer than he looked. "I would have stayed with her, but I couldn't. The baby—it made me—I felt it—I couldn't be there."

I nodded, like I understood, even though I didn't. The only thing I was able to wrap my mind around was the fact that something was about to go down.

Something bigger than Maddy giving birth.

"Sora?" That was all I said—no elaboration, no pretense that what she was about to say might not rock me to my core. I waited for her to speak, feeling emptiness bubbling up inside of me instead of anger, exhaustion instead of fear.

I didn't want to hate Devon's mother again, didn't want to look at her and see the bad things, instead of the good. She must not have wanted that, either, because she expelled a long breath and then started talking.

"What exactly did Callum tell you about Maddy?" she asked. "What did he tell you about the Senate?"

Callum had told me that Maddy might be rabid.

I'd discovered she wasn't.

He'd told me that if Maddy wasn't the killer, the Senate wouldn't be able to enact the vote.

"He told me she was safe," I said, realizing even as I said it that those words had never left his mouth.

He'd said that the Senate couldn't enact the vote.

He'd said that they wouldn't be able to cross into our land without permission.

He'd never said they wouldn't come after her. He'd never said that she was safe.

"Maddy's in No-Man's-Land." My thoughts went from my brain to my mouth with no filter. "And once you get there, No-Man's-Land is fair game."

The other alphas couldn't cut through my territory to get

to Maddy, but they might not have to. By definition, any slice of No-Man's-Land fell between two territories—maybe more. Maddy's cave was in the mountains, and the mountains were accessible from Cedar Ridge territory, from Shadow Bluff, and from Vallée de Glace in the north.

It might not be easy, but it was doable, and Callum had never said Maddy was safe. He'd just listened to me say it.

He'd let me believe it.

"Two other alphas have access to that mountain," I said. "If they realize she's there . . ."

Maddy had been hiding out in No-Man's-Land for months—but this time, there was a trail of bodies, including one in Winchester, that could lead the other alphas straight to her door.

Looking at Sora's poker face and seeing Callum's, I knew suddenly that the Shadow Bluff alpha wasn't the problem, and neither were our neighbors to the north. Shay had called the Senate meeting. He was the one who'd been building alliances.

"He's coming for her," I said. "Shay got passage—from Shadow Bluff or the northern packs, from someone who has access to that mountain."

And Callum knew.

This had nothing to do with the Shadows. Callum's ability to sort through possible futures would have been operating full force. He'd seen this coming. He'd known Shay might come after Maddy, and he hadn't said a word.

"Callum has his reasons," Sora said, but I doubted that she

knew them—I doubted he would have shared them with her any more than he would have shared them with me.

This was what Callum did, who he was. He played God. He played me. He let bad things happen.

You need to be human for this.

I'm sorry, he'd said. *For something that might happen and might not.*

I swallowed down the words that wanted to come and instead gave Sora a small, flippant nod.

"Thanks for the heads-up." My words came out sounding tired, not sarcastic.

Damn it. I didn't have time to be tired. I didn't have time to celebrate Wilson's permanent death, to sob with the memory of holding a gun to Sora's head, to rail against Callum for playing with us like we were dolls.

I stuffed my feelings back in their little steel box, and I turned to the others: to Lake, who hadn't taken her eyes off Griffin, to Chase, still in wolf form. I turned to Jed and Caroline, both ready to fight at a moment's notice.

"Let's go."

CHAPTER THIRTY-FIVE

IT'S GOING TO BE OKAY. IT'S GOING TO BE OKAY.
I didn't bother blocking my thoughts off from the others—to the point where I wasn't sure whether my silent mantra, as we climbed the mountain, was for my benefit or theirs.

We would get to Maddy in time, and even if we didn't, I had to trust that she could hold her own. Shay wouldn't physically harm her—she was too valuable, the *baby* was too valuable.

Shay would try to claim her. He'd dig his fingernails into her skin and try to force his mind into hers, instating a bond that would tie her to the Snake Bend Pack.

To him.

But Maddy was Resilient. She could fight him. She could resist.

I just had to hope that she would be able to hold on until I got there, that giving birth wouldn't have taken too much out of her. I had to trust that, push come to shove, her survival instinct—and her instincts as a mother—would be enough.

It's going to be okay. It's going to be okay.

We were getting close. I nodded to Chase and Lake, let them go. Faster than my human eyes could track them, they ran.

We were going to get there.

Maddy was going to be okay.

And then I was going to kill Callum.

"Wolves." Caroline said the word out loud, and I was reminded for the second time that day that she wasn't a part of our pack. She wasn't a part of this.

Yet, here she was.

"How many?" I asked, unwilling to distract Lake and Chase from their task with that question.

"I don't know," Caroline replied, her baby blues narrowed in concentration. "They've got a perimeter set. The wind's coming out of the north. I can go around back, scope it out."

I glanced at Jed, and he nodded. Caroline was impossible to track—even with werewolf senses, they wouldn't hear her coming.

Like a thief in the proverbial night, she was gone, blending perfectly into her surroundings, stalking through the rough mountain terrain, a girl on a mission.

I turned to Jed. Darkness fell over his eyes, and that was the only signal I needed. I reached for my own Resilience, called up the power, and ran.

One second I was at the base of the mountain, and the next thing I knew, I was at the mouth of the cave. I saw Chase first, then Lake, both in wolf form. Their clothes littered the cave floor. Their hackles were raised.

Opposite them, Shay Macalister was smiling. He was bent at the waist, too large to fit fully inside Maddy's den.

"Leave. Me. Alone."

Maddy's voice was wispy weak, but full of emotion. I stalked into the cave, past Chase and Lake, right up to Shay, and that was when I saw her.

Maddy was lying on her side, her face ghostly pale, blood smeared on her dress. And there, in her lap, was a baby.

A pup.

The newborn must have Shifted during labor, or soon thereafter, because there wasn't a hint of baby-pink skin to be seen—only short, spiky fur, sticky and standing straight up.

Her baby eyes were closed.

"You're mine," Shay said, leaning over Maddy, kneeling next to her, his voice vibrating with power and want and need.

"No. I'm. Not."

Maddy spat at him, on him, but she was too weak to move. She couldn't move.

"Maddy," I said, wary of coming to stand within Shay's grasp, but knowing I had no other choice.

If he kills me, I thought, *Callum will kill him.* Right now that was cold comfort.

"Maddy?" I reached out to touch her cheek. Shay growled, but there was nothing he could do about it—first come, first serve, and he hadn't managed to break his way through Maddy's defenses yet.

She was fighting him—but she might not fight me.

"Mads?" There was a question in my voice. She hadn't wanted this—not last winter, not when she'd left us in the motel room.

She nodded.

"Yes," she said, reaching out and taking my hand, pressing my nails into the flesh of her neck. I felt my fingers curling, felt myself digging in deeper, drawing blood. Then I took all that I was—all that my pack was—and I threw it at her.

Chase and Lake and me.

Devon, at home with the kids.

Lily, Katie, Alex, Ali, Mitch.

Phoebe, Sage, and all the rest.

This was what we were. We were a pack made by choice. We were *family*.

Power exploded out of me. The air hummed with it. I stopped breathing. Maddy stopped breathing. When we started up again, we breathed as one.

Pack. Pack. Pack.

She was mine.

I turned to Shay, expecting to see rage marring his features—so like Devon's I wanted to hurl—but the only thing on Shay's face was a smile.

I didn't realize I'd let go of my Resilience until it flared back up. This cave was too small, Shay was too big, too strong, and he was smiling.

We have to get out of here, I told Maddy, the words flowing freely from my mind to hers, as if she'd never left, as if it had always been this way between us, this easy.

Eyes on Shay's, I hooked my arms beneath Maddy's armpits. I pulled her backward. She scraped her heels against the floor, pushing, propelling herself out toward the mouth of the cave, toward morning's first light, toward freedom.

Shay followed, but stopped when Chase and Lake came to stand in front of us, their lips curled upward, mouths open, canines gleaming.

Maddy was ours. If he attacked one of us, if he made a move against us, my wolves could attack him—and if his pack didn't want to face the wrath of the Senate when it was said and done, they'd leave him to fight us alone.

Us, I thought, and reflexively, I scanned the woods for Caroline and found her, poised behind a rock, twenty yards away, gun in one hand and crossbow in the other.

"It's over, Shay." I shut my fear away—didn't give him the chance to smell it. He couldn't fight me, not unless he wanted to start something that Callum would end.

"It is over," Shay agreed amicably. "And you, my dear, have something that belongs to me."

At first, I thought he was talking about Maddy, but then a garbled cry escaped her throat, and I realized that he wasn't talking about the girl.

He was talking about the pup.

No. A child was born into his or her mother's pack. There

was no Marking, no claiming. It was automatic—but Maddy's child was born in No-Man's-Land. She was born to a lone wolf.

I'd claimed Maddy after the child's birth, not before.

With horror, I realized the implications. Maddy had fought Shay. She'd resisted. She'd been able to. But the baby—

"No," Maddy said, the word halfway between a howl and a growl, not human in the least. "You can't have her. You *can't*."

Shay walked between Chase and Lake, like they were nothing. To him, they probably were. He knelt, and as bile rose in my throat and my dry eyes burned with tears that wouldn't come, he ran one hand gently over the sleeping pup's head.

Maddy trembled, on the verge of a Shift. Shay gestured to someone behind us, and another Were came to stand beside him.

"Careful," Shay told Maddy. "You might hurt her if you Shift."

The Snake Bend alpha stood and faced me, my body dwarfed by his massive dimensions. "The little one is mine," he said, "and there's nothing you or your reinforcements—" he jerked his head toward Caroline, leaving me to wonder how he'd known she was there—"can do about it."

Shay paused. "Of course, the pup might not live long without her mother. She might just waste away . . ."

Maddy stifled a sob, and I saw the trap Shay had laid. He'd claimed the baby. It didn't matter that I'd claimed Maddy—faced with the choice between watching Shay walk off with her child and going with him, to ensure the child lived—she'd choose the latter.

Every. Single. Time.

"The Senate will never let you do this," I said roughly. "You can't kill a pup."

"A female pup," Shay corrected. "With no twin. She's a little miracle, isn't she? And by the time you manage to call the Senate, she'll already be dead. You wouldn't want that, would you, Bryn? You wouldn't want this girl's baby to die. You wouldn't hold her here, when she wants to come with me—don't you, Madison?"

Bryn, please. Maddy met my eyes. I wasn't sure if she was asking me to do something to stop this, or to let her go. I had seconds to decide, seconds, and all I could think was that Callum had let this happen.

"If you don't believe I'll do it, ask your friend with the gun." Shay smiled in Caroline's direction. The Were he'd beckoned forward—a man I recognized as his second—reached for the baby.

"The little girl with the good aim should know better than anyone—" Shay flashed a smile, full of fang—"I have no problem taking a parent away from a child."

I remembered—too late—that Shay was the werewolf who'd given Caroline her scars. He was the one who'd killed her father. He was baiting her.

"Caroline, don't—" I didn't get the rest of the warning out of my mouth before the sound was swallowed up in gunfire. Dully, I surveyed the damage.

A bolt, directly through Shay's throat. Six silver bullets, clustered in his second's heart.

Maddy pulled her baby backward and scooted away from the man who'd had his hands on the pup when Caroline had fired.

A purebred werewolf might survive a cluster of silver bullets straight to the heart, but regular Weres reacted to silver like poison. Shay's second-in-command might have been able to heal from a single bullet wound. But six?

Shay kicked the man's body dispassionately to the side. "Now this," he said, ripping the bolt from his throat, "is an interesting development."

Beneath the roar of alarm in my mind, I heard Chase's voice.

Wolves, Bryn. Lots of them.

Caroline had told me that Shay had his Weres poised along the perimeter, but I'd had no idea how many. One by one, they stepped from the shadows—from behind trees and rocks, from nearby caves.

They ran in from town, from Shadow Bluff territory, from all sides.

There weren't just a dozen of them, or two. Shay hadn't just brought his guard. He'd brought his entire pack.

Even with Caroline, even with Jed, even if Griffin could break through whatever it was about the baby's birth that had pushed him away—we were still outnumbered.

And Shay wasn't the type to take an attack lying down.

CHAPTER THIRTY-SIX

~~~

As the Snake Bend Pack closed in on us from every direction, I half-expected Caroline to sprint for the hills, to settle down in a sniper's nest, from which she could pick them off one by one—but she didn't.

It took me a few seconds to realize why. She wasn't the only one with a gun. The pistol looked out of place in Shay's massive hands, but he clicked the safety off and pointed it just to my left. A pair of werewolves pushed Jed roughly toward Shay—and the gun.

The old man could have flashed out.

He could have fought them.

But he didn't—because he realized what Caroline did not. This situation was volatile. The Snake Bend Pack was the third largest in North America, and if Shay hadn't brought his entire pack here, he'd certainly brought most of them—and all of his fighters.

"Come on down, Caro," Shay called. "Unless you'd prefer to be responsible for the death of your mentor, as well as your father."

He called her Caro, the way Devon did. He even sounded like Devon when he said it.

"Let's have us a little chat, shall we?" Shay continued jovially, as Caroline came to stand beside me, her eyes diamond hard, weapons well within grasp. "As a gesture of goodwill, I'll even have my wolves Shift to human form. I'd appreciate it if you would do the same, Bryn."

All around us, the sound of Shifting echoed off the mountain, but this time, I didn't feel the call or the power. All I felt was dread.

Caroline had shot Shay.

She'd killed his second-in-command.

He was going to kill her. She was Ali's sister, and Shay was going to kill her. There was nothing I could do to stop him. She was a human. She'd killed a werewolf. She was a threat, and as far as Senate Law was concerned, Shay would be within his rights to put her down.

"Well, Bryn?" Shay smiled, and I realized he was still waiting for me to order my wolves to change to human form. I nodded to Lake and Chase. She Shifted back to human form. He did not. Instead, he came to sit at my feet, the warning clear in his eyes.

"Interesting," Shay said again. "I didn't know the Cedar Ridge alpha had taken a mate."

That wasn't a word Chase and I used—but the second Shay said it, I felt a spark of recognition from inside Chase's wolf form.

Yes, it seemed to say. *Mate. Bryn. Mine.*

Shay didn't leave us in silence for long. "Do you know the difference," he said, relishing each word like a delicacy, "between a Rabid and an alpha who kills humans when the need arises?"

He didn't give me a chance to answer.

"It's a matter of subtlety. Restraint. Proper disposal of the bodies." His teeth were so white that I wondered if he'd bleached them, but I couldn't stop thinking of Callum telling me that the future was coated in blood. Now Shay was talking about disposing of Caroline's body.

"Was it subtle when you killed the leader of a psychic coven?" I asked, my voice deceptively calm. I searched for leverage, a loophole, anything that might give me an advantage over Shay. "Was exposing yourself to an entire group of humans and leaving their hatred of werewolves to simmer for years *subtle*?"

This was the card I was holding in reserve. The only one. Shay hadn't just killed Caroline's father—he'd left a witness and allowed her to spread the tale to others of her kind for years. As far as blackmail material went, that might not be enough to save Caroline—but I had to try.

"What are you suggesting?" Shay asked.

I met his eyes, steel in mine. "I'm suggesting that you don't want the Senate looking into Caroline's death. They might wonder why she attacked you, and I don't think you'd want them finding the answer."

Shay was silent for one second, two. "You're assuming there

will be an inquiry." He paused, his lips curling upward, his eyes narrowing to slits. "There won't be."

Shay was right. Caroline had fired the first shot. There wasn't a Were on the Senate who would dispute Shay's decision to kill her, so long as he didn't risk exposure to do it.

She was only human.

"I'll call the Senate myself," I promised, letting Shay see the truth in my eyes, letting him smell it on my breath. "I'll demand an inquiry. And once I present my case, once I tell them what I know—how sure are you that Callum will be on your side and not mine?"

I waited for Shay to call my bluff. If Callum had wanted to prevent this, he could have. I fully expected Shay to point that out, to tell me that the Senate was a *democracy*, and that—at the moment—Shay was playing by their rules.

But he didn't.

"Is she yours?" Shay flicked his eyes toward Caroline, and I sensed a split second of hesitation on his part. *"Is the human yours?"*

Caroline wasn't a member of my pack, but if I admitted that, Shay could and would kill her without repercussions. Since she'd attacked first, it wouldn't even be a Senate matter, not the way Rabid kills were, and all that my calling the Senate would accomplish would be pissing the other alphas off.

But if Caroline were mine—if I claimed her as part of my pack, the way that Callum had once made me a member of his—then that would complicate the situation—for Shay and for me. If he killed her, I'd have the right to call his actions into question, and even if the Senate ultimately ruled that he'd done nothing wrong in killing her, I'd be in position to bring up the fact that Shay had murdered her father—and why.

Shay wouldn't want the Senate asking questions, not about that.

But if I claimed Caroline as my own, that would mean that a member of my pack had just killed a member of Shay's. He'd still have the right to take blood for the blood she'd spilled. If he demanded Caroline's life and I refused to hand her over, he'd have the option of taking her transgression out on me.

Beside me, Caroline didn't say anything. She didn't move. She didn't even look at me.

She didn't have to.

We'd fought side by side these past few days. She was Ali's family, and that made her mine.

No matter the cost.

"She is." I sounded sure. I sounded *alpha*. I may not have Marked Caroline. I may not have made it official—but she *was* mine, enough that the words would have smelled true.

"Very well," Shay said. "And the old man? Is he yours as well?"

I turned to look at Jed and saw that he was holding on to his control by a thread. If they rushed him, if they threatened him, he might lose it. He might flash out.

I'd have to answer for that, too.

"He's mine as well."

The second the words were out of my mouth, Shay moved, quicker than my eyes could track him. By the time I'd processed the sound of gunfire, a bullet had already buried itself in Jed's forehead.

Shay's guards let go of the old man's body and it crumpled to the ground.

Resilients might have been able to survive some things, but a bullet to the head wasn't one of them. Jed had kept his control, right up to the end. He hadn't fought back.

For me.

For Caroline.

And now he was dead.

Animal justice—an eye for an eye.

Caroline let out a cry that sounded more feral than anything I'd ever heard from a Were. She would have launched herself at Shay, attacked him all over again, but Lake caught her from behind. She held Caroline's arms to the side, held her back.

I couldn't think about Jed and the hole in his head. Not about the things he might have taught me, or what he already had.

I had to be the alpha.

I had to follow the old man's example and keep my instincts in check.

Control.

"So we're even," I said, meeting Shay's eyes. "Caroline took one of yours. You took one of mine."

This hadn't been the plan. When I'd claimed Caroline, I'd assumed that Shay would take her transgressions out on me. Not on the rest of the pack. Not on Jed.

"Even?" Shay closed the space between us, coming to stand right next to me, right next to Chase. "That," he said, jerking his head toward Jed's body, "was because she shot me. There's still the matter of my second's death to settle."

Jed's life in exchange for a wound that was nothing more than an inconvenience for Shay? That wasn't an even exchange. It wasn't even close, but if I brought the matter up before the Senate, they would probably support Shay's assertion that killing one of my pack's human members was reasonable compensation for another Cedar Ridge human's attack on the alpha of the Snake Bend Pack.

Jed was only human, and preserving hierarchy and inter-pack relations was worth more to most werewolves than human life.

"The death of a werewolf at the hands of a human." Shay caught my gaze and held it. "That's not a debt I'd like to pay. If I were you, I'd save myself some trouble and put a bullet in the girl myself."

If I killed Caroline, Shay would end this—but he knew I wouldn't do that. He was *hoping* I wouldn't do it. I'd bet everything on the assumption that Shay wouldn't want me to expose his past deeds to the Senate, but clearly, I'd overestimated my hand.

He'd *wanted* me to overestimate my hand.

He'd laid a trap for me, and I'd walked straight into it.

And now Jed was dead, because of me.

"If Pack Justice demands blood," I said, putting my body physically in front of the others', "you'll have mine."

A few hours earlier, I'd been willing to sacrifice Sora for the greater good. What kind of person would I have been if I weren't willing to sacrifice myself? Shay wanted a life in exchange for his second's? Fine. He could damn well take mine. If I didn't fight it—didn't fight *him*—it wouldn't constitute a challenge. Devon would inherit my pack once I was gone, and Shay wouldn't be able to touch them.

Any of them.

Shay smiled again, like he'd known all along that I'd offer my life up to save theirs. But he made no move to hurt me. Instead, he made a tsking sound under his breath. "Didn't Callum teach you anything about Pack Law, Bronwyn?"

He was calling me Bronwyn. The way Dev did. The way *Callum* did.

"You can't trade a human's life for a wolf's," Shay told me, violence creeping into the edge of his voice, reminding me that a human life was nothing to him. "And unfortunately, *you* aren't a wolf."

He wouldn't accept my life for his second's. For all I knew, maybe he *couldn't*.

An eye for an eye.

One second, Shay's gaze was boring into me, and the next, he had Chase on his back and on the ground.

You can't trade a human's life for a wolf's.

No.

I couldn't hang on to the here and now, couldn't keep the rage from bleeding over everything—red, red, red.

This was what Shay wanted. He wanted me to attack him, wanted me to give him an excuse to kill me, one that would be absolutely and 100 percent above reproach in the other alphas' eyes.

In Callum's.

If I attacked Shay now, that would constitute a challenge. If I broke Pack Law and challenged him, if he killed me as a result of a direct challenge, he'd inherit my pack. And the Senate might actually let him keep it.

This was the plan, I thought. *All along, this was his plan.*

Shay wanted me to lose control. He was goading me, the way he had Caroline—and none of that mattered, because this was Chase.

Protect. Protect. Protect.

Strong arms wrapped their way around my torso, holding me in place. Caroline? Lake? Did it matter? Did anything?

I needed to get to Chase.

I needed him.

But Chase just met my eyes. I felt him, felt his calm, felt the warmth of his body in bed next to mine when I woke up each morning. I felt myself fighting with him in the forest and knowing that I would always be his first and last and only. I felt my lips on his, his breath on my face, our hearts thumping as one.

I felt *him*.

I loved *him*.

Stay. One word, from his mind to mine. The only order he'd ever given me. The only thing he'd ever asked.

I couldn't.

I didn't want to.

But I did—and in that last second, so much flowed from his mind to mine: everything he'd never gotten the chance to tell me about his past, his scars, his certainty that his entire life—the good, the bad, and the inhuman—had all been leading to one place.

One person.

Me.

Love you, he said. It sounded simple when he said it. It always sounded so goddamn simple.

Shay's fingernails grew into claws.

He thrust them through Chase's rib cage.

I love you, I love you, I love you, I told him, over and over and over. *Forever.*

I couldn't close my eyes. I couldn't look away. But I did what Chase had asked me to. I stayed put, and I watched, and Shay Macalister ripped out his heart.

An eye for an eye.

A wolf for a wolf.

CHAPTER
THIRTY-SEVEN

TIME SLOWED FOR ME. MAYBE IT STOPPED. THE WORLD just faded away. Nothing mattered. Nothing was real. Shapes blurred together. The smells, the taste of the summer air on my tongue—gone.

All gone.

The only sound I could hear was a strange and gut-wrenching keening: a strangled sob, a whimper, a scream.

It took me a few minutes to realize it was me.

Shay just stood there, smiling, like for the first time in a long time, all was right in the world. Like my pain was his bliss.

Chase. Chase. Chase.

I thought his name, over and over again, but I didn't feel it, didn't feel him. The bond we'd shared, the connection, his thoughts, his feelings—

There was nothing left. Nothing of him, and nothing of me.

I should have done more. I should have fought for him. I should have *died* for him. I would have. I wanted to.

There were never any answers. If I'd been faster, stronger—if I'd been smarter, if I'd been *more*, he would still be here: warm against my side, calm in my mind, loving me the way I loved him. Loving me better.

But he was gone.

My ears roared. I pulled away from Lake's grasp. She let me go, and I struggled to stand straight.

It didn't matter that the rest of the pack was there, in my head. I was alone, would always be alone now. I had to fight the urge to wrap my arms around my midsection, like I was the one who had been gutted, like everything inside of me was in danger of spilling out.

If death was numbness, I'd died when Chase had—but by some cruel twist of fate, I was still here. I was here, and he was gone, and that wasn't the kind of thing I could fix.

"*Now* we're even," Shay said.

I was empty inside. Hollowed out. Dead. But something about Shay's words cut through the shock and the horror and the pain and brought another emotion to the surface.

Rage.

It sparked. Caught fire. Spread through my body, through my blood. There was no red haze, no instinct, no Resilience. There was only me and a certainty that Shay had started something that I would end.

If he wanted to play, I would play—and the name on his lips when he took his last breath?

It was going to be mine.

"We'll be going now," Shay said. "My wolves and I."

I knew he didn't just mean the legion surrounding us in the woods. He also meant the baby, the pup, the little girl, who he would never see as a person so much as a prize.

She was awake now—so fragile, so small. Maddy cradled her body against her chest. Through the bond, I could feel a need rise up inside of Maddy, one that put my own desire to *protect* those I loved to shame.

Maddy wouldn't just die for her daughter. She'd deliver herself to hell to save her even a single second of pain. She'd do horrible things, and wonderful things, and everything in between—and she wouldn't hesitate, not even for a second.

"I take it you'll be coming, too?" Shay asked Maddy, pretending politeness, as if the girl who'd just given birth wasn't covered in dirt, bloody, heartbroken, and nearly feral.

"You'll understand, of course, if I require you to switch packs before traveling with us." Shay leaned forward and blew out a light wisp of air into the baby's nose before turning his attention back to Maddy. "Since Bryn would likely take my head on a platter, I can't risk having a Cedar Ridge wolf running amok among our ranks."

He thought he'd played this—played us—so perfectly. He thought he'd won, but it was obvious then that Shay Macalister had no idea what I was capable of, or how long I was willing to wait.

I was human now, but I wouldn't always be. The odds were on his side, but someday, somehow, that would change.

Bryn. Maddy's voice was quiet in my mind. I didn't make her ask me for anything. I didn't react to the unspoken request or Shay's machinations in any visible way.

All I did was let Maddy go.

I pulled my mind from hers, unable to do anything else.

There were rules—rules about who we could kill and how and why. Rules about a human life not measuring up to the life of a werewolf. Rules about retribution and inter-pack relations, Senate meetings and territory.

The rules said the baby was a member of the Snake Bend Pack.

The rules said her alpha mattered more than her mother.

We all knew that Shay wasn't bluffing. He would take the baby, knowing that if Maddy didn't follow, the pup would likely die. Given King Solomon's dilemma, Shay would have cut that precious bundle in two, because that was the kind of monster he was.

Face streaked with tears and dirt, Maddy stepped forward and offered her mind up to Shay, allowing him to Mark her, to violate her, to possess her in every conceivable way. I felt the change, saw it fall over Maddy's body with the weight of chains. The pup in her arms stirred, pressing clumsy feet against her mother's stomach.

Foreign. Wolf.

Maddy wasn't Pack—not to us, not anymore. The rules said she was Shay's now. The rules said that no one else could claim her unless he willingly let her go—and he would never, ever let her go.

That was reality. That was the truth. Maddy was gone. Chase was dead. The rules said the only way I could attack Shay with impunity was if he offered up his own life or attacked me first. Personally. Directly.

Rules had let him kill Chase.

Rules had let him send Lucas into my pack to kill me.

I hated the rules. I hated them, hated that I was a part of this world, that Callum had ever saved my life, that I had grown up thinking this was *normal*, and that the only slice of normal I'd ever had was gone—without warning, forever. I would never, even for a second, get to be *just a girl* again, and Chase would never get to *be*.

Because of the rules.

"You never stood a chance," Shay told me, in a voice best reserved for lovers whispering in bed. "Look around, Bryn. Everything you see is mine—and what isn't now"—his eyes lingered on Lake—"will be soon."

I looked around. I saw his pack, his numbers. I felt their power, the way he'd meant for me to. I thought about what we had lost, and I thought about the rules.

That's when I realized—what Shay had done. What I could

do. The possibility took root in my mind and filled the emptiness inside me with one purpose.

One plan.

"Until next time," Shay said, directing the words at me
before turning to Maddy. "Time to go, Madison. We'll
have plenty of time later to discuss your reluctance to give me
my due."

Shay was still putting on a show for me, letting me know
that while he wouldn't kill her, he would hurt her—because
she'd chosen me, twice. Because the rules said he could.

One purpose. My heart beat with it. Each breath in and out
of my lungs fueled it. *One plan.*

I hadn't found a way to save Chase. I was too human. I'd
stood there and let him die because he asked me to. Because
I hadn't seen another way. Because Shay had come here with
a plan, and I hadn't.

One purpose. One plan.

Shay turned to go, jerking Maddy alongside him. The rest
of the Snake Bend Pack pulled in to follow. I felt the brush
of fur against my ankles and legs as they passed. I heard the
snapping of teeth, and I let myself think the words that had
knocked over a long line of dominoes in my mind.

He brought his entire pack.

I waited until they were out of sight, all of them—
Shay, Maddy, the Weres in wolf form and the ones who'd
chosen to run as humans. They disappeared to the west,

through Shadow Bluff territory, and I absentmindedly added the Shadow Bluff alpha to my list.

The list of people responsible for the bodies on the ground.

The list of people I would never forgive, never forget.

Wordlessly, I knelt next to Chase's body. In death, he'd Shifted back to human form. His face was frozen in an expressionless mask. His eyes were open, his body a bloody mess.

I brought my hand to his cheeks. I closed his eyes. I expected to feel something, to feel him, but I didn't.

I love you. I love you. I love you.

Gone.

I straightened and stood. No crying, no tears, no asking God why. All that mattered was taking from Shay what he'd taken from me.

The thing that mattered most.

Lake opened her mouth to say something, but no words came out. Caroline was equally silent, her eyes bloodshot, dead. Maybe I should have blamed her for this, added her name to the list. She was the one who had fired the shots, she was the one who'd gotten under my skin enough that I'd put my pack on the line to protect her.

But there were only three of us now—three teenagers, alone on a mountain, our dead scattered like petals at our feet.

"We should put the bodies in the cave," I said. "We won't have time to bury them."

"What?" Caroline sounded like I felt. I was half-surprised she didn't take a swing at me.

"We'll come back," I told her. "But right now, you and Lake need to move the bodies, and I need to call Devon."

Lake reached out and touched Caroline's arm. Caroline continued glaring at me, but she didn't voice an objection. She must have seen that I had a purpose.

A plan.

"And after you do that, and we do this?" Lake asked.

I didn't smile. Not yet. Maybe not ever again. I just ground my teeth together, got out my phone, and answered Lake's question.

"Then," I said as I dialed, "we're going to catch a plane."

CHAPTER
THIRTY-EIGHT

IT TOOK US AN HOUR TO GET TO THE CLOSEST AIRPORT, a tiny little strip of a thing that didn't fly commercial. I'd been willing to commandeer a plane by force if necessary, but there was no need: pilot, plane, and a small white envelope bearing my name were waiting for us when we got there—courtesy of Callum.

He'd known we'd come here, and he'd known where we'd be headed—and why. Any doubt I might have clung to that he hadn't foreseen Chase's death—hadn't already *apologized* for it—evaporated.

There wasn't an apology in the world—before, during, or after—that could make this right. A plane and a pilot and the Stone River alpha's reassurance—via note card—that he would be glad to send Devon's father to stay at the Wayfarer in his son's stead did nothing to change what had happened.

What Callum had let happen.

I didn't bother calling him. I sent permission for Lance to

enter our territory via text. Then I closed my eyes and waited—for the plane to land, for Shay to realize that he'd pushed the wrong girl too far.

Devon met us near the northern border of Shay's territory. I was betting that to get to Maddy's hideout, Shay would have had to take his pack north, up and around Cedar Ridge, and then down into Shadow Bluff territory and over. Even at werewolf speed, the return journey would take time—more time than it took Devon to get here from the Wayfarer, and more time than it took Lake, Caroline, and me to fly.

In a fair race, I wouldn't have been able to outrun Shay, but werewolves had a tendency to forget about things like planes, and I was done with *fair*.

Now was the time for playing dirty.

"This is what you want?" I asked Caroline.

"It is."

I didn't ask her if she was sure—didn't need to be told that the answer was yes. Digging my fingernails into her flesh, I made good on the assurance I'd given Shay in the mountains: Caroline wasn't just any human.

She was ours.

With little ceremony and only Devon and Lake as an audience, I made Caroline a member of the Cedar Ridge Pack. I tied her mind to mine, to the others. I Marked her, the way that Callum had once Marked me.

She didn't flinch, and I got the feeling that Caroline would have gladly gotten in bed with the devil himself if it meant taking Shay down a notch.

Hurting him, the way he'd hurt us.

"So that's it, then," Caroline said. "I'm one of you."

I got a vague and fuzzy sense of her thoughts on the other side of the pack-bond—not nearly as clear as they would have been if she was a Were. I heard enough to know that this was not a place she'd ever expected to be.

Welcome to the club.

She started at the sound of my voice in her head, and I figured it wouldn't be long before she learned to shut me out, the way Ali did, the way I'd shut Callum out, growing up.

Let's do this.

Even with the addition of Caroline, four was a small number to represent our pack, but Devon was my second-in-command, and at the moment, he was bleeding power, anger, *pain*.

Our eyes met, and his took on the sheen of tears. He crossed the space between us and opened his arms. I'd been intent on staying strong, on keeping my emotions in check, but seeing Devon undid something inside of me. He'd been there when Callum brought me home to the Stone River Pack. He'd been the reason it had started to feel like home—and he'd been with me every step of the way since then.

It was killing him that this time, he hadn't been there, that I'd been gutted, and he wasn't there to stop it.

Without thought or hesitation, I launched myself into

Devon's grasp. I buried my face in his shirt—purple silk that smelled like him, felt like him. I didn't cry, but my body shook like I was sobbing.

Devon murmured to me, held me, hurt for me. Through the bond, I could feel his emotions, and I felt him feeling mine. We only stayed that way for three seconds, maybe four, before I stepped back, sending a death glare around the group, daring them to comment.

No one said a word.

I went over the plan—again and again. It was simple, but we couldn't afford for anything to go wrong.

We were going to do this by the rules.

Eventually, Griff joined us. He didn't ask what had happened or what had brought us to Snake Bend territory. Maybe he'd been watching. Maybe he'd tried to see Maddy again and had realized she was with Shay.

Maybe he saw all he needed to see in Lake's eyes.

"We have a plan?" he asked.

Two werewolves, two humans, and a ghost up against the third-largest werewolf pack in North America?

"Yeah," I said. "We have a plan." I outlined the details, the rules. "Think you can handle damage control?"

I hadn't counted on Griffin's presence, but having an ally who was impervious to the fangs and claws of our opponents wouldn't hurt—though if things went according to plan, there wouldn't be much of a fight.

"We're really doing this," Lake said. It wasn't a question, or a complaint. She punctuated that fact with a low whistle. "This is big."

She was right.

This wasn't defense.

This wasn't waiting for Shay's next move.

This was war.

CHAPTER THIRTY-NINE

DEVON AND LAKE SMELLED THE SNAKE BEND PACK coming long before I felt their presence registered to the part of my brain that was alpha.

Foreign. Wolves.

Foreign. Pack.

Devon, Lake, Caroline, and I spread out in a line. Behind us, Griffin faded from view: invisible, but present. Our secret weapon.

Shay came around the bend first. I saw surprise in his eyes, then delight. Apparently, he thought I'd done something stupid.

He hadn't seen stupid yet.

"You," he said, stepping over the border and relishing the words, "are trespassing."

"No," I said, my voice an exact echo of his. "You are."

It took a moment for my words to sink in.

"Take a deep breath, Shay." I gestured around. "Does this smell like Snake Bend territory? Does it *feel* like it's yours?"

I hadn't been able to ship my pack off to Callum's for safety because territory was only territory as long as it was occupied and protected.

"What I don't understand," I said, "is why you took your whole pack after Maddy." I pretended to mull it over. "You must have made deals with the other alphas—the ones whose territories border yours. You wouldn't have just left your land completely unprotected unless you were *sure* no one else would come after it."

I shrugged and smiled. "Whoops."

Shay had never seen me as a threat. He'd never even considered the possibility that I might strike back.

"You think that four children can stand against my entire pack?" Shay's lip curled upward in disgust. "You think I'll let you take what's mine?"

I smiled. "I don't think you have a choice."

Shay had left his territory. His pack had left their territory. He'd gone after Maddy with everything he had, stacked the deck in his favor in the event of a confrontation with my little ragtag group.

He'd done it to intimidate me.

To remind me that he had the power.

That I was nothing.

Well, look who was nothing now.

"While we were waiting for you, the four of us went for a little run in the woods," I said, my voice downright chipper.

"And our peripherals? The ones you've been more or less stalking from your side of the border for the past year?" I turned to Devon. "Remind me where they are again?"

"Well," Devon said, tapping his chin thoughtfully, "I believe that Phoebe is in Minnesota, and Sage is running the border in Iowa, and Jackson was just telling me that he'd always wanted to see Missouri . . ."

The plan had never been just to take North Dakota from Shay. I wanted it all.

The man I'd taken it from stepped toward me, every muscle tense, violence and rage battling for supremacy in his eyes.

"Nuh-uh-uh," Devon told him. "Our alpha's really been very understanding about the issue of trespassing, but I'd suggest you stay where you are."

Shay's pack had been quiet up until now, but I could hear the murmurs starting—growls and grunts and human words, hushed to whispers.

They were the third-biggest pack in North America, and now they had nowhere to go.

"Seven people cannot claim a territory." Shay spoke through clenched teeth, and his jaw trembled. He was fighting the urge to Shift.

If I kept pushing him, Senate or no Senate, Callum or no Callum, rules or no rules, he was going to kill me.

I summoned my knack, channeling every fear I'd ever felt into this moment.

Let him try.

"Is that what your instincts are telling you?" I asked Shay facetiously. "'Cause that's the funny thing about werewolf laws—it's not about numbers per se. Four people can be a pack if they're bound as a pack. A human can be alpha, if she's the one the others look to for leadership. And seven people *can* claim a territory, if they represent enough of the pack."

Cedar Ridge had twenty members. Counting the peripherals, there were seven of us in this territory—including the alpha, the second, and the strongest female. That was more than enough. We *were* the pack, and standing there, flanked by the others, I could feel the power humming between the four of us.

Pack. Pack. Pack.

The bond that connected us to each other was the same thing we'd used to mark the land. It was why this place smelled like us, felt like us.

It was why the Snake Bend Pack registered as foreign to our senses, when this land was once their home.

Pack. Pack. Pack.

Ours. Ours. Ours.

"It's been nice chatting," I told Shay, "but you have five seconds to get the hell off my land."

He lunged at me. I saw it coming, and my knack, already active, already waiting, came online full force.

Fight. Fight. Fight.

Run. Run. Run.

Survive.

One second he was flying at me, human teeth bared like fangs, and the next, I ducked out of reach. I felt air against my face, felt his teeth snap an inch away from my throat.

His human hands encircled my neck.

I can't breathe.

I fought—fought dirty, fought hard, rode the power like it was a wave. I had to get out, had to get away, had to stall—

Shay's body flew backward. A growl echoed all around us, and phantom claws dug into Shay's flesh.

Thank you, Griffin, I thought.

In retrospect, it was a really good thing he was there. Flashing out let me push my body to its limits—but the limits themselves were still there. I would never be as strong as a werewolf. I would never be as fast.

Luckily, being attacked by an invisible opponent took Shay off guard, and in the moments it took him to recover, Devon came to stand directly in front of me.

The message was clear: you want her, you go through me.

Dev? I knew what he was thinking, knew that the moment Shay had attacked me, there was no other way this could end.

Devon reached back to grip my hand, briefly, then dropped it, settling into a position that Callum had taught him, the same way he'd taught me.

"You're trespassing on Cedar Ridge territory. You just

attacked the Cedar Ridge alpha." Devon's voice was loud and deep, and the words sounded like they were spoken through him as much as by him. "You've just saved me the trouble of having to transfer to your pack to kill you."

Inter-pack aggression wasn't allowed. An alpha could only be challenged from within—but Shay had broken the rules first, and there was nothing more animal, nothing more basic, than retribution.

He'd attacked me. Devon could kill him. End of story.

Shay's pack—spread out along the border like the crowd at a concert—responded to Devon's words like an intense electric shock. Some of them Shifted. Some of them growled.

None of them came forward to help their alpha.

"You really think you can take me?" Shay asked. He climbed to his feet, dripping blood from wounds that were already healing. "Take us?"

There were so many of them, too many, and if Shay ordered them to fight, they'd have no choice, Senate or no.

Callum would kill them—kill him—but by that time, Devon would be dead.

No. I couldn't lose him. I couldn't lose him, too.

"Are you saying you can't take me on your own?" With the skill of younger siblings everywhere, Devon delivered the taunt with one arched eyebrow. "Are you saying you're scared to accept the challenge of fighting me head-on?"

That was the magic word.

Challenge. Challenge. Challenge.

I could feel it, in the air. My pack could feel it. The Snake Bend Pack could, too. Devon wasn't one of them, but he'd challenged their alpha.

There was a reason that people from different packs weren't generally allowed to challenge each other.

A challenge to the alpha was always settled with a fight to the death.

Driven by instinct, the Snake Bend werewolves circled the two brothers. Lake, Caroline, and I joined them, and I found myself standing directly between Griffin—who'd chosen to manifest—and Maddy, who appeared to have survived the journey unscathed.

Challenge.

Devon and Shay were standing four or five yards apart, mirror images: taller, bigger, broader through the shoulders than any normal Were. Dev looked old for his age—maybe twenty—and Shay looked less than a decade older, despite his many years.

Fight. Fight. Fight.

I couldn't interfere, couldn't fight beside Devon, no matter how much I wanted to. All I could do was open the bond between us as wide as I could, willing my strength to flow into his body, willing my love to spare him from harm.

Without any forewarning, Shay attacked. The space between them disappeared to nothing, and an iron-hard fist crashed into Dev's jaw. He fought back, and I focused on the fight, pushing out any thoughts that might distract my best friend from the battle at hand.

The two warriors were nothing but a blur. I couldn't make out where Dev's limbs ended and Shay's began. I heard each impact more than I saw it. I smelled blood in the air. I felt energy, running electric through the rest of my pack.

The rest of Shay's.

Tell Devon that he's the only thing I ever did right. Sora's words echoed in my mind. *You're it for him. You always have been.*

In the circle, Devon was on the ground. He was still. Bones broken, bleeding, he spat. He struggled against his own body—he fought to stand, to keep fighting.

I'd never done a thing to deserve Devon.

All that I had, all that I was—I gave it to him, the way he had always, always given everything to me.

Shay Shifted—not entirely, but in monstrous parts. His mouth grew into a muzzle, his fingers into claws. His spine broke itself, his body caught in between the human's form and the wolf's. There was no beauty in this moment, nothing natural or animal or right.

This was Shay, looking as monstrous on the surface as he was at his core.

He loped toward Devon. He swung one massive hand back to strike the death blow.

Devon rolled forward, into a squatting position. He met Shay's eyes, and instead of dodging the blow, he sprang toward it, Shifting midair. The change was fluid and instant. As monstrous as Shay was, Devon was beautiful.

Powerful.

And unlike Shay, he had something to fight for—someone. As Dev's wolf body collided with his brother's, as the two of them fell to the ground and Devon grappled for position, as his jaws closed around Shay's neck, the only thing in his mind was me.

Looking eerily like his mother in posture and motion, Devon went for Shay's throat.

Teeth bit through inhuman skin—deeper and deeper. Shay fought, his claws digging into Devon's stomach, but Dev never let go.

He bit until he hit bone.

He bit through bone.

He didn't stop—not when Shay's arms dropped to his side, not when he stopped moving, stopped fighting.

My best friend tore his brother to pieces, and I watched.

Devon, who couldn't stand to have dirt under his fingernails, bathed in his brother's blood. By the time he stopped—stopped fighting, stopped the bloodlust, just *stopped*—there was nothing left of Shay: nothing scary, nothing evil, nothing dark.

He was nothing.

Dev Shifted back to human form. Naked as the day he was born, he spat on the ground and—God bless him—asked, ever so politely, if any of us had a mint.

I choked—on hysterical giggles. On tears.

Devon was alive.

The man who'd killed Chase—*Chase, Chase, my Chase*—was dead.

And finally, finally we were free.

All around us, the Snake Bend Pack howled—a horrible, keening sound, a soul-wrenching send-off for a man who'd brought them nothing but pain.

Challenge. Challenge. Challenge.

The call was fading; the moment had passed, but something else was rising in its place: something that brought the wolves' howls to a close.

Something that brought them to their bellies, to their knees.

I couldn't hear it. I couldn't feel it. But I knew what it was.

Devon had killed the Snake Bend alpha. Shay's second-in-command was already dead, and the most dominant werewolf present was Dev.

Dev, who wasn't a member of the Snake Bend Pack.

Dev, who was a member of mine.

I looked at the Weres—a mixture of men and wolves—on the ground. I saw them gazing up at Devon, and I knew. Leaving them to fight it out for dominance would be asking for trouble.

They needed someone to take Shay's place—and Devon was the one who'd delivered the killing blow.

Shay's dead. They're fair game. You could claim them, Devon told me silently, but the wolf inside of him said something very different. It longed for something else: something animal and powerful and right.

I nodded—not in response to Devon's request, but in response to the knowledge that this was what Callum had foreseen, this was what was meant to be.

I walked forward on stiff human limbs. I stood next to Devon, so close that I could feel the heat of his body, smell Shay's blood. I lifted my hand to his cheek. I smiled—and then before he could tell me not to, I swiped my fingernails across the surface of his neck.

I let him go.

I pulled myself out of his head, snapped his bond to our pack like it was dried spaghetti.

I heard it break.

I felt it, felt his absence, like a hole in my own body.

"Bronwyn," he said, but I shook my head, didn't let him finish.

"Go," I said. "They're waiting. For you."

All around us, the Snake Bend Pack watched in silence, their eyes on him.

"All I ever wanted," Devon said softly, "was to stay with you."

I didn't reply, because Devon, of all people, understood—what we wanted didn't matter. My first allegiance was to my pack—and from this point forward, his would be to Snake Bend.

"You stubborn, impossible, backhanded little wench."

From Dev, that was the equivalent of *good-bye*.

He turned. He walked toward the Snake Bend wolves. And then he claimed them. I could see the power, shining in his eyes, could see the moment they accepted him, the instant their world realigned itself with Devon at their center.

Alpha. Alpha. Alpha.

I couldn't hear his thoughts or theirs, but I could see the call spreading from wolf to wolf. I could see them waiting for their alpha's signal.

With one last glance over his shoulder at me, Devon gave into the call of the wild. He Shifted—and as a pack, one incredible, immovable, unfathomable force, they ran.

EPILOGUE

~

"BUT WHY?"

I tried to summon the part of my brain responsible for political dealings. It was all about patience—and control.

"Because," I replied calmly, "Rose is too little to play Fuzzy Wuzzy Death Ball. She's just a baby."

Lily did not seem overly impressed with my reasoning. Katie and Alex had been following her around since they were barely a year old themselves. Lily wasn't disposed to wait for Maddy's baby to outgrow infant status.

Despite the similarity in their names, the four-year-old hurricane and Maddy's little daughter were about as different as two pups could get. Rose was quiet, even when she cried—and she rarely cried. She was wide-eyed, observant, peaceful—and sometimes, I would have sworn she was looking at things no one else could see.

We still didn't know—what her knack was, why the Shadows were drawn to her, how she'd brought them back. But you could tell, just by looking at her, just by holding her, warm and solid in your arms, that she was different.

Impossible.

A miracle.

A female born alone.

None of which made her capable of playing the rough-and-tumble game Lily had fashioned for herself and the twins.

"Get some of the older kids to play," I told Lily.

She made a face. "They *cheat*."

Since I was highly skeptical that Fuzzy Wuzzy Death Ball actually had rules, that seemed doubtful. More likely, Lily just didn't like playing with anyone she couldn't boss around.

"Go," I told her, cutting off another "why" with a gentle nudge to her side. "Go on."

After a long, considered moment, Lily went, leaving me in the woods alone.

No Devon.

No Chase.

Just me.

That wasn't technically true, of course. Lake was still around, ready to kick my butt out of moping anytime she suspected the dark place might be beckoning me on. Griffin assisted her in that effort, though I suspected he ran interference on my behalf just as often.

Then there were the newest members of our pack. Maddy—and baby Rose—and a handful of adult males, handpicked by Devon for their fighting prowess and their loyalty. Before

I accepted them as part of Cedar Ridge, I'd run their names by Mitch. Having interacted with them more than once over the years, he'd given the transfers his stamp of approval, and Callum had sent me e-mails, encouraging me to accept Devon's offer of extra muscle.

I hadn't replied.

There were twenty-five of us now—enough to cover a wider territory than we'd held before. With a civility unobserved in any alphas before us, Devon and I had split the former Snake Bend territory the way we'd split candy bars when we were little. North Dakota was mine; the lower states his.

Together, we had more people, more land, and more females than most other packs could ever even dream of. I didn't kid myself that the other alphas were unaware that the Cedar Ridge and Snake Bend packs, though separate, would fight any enemies as one.

I also didn't ignore the obvious, that this was the future Callum had been aiming for all along. This was the reason he hadn't warned me that Shay might come after Maddy. This was why he hadn't prevented Chase's death, why I woke up each day alone, feeling like half my body was missing and a chunk of my soul had gone dead inside.

Callum had his reasons. I understood—I did. I saw his thought process with crystalline clarity; I recognized that the outcome—Shay dead, Devon the alpha of his own pack, the other alphas sufficiently warned about what might happen if someone came after me—was the best any of us might have hoped for.

But Chase was still dead, and that, I couldn't forgive. Not now. Not ever.

You can't trade a human's life for a wolf's.

If Callum had Changed me when I asked him to, Shay would have had to go through me to get to Chase. I would have had the option of offering my life up for the wolf Caroline had killed. With my life on the table, Shay wouldn't have been able to go after anyone else.

You need to be human for this, Callum had said, and I was. I'd waited. I'd been patient. But Chase was the last person who would die because of what I was—and what I wasn't. He was the only one who might have been able to talk me out of it.

He was my why.

I went back to the house and dressed in simple clothes: a light sweatshirt, cotton shorts. I told Ali I was going out.

"Won't you get cold?" she asked. Summer had given way to early fall; already, there was a chill.

I shrugged. "You know me," I said. "I'll survive."

There was a pregnant pause as she looked at my face, really looked at it. There was nothing to see there, no hint of things to come.

She let me go.

I drove to the border and waited. I didn't call Callum, didn't give him an ultimatum, but if he didn't show, I'd order one of the new Weres to attack me. Loyal or not, protective or not, they wouldn't be able to disobey.

"Five minutes," I whispered. "You have five minutes."

I didn't, wouldn't say his name.

I sat down on the ground. I offered my face up to the sky. It was dark and overcast, but I basked in it, the same way I would have if there were sun. These were my last human breaths.

My last human sky.

A hundred years from now, would I look back and remember the way the colors looked? Would I recall what it was like for goose bumps to dot my flesh, to hear nothing, smell nothing, to know that there was no one and nothing in my body but me?

I didn't care.

What good was being human, if it meant watching the people I loved die? What good was it pretending that I *was* human, when life just kept peeling my humanity off in strips?

Crunching gravel alerted me to Callum's approach. I looked at him, expecting to feel a stab of betrayal, anger, hurt, but for the first time in memory, I met Callum's eyes and felt nothing.

Whatever we'd had, whatever bond we had forged, whatever memories we'd shared, however much of the person I'd become that I could trace back to him—he'd killed it, as dead as Jed and Chase.

"Bryn." That was all he said, just my name. Everything else went unspoken, evident only in his tone. From the day he'd found me until now—every interaction, every time he'd dried my tears, the times he'd been the one to make me cry. I'd loved him, and I'd hated him, and it had all been leading up to a single moment in time.

Now.

"You made me a promise once," I said, my tone as flat as his was brimming with everything that had passed between us in the past thirteen years. "I've come to collect."

He didn't push me. He didn't reach out to touch me. His eyes locked onto mine, a perfect match for the tone in his voice.

"You're certain?"

I stood, faced him, held my arms out to my side.

"Go ahead," I said. "Kill me."

Kill whatever humanity I had left.

He turned his back on me and began Shifting. I heard each snap of bone, as flesh rendered itself into something new. I thought of my parents, the scars on Caroline's arm, Lucas trying to rip out my throat.

I thought of the chunk the Shadow had taken out of my flesh. I thought of a thousand cuts on my body, needles digging into flesh, the smell and taste and feel of blood.

Callum turned back around. On four legs, he padded toward me. His eyes met mine. I nodded.

He leapt.